My Sweet Vidalia

For my dad,
who taught me to always measure twice.

Still / adv.

existing even at this time

My MOMMA BELIEVES ALL BABIES to be gifts from God, no matter what. But for as sure as she was in that truth she understood how, time to time, one or another of them cherubs might get lost or redirected.

Momma reckoned only the bravest of the brave dared commit to this earth, and that, irregardless of pronouncements otherwise, I was one of those.

"*Still—*" was all she'd heard. Why, she wished it so hard I could almost see my reflection in her eyes.

"The body doesn't always have a choice," she whispered. "But the spirit does. Ain't that right, baby girl?"

MY NAME IS CIELI MAE Jackson, birthed in 1955 on the Fourth of July to Vidalia Lee Kandal Jackson, seventeen, of Willin County, Georgia.

Of importance in this telling is that upon First Breath any omniscience is expunged. Annulled. Poof. Gone.

In plain-speak, had I but gasped, wheezed, panted, or sighed, even one little sigh, I'd have no recollection of events past, present, or to come. As I never did pull that first breath I see most all of what was, what is, and what could be.

I cannot say what might have happened had I come unto Momma by way of more common channels—I can only tell what did happen—because I did not.

CHAPTER ONE

F IXED BETWEEN BREASTS AND PLUMPED belly, that tattered apron bound her despite its ties dangling loose by her sides.

Glancing sideways at the crumpled cap and shredded gown, she tsk-tsked. She did what she could to keep from thinking ahead but every now and again, well, my momma-to-be just couldn't help herself.

In late March but a few months shy of her high school graduation she'd dropped out. This was not unusual for a girl in these parts back then. Truth be told, most folk supposed it peculiar she had made it that far.

Irrespective of a quirky set of values and a staunch dedication to her studies my Vidalia had got herself caught. A former A+ student, she was even more confounded by the misunderstanding than the predicament itself.

JB Jackson had sworn to her there wasn't no way she could get pregnant so long's he was on top and she took nothing to drink until two hours after. Somehow she'd trusted him over what she suspected.

AND SO IT CAME TO PASS that way across town, as a gaggle of her former schoolmates, survivors of Willin County High School's class of 1955, received their diplomas, my momma I-do'd and JB, well, he I-reckon'd.

Preacher Tidwell raced through his part of the ceremony intent only on a strong enough finish. Memaw Veta Sue looked on indifferent and Pawpaw Clyde Royce Kandal mopped at a sweat-brimmed brow with the sleeve of his faded work shirt while Granny LuLa culled tobacco from her teeth with a good-as-new toothpick.

It was barely noon when, through a spit of stale rice, Pawpaw watched his new son-in-law dump two quarts of white lightning into the clouded plastic punch bowl of cherry flavored Kool-Aid.

Pawpaw backed away, his face tight.

"Paw!" my Vidalia exclaimed, sidestepping a collision just in the nick of time. "Something a' matter?"

"Here now, Vida Lee," Pawpaw whisper-warned, pulling her aside. "You best keep this."

My Vidalia looked back over one pale freckled shoulder exposing a slender neck, chalk-like and smooth but for the scab meant to've been hidden by her makeshift ribbon choker. Heart aflutter, she slid the short barrel, a J-frame Chief's Special and her only dowry of sorts, into the side pocket of her borrowed wedding smock.

Her palm absorbed the warmth of the pistol's wooden handle while her fingers lingered over the chill of its blue steel frame. Though my Vidalia had never taken aim at more than a rusted tin can or a rattler, she'd been a crack shot worth reckoning even as a child.

On impulse, she planted a quick kiss on Pawpaw's whiskered cheek.

Pawpaw gave the scruffy spot a pat, nodded once in her direction, and turned back to rejoin the others.

Memaw Veta Sue stood by, prickly and stiff. Shoulders squared, elbows snug to her sides, hands clasped below an ample bosom. If she relaxed she might give way like a silk slip from a bowed hanger.

"We done our due here, Mister Kandal," Memaw told Pawpaw with an elbow prod to his side. "We best be getting home now."

Memaw Veta Sue hadn't always been as unflappable. Why, she herself had come undone but a few years after birthing my Vidalia.

But Memaw's unraveling had less to do with the child she'd had than the one she didn't. More to do with an unloving life than the one she might've had. Despair, brought on by grace discarded, had taken hold of her mind and hardened her heart.

Since then, time, with its own peculiar set of powers and peccadilloes, pressed Memaw into a being of a cold brand of sturdy. Untouchable. Unreachable.

"Lie down with dogs, Vida Lee, you're gonna wake up with chiggers,"

Memaw Veta Sue admonished her only child. Seemed to me she was a pinch late with that advice. My Vidalia pushed out a contorted smile. Fixing a hungry gaze upon her folks, she shrugged. "Well then, Maw. Paw. I surely do thank y'all for coming."

My Vidalia shook Pawpaw's hand and then, with her own still outstretched toward Memaw Veta Sue, caught one of her white rubber flip-flops in the hem of that frayed pinafore and took a tumble. It broke my heart to see Memaw step back, steeling her hold only on her own self.

Watching her walk away my Vidalia murmured, "I love you, Maw," under her breath. And she did love her. She just couldn't trust her was all.

CHAPTER TWO

ALMOST BEFORE WE KNEW IT there we were starting in on July. Me and my Vidalia. Me and my momma-to-be.

It'd been six and a half weeks since the wedding. In all that time we hadn't seen more than a glimpse of her folks. Back there in that ramshackle vault, standing over the sorely stained, badly-nicked kitchen sink, looking out from the wrong side of that open window, my Vidalia shook her head ever so slowly. She liked to believe such a motion might dislodge any leftover supposes.

Scabs of dried caulk pocked the knotty pine-look panel surround. A nasty gray bled through a slipshod, watered-down whitewash. Just looking at the state of it all left my Vidalia with a bad case of the prickles. She wondered why JB had forbade her from asking their fair-weather landlord to hold off some on those touch ups, and I wondered why she'd heeded him. Even in her condition she'd have done a better job than Mister Heyhey.

Pawpaw Clyde Royce hadn't taught my Vidalia much else of value, other than the basics of a sort of carpentry, but he did instill a proper understanding of preparation as crucial to final product—more so even, than the quality or quantity of any cover-up slopped on down the road.

The post office, situated just across the street on Main, closed itself to business each weekday afternoon at three o'clock. At least that's what the sign said. Some days though, things ran amuck with certain persons needing extra services or something done over, after the hour. That was all fine and good as, for the most part, no one in this town ever seemed in much of a hurry to get things right the first time around.

My Vidalia usually always finished her chores early so she might sneak out and set herself on the tipsy porch, one floor up. Ever since the first floor tenant, a just-jilted Corilyn Muckle, made her hasty departure in the middle of one starless June night some weeks past, that porch with its blue painted ceiling had been my Vidalia's most favorite place in this world.

From there she could see weeds running riot as hardy stalks of thistle and pokeweed burrowed through crusty earth. From there she could see the peeling, painted gate of pig iron, like gnawed licorice, feigning guard. From there she could see a gritty mist of cinnamon clay-dust and intermittent streams of candied apple and apricot sunlight.

From there she could see JB coming.

CHAPTER THREE

PERCHED UP ON THAT TIPSY porch my Vidalia delighted in waving howdy-how-are-you? to those folks entering and exiting the postal service building just across the road. All the while her fingers raced knitting the tiniest of booties and the softest of blankets from discarded yarn scraps, foraged and reclaimed.

And she hummed. Up there she could hum to her heart's content with nobody telling her she couldn't.

Though my Vidalia didn't near know many, she'd fret over each and every one of those poor postal workers sent out to suffer a day's work under a searing Southern sun. How could she be sure they'd make it back without collapsing from the heat stroke?

Hell-bent on protecting my momma-to-be from any other evils of this world, JB didn't abide by such concerns and interminglings. That he was off running whenever he got a wild hair to do so, calling himself a working stiff when he was nothing of the sort, was of no consequence. She never had to ask if he was up to no good, if he was coming home. She knew, like any other catfish bottom-feeder, eventually, he'd drift to surface.

Without a penny in her purse, her steady worries, along with an inconstant strain of pride, disallowed any venturing. Why, she couldn't even go to Parson's Grocery & Emporium just around the corner. Especially not after what JB had done to that poor clerk.

Finishing up his shift, the oldest Barnett boy had caught sight of my Vidalia waiting on line and offered to help her home with her bags. After all, they'd almost graduated together.

My Vidalia and her stoop-shouldered knight traipsed along rutted roads and sidewalkless streets, dodging stray cats, headless dolls, and rusted bicycle parts.

Having reached their destination she placed a finger to her lips motioning for him to stay put for just one minute while she checked on something inside.

The coast clear, my Vidalia let out a sigh and beckoned the boy to come on in. "I ain't seen nobody from school, Jasper," she'd said with an excited nervousness. "Not in such a very long time."

After placing her parcels down gently on the metal-topped table, Jasper wiped the sweat from his brow with a paper napkin and took a quick swig of a near-cold, near-fresh lemonade she'd offered up in gratitude. The two laughed, exchanging pleasantries and whatnot. Jasper was about ready to head on home when JB arrived on the scene.

My Vidalia took one long look at him and started in gnawing at her fingernails. JB took one long look at my Vidalia gnawing at her fingernails and sucked in his cheeks. "He didn't do nothing, JB!" my Vidalia shrieked. "I swear to Jesus!"

But like a starved dog in a meat house, he charged that poor Samaritan.

JB wouldn't leave the boy be, pounding him up one side and down the other, and he wasn't planning to take it any easier on my Vidalia either.

At that moment, Gamma Gertrude Jackson happened by on her way to the River of Hope Springs Eternal Church and Pool Hall for prayer meeting. "Pisshit!" she'd mumbled under her breath.

Those Wild Women of God would have to wait.

Gamma Gert elbowed her way through the crowd, crammed shoulder to shoulder at the top of the stairwell, daring that audience of namby-pamby onlookers, "Y'all ain't got none of your own bidness to tend to?"

She rushed down those stairs breathing hard, put out over, yet again, being made late for her meeting, hushed into her boy's ear some such about hadn't he ought to know better by now! and that she wouldn't be surprised a'tall if Sheriff Truith wasn't on his way.

"You got your stupid head on today, son?" she demanded. "That fella ain't got nothin' but sugar in them britches."

Gamma regained herself some, slipping into a more familiar kind of survival mode before turning to the young victim.

"Boys, boys," she chided, winking at young Jasper. "I 'spect all we got here is a missed understanding."

Gamma picked up the young man's newly crooked wire rims, now missing one lens, and kicked up some red dust.

"Here it is!" she shouted, grabbing up a clouded piece of glass. She finagled the lens back into its mangled frame, spit on her shirttail and polished up the boy's bifocals, helped him to his feet, and dusted off his seat.

"Never you mind about telling nobody about all this." Gamma winked as she stuck a crumpled-up George Washington—more than he'd make in a month of tips—into the boy's white plastic shirt-pocket protector.

Gamma had winked so many times that afternoon I feared she might be developing some kind of a nervous tic. "And son," she went on with a slight nod in young Jasper's direction, "you tell your mama Gertrude Kaye Jebbitt Jackson sends her regards. And that me and the others been missing her at meetings."

The boy wobbled away still trembling, but bless her heart, Gamma stayed put until my momma calmed. And JB? Well, now. He passed out, which was just fine by me.

From then on JB saw to it my Vidalia's change purse stayed empty, as well as the cupboards, and their due bills unpaid. "No sense tempting the devil," he declared from high atop his sawdust soapbox.

Yet he'd fritter away whatever little monies Gamma Gert spared them. And when that ran out he did the same with whatever he'd conned from those wealthy widows in Leland, the next county over, where his reputation was not an issue.

But even right here in Willin there always seemed to be some working girl desperate enough to loosen her purse strings in exchange for the affectations of the charming-when-necessary scoundrel, too good looking for anyone else's benefit.

CHAPTER FOUR

The SKY RUMBLED AND A lightning bolt flashed us a fiery grin. There we were, still in that same spot. Just standing over the sink in front of that wide-open window.

Worrying in her head, my Vidalia rooted a hopeful gaze on the bottommost rung of the steely stairwell. She finished topping off the last of her delicate crusts for sweet tater pies for tomorrow's church picnic and transferred the dented but fulfilled tins to the sill and then, one at a time, she licked her fingers clean.

Pearls of sweat trickled down from the nape of her neck, merging in a rivulet between her swollen breasts. Crossing her right arm over her puffed middle, she giggled, cupping in her palm the tender spot where my heel pressured her from the inside out. Meanwhile her left hand gently shooed an unsuspecting housefly from the molasses-coated sticky strip overhead and out the window.

By and by JB made his descent. His feet plodded, uneven, too disconnected from his brain to allow any amount of grace.

Stumbling on the second-to-last riser down, he pitched forward, missed the next step, and smash-crashed into our door. He'd popped the weary thing off its rusted hinges, tripped over the warped portal, slipped on the worn welcome mat, and landed butt first in a muddle at her bare feet.

My Vidalia gripped the edge of the chipped basin, jerked back from her shoulders on up, and peered down into an interminable darkness.

A set of eyes as dank and bleary as Mississippi floodwater met her gaze with a tar-like indifference.

"Stupid ass stairss," he slurred. "Shee-it."

"Where you been?" she asked, a dazed look taking her over. "I was half out of my mind with worry—"

Oh, she'd fretted all right. Not that he hadn't come home, but over what state he'd be in when he did.

JB mumbled, sloppily hoisting one deadweight limb then another.

"I'm thirssty," he said in a half-stand, leaning hard on his esses.

Her full lips stretched so taut she appeared simpleminded as she moved to retrieve a pitcher from the icebox. Making an over-polite offering of sweet tea, she plucked a misshapen butter knife from her front pocket. "Let me see if I can scrape some ice out this old thing."

Uprighting each mug on the drain board, she rejected one cup after another. My Vidalia always turned the cups upside down, even in the cupboards. "Maw Veta Sue says it keeps critters from getting inside," she explained to JB, as if he cared. Finally, and with intent, she poured and served.

JB looked back and forth from the mug to her face. "This one here's got a crack."

"Just only on the outside," she said back, in her softest voice.

"Just only on the outside," he repeated in singsong.

She'd heard the smirk in his voice and did her best to reassure, but grabbed up a new cup just in case. She glanced back at him over her shoulder one more time before emptying the contents of the one into the other.

JB pursed his lips and hollowed his cheeks. He rubbed the chapped knuckles of his two balled fists against his thighs, up and down, faster and faster, just about starting a fire, and leveled a hard stare on the back of her head as she added a desperate scuff of frost from the attic of the grumbling pink Frigidaire to his cup.

"Like I'm gone drink that now?" he sniggered. With a flick of his finger, like a matchstick on a tinderbox, he knocked the tumbler from her hand.

My Vidalia eeked out a half smile lowering herself gently into a kneel-squat and began sopping up his mess with the skirt of her once white bib apron.

"Aww, JB," she said in a dead voice, shaking her head slowly. Grabbing onto the table edge, she managed to pull herself to standing. "There ain't but a swallow left in the pitcher—"

"Hmmph. If that don't beat all," he sneered, so full of himself I thought he might explode right there, granting her even more of a mess to clean up. He smacked the table hard, and my Vidalia just about jumped out of her skin.

"I'm sorry, JB. Please don't be ugly to me. I'd make more," she said, still trying to keep her sounds neutral. "But I'm out of sugar for the sugar water. And we're late on our due bill at the grocery again."

"What the hell?" His dander rose up with his voice, all gravel and spit. My Vidalia froze in place. Her forehead prickled and an odorous sweat streamed out from her armpits and the underneath of her dress.

As JB's knuckles resumed their grinding attrition, my Vidalia's bottom teeth gnawed at her upper lip while layers of her soul peeled away, one by one.

"You set," she said, exacting a smile onto a broken mirror. "Let me just run upstairs and see if Miss Dandy could loan us some—"

"Shee-it, Vida Lee. I ain't got all day."

"'Course you don't," she murmured. She grabbed onto a chair back, staying her hands, bracing herself against incoming attack.

"I don't like that old biddy."

"But Miss Dandy's a mindful good person. A right fine lady. If you'd just—"

"And I don't want you talkin' to her no more."

Wringing her chapped hands, my Vidalia hushed on as sweet as molasses, "But JB, you ain't even made her acquaintance yet. You don't even know her none."

"Since when d'I need know somebody to know I don't like 'em?"

My momma-to-be lowered her head and turned from him. "But that, that just don't seem fair," she murmured, half truth, half question.

⟵⟶

TWO FLOORS ABOVE US, BY way of the old, processed iron staircase, Miss Pickett Dandy appeared a risk worth the taking. Unless Gamma Gert happened to come around for a chitchat, my Vidalia had no one else. Oh, she talked to me on a regular basis. But still in her belly, I was unable to uphold my end of any conversation.

That weekend just past, a new resident, one my Vidalia meant to befriend, had begun moving in on the first floor between us down in the cellar and Miss Dandy up on high.

Over and again Gamma Gert had tried to impress upon her new daughter-in-law the importance of using her time more wisely. Why in tarnation should she be troubling her head over the likes of strangers when she had a good man to tend to?

"And, well now," Gamma summed it up, "JB says you need to quit all the woolgatherin' with that Pickett Dandy, too. All she does is fill your head with book talk and highfalutin ideas. My boy don't like that kinda nonsense. You know he don't, Vida Lee, so why d'you keep doin' it?"

Though my Vidalia did try to hold back her excitement over interesting pieces of news, or bits of those thoughts she'd never thought to think before, JB had more than once come home to her joyful babbling.

"Civil Rights? Ethics? What does that ole geezer know about such things anyways? Dammit-all!" he roared loud enough to be heard two stories up and then some. "For chrissake, any fool can see all men ain't created equal."

I was especially thankful that, somehow, his threats didn't interfere any with the kinship between Miss Dandy and my momma-to-be. That maybe she had at least one person of this earth looking out for her better interests.

"OKAY, THEN. I WON'T TALK to her no more," my Vidalia said back flatly. She removed her wetted apron and slowly, but not too slowly, shook her head. She then slipknotted the loose ties together and hung her apron from the bent nail above and to the left of her workspace.

"But just only this one last time, I'ma run up there, if it's all the same to you, JB. For sure she'll loan me one more cup of sugar. She always says she don't mind none."

"Dang it, Vidalia," he whined, bringing a closed fist down hard onto the already sorely dented enamel tabletop.

"I swear. I'll be back directly," she promised, pushing her voice up just enough to drown out the loudened thumping of her heart.

"Aw, forget about that ole bitch. You come on over here. I got somethin' for ya."

"But JB," my Vidalia whined back, forcing a flirtatiousness. "You said you was thirsty."

He sniggered, undoing his belt buckle.

"Well then," she said. She cleared the lump of coal half-formed in her throat and brushed one hand against the other. "How about I just freshen up a bit? I'll try'n find that lace nightie you like so much."

"G'wone then. But make it snappy," he said, looking down at himself. "This ain't gone last all day."

Oh, my Vidalia knew his ways. And truth be told, she'd rather take a few punches later on than, well, you know.

She dillydallied in that back room just long enough. When she emerged on tiptoe balancing the laundry bushel on one hip, JB was out like a burnt lightbulb. And that was a good thing. A real good thing. Those forbidden books laid well hid in the basket under a stack of neatly folded and freshly laundered towels and bed linens, but she still wasn't sure how she meant to explain leaving the premises with a mess of already clean laundry.

My Vidalia paused but a quick second, like a parent worrying over a fretful child at rest. With a sigh my momma-to-be sidestepped the sagging floorboard she knew would creak and headed for the stairwell.

CHAPTER FIVE

By THE TIME JB REGAINED any sense of mindfulness my Vidalia was back at the sink shelling peas. Miss Dandy had insisted the pods would surely go bad if she didn't take them off her hands right then, and wouldn't it be a pity to waste such when there were babies starving in the backwoods?

The last batch of library books had been returned to their rightful borrower, and now, hidden beneath the laundry pile, snug in a brown paper bag, was the latest edition of The Book of Common Sense Child Care written by some world-famous baby doctor.

Whenever JB wasn't home, Miss Dandy and my Vidalia talked long hours into the night. They'd hash over the importance of being a good parent and a sound example to the community. And about how my Vidalia wanted me so bad she could taste it. "It's like nothing else much matters no more," was how she'd put it.

Miss Dandy had checked out that baby guidebook at my Vidalia's behest, mightily enjoying the dustbowl she'd stirred by her association.

Why, Miss Dandy made her way down the library's front steps with her nose in the air and her back straight as an arrow aimed heavenward. Townsfolk joked Pickett Dandy had a stick up her butt. My Vidalia maintained Miss Pickett had the good posture, that's all.

Finally come to, JB looked around some. Pulling on one ear, he willed himself up from the saggy spoon rest of a couch.

He unbuttoned his blue jeans and commenced to stretching like a tomcat readying for conquest. When he pulled his unbuckled belt free of its loops it dropped to the floor, landing with a loud *ka-plunk*.

JB strutted toward my Vidalia, leading with his chin, a cock-eyed squint fixed on her half-moon middle. "Now then," he said in his most nettlesome way. "Didn't I tell you to get rid of that there?"

Grabbing her by a scabbed elbow, he pinched one arm behind her back and pressed her belly hard into the chipped porcelain sink.

"But you didn't mean it—" she whispered. The timbre of her voice sang to the raw truths beyond her words.

"The hell I didn't!" he yelled, spit flying.

She twist-turned to face him, still trying to disbelieve. Even then and there, even with her lower half pinned against the sink.

"Dang, girl. Wipe that stupid look off your face—"

"But JB, we're husband and wife now. You heard the preacher. We're meant to procreate. You don't really mean to hurt our baby. Do y—"

Shush, Momma. Shush, I wished I could've told her.

"And how'd I even know the thing's mine?"

"Jamerson Booth Jackson, you know better'n that. I ain't never even been with nobody 'sides you—"

Oh, he did know better, but he commenced to pummeling her anyways. Up and down, up and down. Why, he pushed her so far beyond fleshly boundaries that she brought forth wails from a place so deep inside, even I was unaware of its existence.

It was too soon. We both knew it was too soon.

I paddled against those choppy waters with the strength and prowess of an Olympian while my Vidalia did her best to hold on. But still, it was not enough. Our hopes dissolved into a *whoosh* as the waterfall from between her legs saturated the already-warped floorboards beneath us.

After a time she quieted, focusing on depleting his efforts and rebuilding her stores. Amid that rot and squalor, the sharper edges of his vengeance dulled, JB's head cleared some and he readied himself to take leave of us.

"What's to eat?" he asked as if he hadn't just beaten his pregnant wife to a pulpy mess. Eyeing the pies left cooling on the sill, he stretched out his neck, relieving the new kink in his back. "Well, now. Lookit here," he said, wiping the spittle from his chin with a palm stained the color of beetroot juice. "You don't do much right but you always did make a fine pie, Vida Lee. I'll give you that much."

He went ahead, scooping up portions from each of the overfilled pie shells she'd prepared for the River of Hope Springs Eternal's Fourth of July picnic. He plowed through what he could and chucked the moist remains, even her special tins, out that open window.

"Jesus H. Christ on a popsicle stick. I. Don't. Want. No. Baby!" he yelled in her bloodied ear. That screen door, so many times repaired and remounted, slammed behind him, wagging tentative in familiar defeat, while just kitty-corner, yellow jackets swarmed the fragrant discards of her delicate labors.

CHAPTER SIX

MOMMA'S CRIES HAD GUTTED THAT black-and-blue dawn terrorizing our new first floor neighbor. Just coming off the hoot owl shift, all Johnnie Faye Falfourd wanted was to peel off her garters and snagged nylons and crawl back under her auntie's patchwork quilt.

Avoiding the more rotted of the wooden planks upholding that slanting side porch, Johnnie Faye hid herself from the moon's glow. Unafraid, a woody bougainvillea reached out to her in the darkness, but that poor gal didn't dare stir from the shadows until JB was long gone.

"Ma'am. Miss Dandy?" Johnnie Faye whisper-shouted heavenward, tossing handfuls of pebbles at the second story window where an uncertain light flickered. Blubbering and too tired to wait any longer, she pitched up a rock.

A shard hit Pickett Dandy, half asleep on her slipper chair, grazing her left temple. The fuzzy screen of her black-and-white television console glowed alternately in black-white, white-black.

"What in hell's bells!" Miss Dandy sputtered. The spinster straightened, pulling her deep-purple dressing gown closer. Jamming her arthritic feet back into a worn pair of white chiffon boudoir slippers, she grabbed up a tire iron, her kitty, and her spectacles, and shuffled over to the shattered window. For the first time in her lifetime that former suffragette didn't know what had hit her. Even with her bifocals in place, she could barely make out the quivering figure below.

Miss Dandy crammed her hearing aid into her right ear. Heeding the surging sounds of sorrow in the swelled night air, she reckoned what all had gone on during her repose. Letting go of her cat, she snatched up the telephone receiver with her right hand, and pounded the tabletop with her left fist, spit-damning that dirty, no-count, sonofabitch to rot in hell. Within the same strained breath she praised Jesus, thanking the Good Lord her party line was not in use, and that Doc Feldman's nurse had the good sense to answer on the first ring.

Less than half an hour later, still bow-tied and buttoned up, with his starched collar just now starting to wilt, kind-eyed Doctor Feldman appeared at our side. At forty-some years of age, the doc turned up on the skinny side of just handsome enough. What remained of his graying reddish-brown hair, like cigarette ashes aglow, stood on end. As always, he'd lend his lithe but steady hands only as far as my Vidalia allowed.

Doc Lewis Feldman had just finished up his own version of a hoot owl shift at Lafayette General. In those fourteen hours prior, he'd delivered two babies, extracted a butter bean from the left nostril of Linus Cockrell, sutured the hand of Dewey Applewhite, and performed an emergency hysterectomy on ninety-three-year-old Rosamund Ailey whose twenty-two children were in attendance, as well as the remaining five of her seven ex-husbands.

Memaw Veta Sue and Pawpaw Clyde Royce Kandal arrived, having been notified by Doc's nurse and apprised of our piteous situation. Sheriff Truith was on his way.

The doc washed up as best he could and got down to business. He spoke to my Vidalia in the softest of whispers, easing the way for what was to come.

Though he'd administered enough painkillers and sedatives to subdue a steed, neither her will nor mine would be trotted into a surrender. My mission stood firm: I was hers for as long as she needed me, meant to bring a fullness to her life. Meant to initiate the release of any strengths she already carried deep within. To undermine any untruths she'd been misled to believe.

Doc placed my body oh-so-gently upon my Vidalia's emptied belly, and my spirit melded with hers. We'd been upended, but not undone.

Through a jagged hole in that bedroom door, an opening just the size and shape of JB's right fist, Pawpaw peeked in.

"That baby," Pawpaw murmured. "That baby's so small, Veta Sue.

And purple. That baby's purple. I ain't never seen anything so tiny, since . . ." Through the din, his words faltered as fermented sorrows bubbled over the edges of his wishing well. "I don't think our girl's gone be able to handle this all. She don't look so good, Maw."

"We all deal with what needs dealing with, Mister Kandal. I 'spect the girl will do what needs doing. Just like the rest of us." With that, Memaw's glare settled elsewhere.

Doc Feldman returned a paled face.

"Now might be a wise time to put things into some rightful order," Doc said, guiding his voice through a hard swallow, "before our Vidalia here awakens and learns of what has happened."

As if on cue, Gamma Gertrude Jackson rushed the scene. Without batting one eyelash, she edged right on past Memaw, Pawpaw, and Doc.

Weighted and uncomfortable, his Sunday-best overalls whisked on over long johns, Pawpaw flinched like he'd been asked to pay in advance for something he didn't want in the first place. His shoulders collapsed. A loosened strap drooped down one arm as his good hand steadied the other not-so-good one.

Memaw still in her dressing gown, stood aside him, poised and unruffled. In a judgmental silence her head cocked from one side to the other and back again, taking slow measure of my other grandma— her counterpart—wrapped up tight in her own straitjacket of skewed loyalties and distorted perceptions.

Gamma Gert's eyes raked over them all. "Shoot the fire and save the matches. My boy didn't mean nothin'. He just don't know his strength is all." Gamma scanned the room, unfazed. Tightly balled fists propped against lopsided hips, she dared the dazed bystanders. "Well, now. You gone help me clean up this mess or stand around like you're waitin' to get your pictures took?"

⌣‿⌐

MOMMA AWOKE SWIMMY-HEADED BUT DETERMINED. She thanked the doc for his efforts and waved off the sheriff who'd arrived in the meantime. "Nice to see you again, Sheriff Truith. I am sorry to be such a bother. Truly I am. I'm a little sore from the birthin' is all. But I expect that's to be expected. Ain't that right?"

Pawpaw Clyde Royce and Memaw Veta Sue stood by like a pair of wrung sponges just waiting on my momma to dismiss them, too. Gamma Gert bustled about scrubbing up clots of dried heartache along with the last layer of stain from the wooden floorboards. Doc gathered up his instruments as if they were made of delicate crystal instead of surgical steel, wrapping each piece in its own muslin casing, reinserting them, one by one, into his satchel.

He had extended to Momma many chances to state the facts as they were but she was too young, too weary, and too unsure, to stand tall in the face of such an offer.

"Please, my dear, tell me what happened. I want to help you," he'd solicited bigheartedly.

Momma stared up at him. Her eyes glistened, grateful but doubtful. There we both were, tucked beneath the new neighbor's auntie's color-blocked comforter with Momma's arms wrapped tight around my spirit. At that point in time she had neither the sense to accept nor the fortitude to counter his offer.

Doctor Feldman would do whatever it took to remain in her good graces. Long-widowed of a sorrowful and childless marriage, he understood all too well how some hurts are just too big to talk about.

Gamma Gert, arms now folded across her chest, one brow raised, looked on, ready to jump in as needed. She'd already worn a rut in the floor planks with her pacing.

Meanwhile, Momma carried on her charade. "Why now, aren't you just the most nicest, most sweetest man," she cooed to the doc. "Fretting so, over little ole me. I truly appreciate your concern. I do. We just need some rest is all."

"Perhaps one day you will trust I have your best interests at heart, Vidalia," he replied, leaving his petition on her table. Why, that man didn't possess the power of his own convictions, and as everybody knows, folk can't give away something they don't own in the first place. "Maybe one day," he murmured, "you will grant me my own absolution."

Then he walked through the door with the hole just the size and shape of JB's fist and out into the front hallway.

CHAPTER SEVEN

JB HAD STAYED GONE JUST long enough.

"Where's my wife at?" he stormed, breathing hard through his nose. He yanked open the old pink fridge and stuck his head inside to cool off some before grabbing a brew, the lone bit of matter in there. "Where is she? And what the hell happened here?"

"Here I am, JB," Momma called out, softly, so as not to disturb me. "In the bedroom."

JB removed the cigarette from behind his left ear and lit it with a match from the counter. He took one long drag, cocked his head from side to side, exhaled a trio of smoke rings, and strolled past Momma's sentries, sweaty brown bottle in hand.

"Mister Jackson," Doc interrupted. With his one hand outstretched, Doc Feldman looked like a school crossing guard caught in a hailstorm. "Our Vidalia has suffered a grievous trauma. It is my belief that she will recover in due time, but the baby," Doctor Feldman stammered after JB, trying to keep his tone doctorly and impartial. "But the baby. Your baby, didn't make it."

"You don't say." JB scratched behind one ear and took a slow pull from the bottle.

"I did the best I could," the wearied doctor offered up.

"You sure about that, Doc?" Sniggering, JB jerked his head back like a drunk rooster.

Memaw then stepped forward. "Damn you to the fires of hell, Jamerson Booth Jackson," she hissed right into his face.

JB bared his teeth.

Quick as a flash both Pawpaw and Doc Feldman jumped in to fill what little space remained between those two.

Staring down at the ashen end of his cigarette, JB flicked the butt to the floor and smashed it into the fresh-scrubbed boards with the steel toe of his work boot. His eyes lingered, sizing up the tired trio. "Here I come, darlin'," he called out over their heads, nodding, his voice dripping saccharine. "I'ma go and see to my bride now, if y'all don't mind."

He then planted himself by Momma's side, like a dog guarding a bone.

If I hadn't known better, I might've reckoned his concerns were for her. But I did know better. Then again, I expect we all did. Why, even after seeing my flesh and bones all snuggled up in her arms, he didn't think to ask how she was feeling or if I was a boy or a girl.

For the rest of that day, with the doc fretting in the parlor, Memaw pacing in and out of the apartment, and Pawpaw reading a Bible in the front yard, JB kept at her.

"I swear on all that's good and true in me, I'm sorry, Vida Lee," he muttered into her swollen left ear. "But girl, you make me do things. Things I don't wanna do. Why d'you have to look at me that way? You know I don't like it when you look at me that way. If there's any fuss made over this, Vida Lee, they're gone try'n lock me up again," he warned. "And if they do, it'll be you who's to blame. Oh, I'll get out. Just like I did before. And then," he said with a devil-wink, "you're gone have somethin' real to fret over."

JB droned on about how she wasn't near ready to be a mama. And that if something happened to him, what other righteous man would ever have her now that she was spoilt and all? It wasn't like her folks were wanting to take her back, now was it?

Why, he went on and on until finally, laying his head against her arm, he'd put himself to sleep.

Momma's hold on me stayed strong. I was her lifeline. Her buoy. She, my anchorage. Although they could not out 'n out see it, they couldn't help but feel it, and so for a while, the others? Why, they just let us be.

CHAPTER EIGHT

Uᴘꜰʀᴏɴᴛ, ɢᴀᴍᴍᴀ ɢᴇʀᴛ'ꜱ ᴘʀᴀʏᴇʀ ɢʀᴏᴜᴘ, the Wild Women of God, offered sympathy and support. Their unyielding loyalty to my gamma aside, they, along with the rest of the townsfolk, did their own share of tsk-tsking behind our backs:

"It's a shame about Gertie's boy. What he done."

"A shame for her you mean."

"Bad things happen to good people—"

"Ain't that the truth."

"They say young Vidalia done lost her mind—"

"Well, thank the Lord she got Gertrude Kaye lookin' out for her."

"If Jesus hisself came down from the cross and told Gert to throw that boy out—"

"She wouldn't do it. Y'all know she wouldn't do it."

"It just don't seem fair."

"Life ain't fair. Who don't know that?"

The Wild Women's bimonthly prayer callings at the River of Hope Springs Eternal Church and Pool Hall commenced with a Baptism of Tears for new members or any constituents in need of refreshing. Purifications by dunking took place at the Go Forth Creek followed by a processional to the pool hall for spirits, vittles, and benediction.

Each woman appealed to her sisters-in-prayer at one time or another and nary a one was denied. Sustenance flowed in proportion to need, not propriety.

They prayed over ornery in-laws, wayward children, and over-zealous revenuers. But mostly they petitioned against cheating-hearted men, and that any straying husband be stricken with the lockjaw, or an agonizing, slow-death version of the clap.

The Women left any other of life's sundry social quandaries and improprieties to be remedied however they all deemed fit, depending on an individual's inclinations. Their creaky, squeaky gate of support, hinged on various theories of right and wrong, swung loose and wide, being more of an evolving system than one set in stone. The undercurrent of acceptance and protection from within this sodality ran steady and impenetrable.

Those Wild Women made no distinction between the Haves and Have-Nots. Though their sisterhood consisted mainly of the latter, all were welcome here.

Gamma solicited their indulgence and the Women responded in kind. Momma was, as a wounded baby bird, taken in under their most colorful and abiding wings.

Loyal to a fault and ever true to her charges, Gamma said and did whatever she thought best to dispel rumors that her son had driven his child bride mad having beaten her badly enough to cause my misbirthing.

"After all, JB never had no decent role model," Gamma'd offer up. "And in the end that ain't nobody's fault but mine."

Now, no one blamed Gamma for her son's misdoings, but surely she could have tried just one little bit harder to hold him accountable.

To her credit Gamma's blind spot wasn't limited to blood kin. She was just about as duly unsighted of my momma's odd behaviors as she was her boy's.

"We shall pray for Vidalia Lee, my sisters. She's sliding down a razor blade barefooted. What the gal's gone through is just a phase," Gamma insisted to her choir. "She'll get through it all though, in her own way. In her own time."

Gamma was right, in her own way. And while Momma busied herself fancying I was her's to care for, I'd set my spirit to figuring, without straying beyond the boundaries of my calling, how I might help her find her own self, and what exactly could be done about the situation at hand.

"But Gertrude Kaye, Vida Lee reckons her baby is still here," Mabel Minor insisted.

"Ain't nothin worse to befall a woman then what befelled our Vidalia." Gamma spelled it out, yet again, for her guard.

"Gertrude? Maybe the girl needs have herself a nice long rest at the Brandywine. Me 'n Mable might could carry her there for you," old Sally Anne Seamens interjected.

"That child gets all the rest she needs. I see to it!" Gamma insisted, attempting for the umpteenth time to put an end to the matter.

"Now, Gertie, dear, we don't mean no disrespect but that girl, why, her head ain't on straight no more. Not since—" Beverly Eberly said, wrinkling her brow.

"We all seen it, Gert. Vida Lee talks to a baby that ain't there."

"There ain't no baby Gert. No baby, a'tall."

"Hmmph. And how do y'all know that?" Gamma demanded.

"Know what?" MabelSallyBeverly, like a three-headed monster, exclaimed in unison.

"How do y'all know there ain't no baby?" Gamma repeated with a heavy sense of calm. "Ain't nobody knows what Vidalia sees from behind her own eyes. Y'all know that's right."

Humbling herself, Gamma Gert concluded her grand sermon on the porch, "My dear sisters, who I stuck with through hell and high waters, can I hear a amen?"

With a fervor of those gone before in their own madnesses and mayhems, any air of dissension subsided and the Wild Women responded in kind, "Amen, Gertrude Kaye. Amen."

OUR TENDING HAD FALLEN TO Gamma Gert by default, and like everybody else excepting my momma, she couldn't see me nor hear me. Just the same, she cared deeply for Momma, always responding most gently and directly to her needs, however questionable or outlandish. Gamma fulfilled whatever it was Momma required, and then some.

Gamma Gert's seat-of-the-pants efforts freed me up to carry out my own mission within the limited terms and time frame to which I had agreed. Why, truth be told, I'd only just overstepped my boundaries but once. And I reckon that particular diversion, which will be spoken of by and by, was somehow acceptable on some higher level and in keeping with what all was expected of me.

GAMMA GERT KEPT MY FOLKS' room-off-the-farmhouse-kitchen clean enough. She laundered their clothing and bed linens as needed, stretching the sheets and covers tight with proper folds and creases in all the right places. She saw to it Momma changed her undergarments regularly and that she bathed at least once a week. Gamma brought Momma breakfast in bed most mornings, and dinner sometimes, too, whenever she fell blue and strayed even further than usual from the here and now.

Day after day, week after week, stationed by my momma's bedside, Gamma pitted hope against common sense as she rattled on about any old thing, from comings and goings on our side of town, to who married who, and who left who for who, to who got caught with their hand in the till, as well as any other late-breaking or life-enhancing scuttlebutt. In her own way Gamma Gertrude loved my momma and truly did not want her left so far behind that she'd never catch up.

Vidalia's phase, Gamma persisted, was just something she needed get through and come back around from. "There ain't no stick big enough to measure what's right or what's wrong for a woman summoned to bury her child," she'd say with a certainty.

Through many miseries and tribulations heaped upon Gamma for the better portion of her life, she'd kept up her own version of The Faith. I expect it helped carry her forward after losing JB's daddy to the wanderlust.

According to legend, Clayton Booth Jackson had deserted Gertrude Kaye, along with their brand-new baby boy, behind a filling station, just outside of Belle Glade. JB was no more than a mere suckling at Gamma's then barely budded, fifteen-year-old breasts. Though it was Clayton Booth who'd left them and of his own accord, it was always his own mama JB chose to hold responsible for their abandonment.

"YOU DON'T NEED FRET NONE," Gamma liked to tell Momma. "It's all gone work out, one way. Or another way." Until such a time, Gamma Gert was agreeable and satisfied to nurture us with her good eye close up on Momma and her blind eye trained on her boy.

Momma and I got on just fine tucked back in that farmhouse so long as JB kept his distance. And he did, for the most part. Oh, he came around now and again looking for affection and whatnot—most especially when his lady friends were busy with their paying customers. Yep, other than those times, we got on just fine.

CHAPTER NINE

JB'S GOOD LOOKS WERE A tool he was not above using under any circumstance.

Ever since he could string words into sentences, his pretty face had been more a ware for barter than a blessing.

The Coggins County High yearbooks anointed Jamerson Booth Jackson Most Likely to Succeed—especially, he liked to joke in all seriousness, with the ladies.

Irregardless of the warnings of his teammates, their younger sisters swarmed him by the bushel. Why, it wasn't even unusual for their mamas to corner JB in alleyways or back rooms. But when he had his druthers, which he usually did, he opted for the young'uns. All things considered, they were easier to discard.

Recruited by some of the finest football universities in the south JB could've blitzed his way into a full college ride, but that all went up in a puff of smoke after the fuss over him and Coach Ledbetter's thirteen-year-old daughter.

Penny Rae Ledbetter did not want to do the dirty with JB, but he thought she did. This confusion, which left the girl with a broken nose, two cracked front teeth, and one busted shoulder, led to his abruptly halted high school football career. And a stint in the Coggins County Jail.

JB had always been in the habit of robbing cradles and looking down at the world from the treetops. Often times the wind blew, but this time the bough broke. Convicted of aggravated child molestation and statutory rape just after turning eighteen, he was sentenced as harshly as the law allowed.

Still, early lessons in pretense served him well as he cut and juked his way through the initial stages of a supposed long-term imprisonment. Most assuring in his proclamations of innocence, JB'd secured quite a following. Bless their silly little hearts, those young ladies from families of certain means had allowed their thought processes to be compromised. JB, with his deadly combination of good looks and junkyard charm, had always had that effect on members of the opposite sex. Most specifically those of the debutante variety in search of a cause.

Prompted by the promises and propositions of a man who would always be the center of his own universe, those well-meaning maidens banded together to set him free. One in particular rallied strong. The local Miss Goody Two-Shoes, Winifred Birdsong.

Convinced Jamerson Booth Jackson had been hornswoggled, Miss Birdsong developed a strong tenderness for the sympathetic convict with his wide-eyed choirboy look. Lovesick and forlorn, the trusting socialite persuaded her own daddy to engage an attorney from Atlanta to find grounds upon which JB's conviction might be reversed. Which, as it turned out, wasn't all that difficult.

Those Good Ole Boys at the Coggins County Courthouse had, once again, shortened the long arm of the local legal assembly. Known to have bandied about their own travesties just under the radar of moral correctness, they'd held JB's trial within the confines of the jailhouse instead of the courthouse. In doing so, without the presiding judge even asking him, the accused, if it was all right, they'd violated his right to a public trial.

When Gamma Gert went and mashed the buzzer to gain entrance and observe her boy's trial, jailer Quinn Harle refused her admittance. "Over my dead body," was what he'd told her. By the time Gert returned with her shotgun tucked under her arm, JB had already been convicted and sentenced.

Coach Ledbetter, in a too-little-too-late attempt to protect, refused to have his daughter subjected to any additional intrusions following the attack. The extent of the "alledged" assault had never been officially substantiated.

As if that all wasn't near enough, the presiding judge, the Honorable Joachim L. Bartramus, was found out to be Coach Ledbetter's first cousin. The arresting officer, his brother-in-law. No rights had been read. No warrant issued.

Jamerson Booth Jackson was released.

To lead a woman on, irrespective of the damages incurred, was a skill worth its master's efforts. In response to JB's feigned regard and false promises, poor Miss Birdsong had surrendered unto him that which she'd held higher in value than the sum of all her own daddy's worth. The anguish experienced over this most intimate loss left her in desperate need of asylum.

The same fall Winifred Birdsong disappeared behind the ivy-covered walls of the Brandywine Sanitarium, JB started a new life with a new job: Head of Field Maintenance for Willin County High. There would be no additional restitution required of him. Unless, of course, he messed up again.

As expected, Gamma welcomed him back. Open armed. Open hearted. "Wasn't no way my boy done what all them hussies said he done."

Certain in her misbeliefs, Gamma cautioned her boy to be ever mindful of his peas and of his cues. "Them Jezabels is waiting 'round every corner, son."

The duo settled quickly into their previous ways. Old habits don't die easy, most especially when their consequences are undermined by reward. With Gamma on alert, providing cover, excusing his every misdeed, JB was home safe. Free and clear. At least, for the time being.

CHAPTER TEN

Bʏ ᴀʟʟ ᴀᴄᴄᴏᴜɴᴛs ɢᴀᴍᴍᴀ ɢᴇʀᴛ had been much overindulged, as well, by her daddy, Grady Bo.

Why, ever since his Jolene left him and their infant daughter behind to pursue her her dream as a bar singer, my great granddaddy, Grady Bo Jebbitt, played a dual role. Almost satisfactorily, he'd raised his baby girl to a version of womanhood.

It was only with a heavy-handed manipulation on her part and against his best judgment that he'd allowed his Gertrude Kaye, at fourteen years of age, to carry on with her new beau of choice. Grady Bo had warned his little darling how this coupling would come to no good in no time, but, as usual, his cautions went unheeded.

JB was the lone byproduct of Gamma Gert's adolescent rebellion. So many years later, and with all I'd learned in the meantime, it still proved hard for me to figure how Grady Bo managed to turn his back on his only child, even with the young JB as part of the package, but he did.

Once he'd figured out the true nature of his grandboy, with his tendencies toward good-for-nothingness, I suspect my great granddaddy just couldn't bear to witness what all was coming. Grady Bo gave over to his Gertrude Kaye the acreage of Purgatory, the fruitful aftereffect of the back-breaking laboring of his hard-drinking, hard-driving Scotch-Irish ancestors—lock, stock, and combines—but left her no funds for managing it all.

It wasn't an easy life for a gal who, until that point, had never had to make do but, bless her heart, she did. Why, Gamma raised her boy in as much comfort as she could afford supplementing the spotty farm revenue with sales of her Special Blends of sugar, water, and cornmeal, which she'd kept hid from the moonshine revenuers in barrels in the stream out back. And then, every so often, when times got especially dire, there would appear in Purgatory's mailbox a roughly assembled, homemade envelope from no one in particular, stuffed with dollar bills and smelling of Grady Bo's chewing tobacco.

And that was how we, Momma, JB, and I, a homeless and penniless trio, had found Gamma Gert, just making do as best she could, in the middle of that Indian summer.

Evicted from our first Main Street cellar apartment, the one across from the post office, we'd moved in with Gamma into Purgatory, where I was neither regarded nor disregarded by her. We were all, more or less, just biding time while carrying out our own melodramas, with JB pretending a search for gainful employment, and me and Momma doing our best to cover up her slow healing.

Gamma Gert insisted she didn't mind none. "Why, it ain't no trouble having y'all here. No trouble a'tall," which ranks pretty high up among the most daring of the boldfaced lies Gamma would come to tell in all her born days.

For sure, she could've used JB's help mending fences, tilling soil, and pulling corn. It should've been him loading and unloading all that stock for transport to the feed store in downtown Ellis. Not her.

But to JB, with his distorted expectations as to what the world owed him, his mama was no more than a lowly innkeeper. Purgatory, no more than a safe place to sleep off the fruits of his follies.

Gamma never did turn him down when he requested a handout, no matter the pretense or reasoning or cost to her. Just like Gamma, Momma never questioned him. Not when he came. Not when he went.

"A watched pot won't never boil, Vidalia Lee," Gamma instructed the young bride. "All a gal can do is turn her other cheek and wait."

Time after time, Gamma received JB back into her fold with a table set for a prince despite having had to've known, at least on some level, of what all he was made.

My momma as well pitched her tents in the dark. Strange as it seems, she'd known nothing at all about JB's past misdoings, thanks in large part to Memaw Veta Sue and her peculiar amalgamation of fears and compunctions.

Veta Sue Dixon Kandal believed first and foremost in the virtue of minding one's own business and spent little time on musings unrelated to her own self.

"I done suffered enough fools and mudslingers in my day, Vidalia Lee. Enough foul whispers to last me my lifetime. And yours, too," Memaw'd informed my momma, still tender and unseasoned.

CHAPTER ELEVEN

From way back when my Vidalia was still in her most formative years, Memaw Veta Sue had branded even the prominent *Atlanta Charter* a scandal sheet. The *Willin County Gazette,* no more than a tablet of sin.

The Kandals had no telephone. No television. Not even a radio.

Why, Memaw frowned upon fraternization in mostly any form excepting church meetings as required by Pawpaw Clyde Royce. Socializing led to small talk, which she regarded about as highly as devil vomit.

Aside from my momma's schoolbooks and any necessary appliance manuals, the Bible was the only text to be found within the walls of the Kandal's cottage.

Just beyond their doors, unsupervised inbreeding yielded an unruly lot. Weeds, vines, and shrubs in sickly shades of green, anemic browns, and wheaty yellows intertwined, encircling the tiny dwelling, compressing its contents like a corset, granting the inhabitants air enough for only a kind of survival.

Pawpaw had adjusted to Memaw Veta Sue's irregularities without much protest which is, I reckon, what married folk do more often than they know. He'd carry on any other of his reading by moonlight keeping her none the wiser, or so he figured, setting himself out back on the split stump, between their tumbledown outhouse and his toolshed, with his pipe, a newspaper, and the slew of do-it-yourself magazines to which he secretly subscribed.

He and little Vidalia Lee worked on that shed regularly and for weeks on end. They'd rid its planks of wood rot and critter damage and restored its rusted-through tin roof, following the step-by-step instructions my momma'd found within the worn and hallowed pages of a past month's *Popular Mechanics*.

Come the last Thursday of each month, Pawpaw and his eager apprentice would walk, hand in hand, the long, twisty dirt paths away from their overrun cabin into town to retrieve their latest subscriber copy.

A retired coal miner with the mind of an engineer, the heart of an architect, and the reflexes of a kindergarten teacher, Pawpaw relished any opportunity to share his expertise. From "Measure twice, cut once," and "There's but two kinds of houses down here, Vida Lee. Them that's got termites and them that's gonna get them," to some more personal in nature.

By and by, ice storms, hurricanes, and even a few tornadoes swept through their remote pocket of Willin County, but that structure stood firm.

Stacked floor to ceiling, clean, well-oiled doohickeys and other contraptions—some handed down, some leftover from his days in the mines—braced the cozy, sturdy space. Ready to go as needed, Pawpaw's selection of hand drills, miter boxes, saws, hammers, anvils, screwdrivers, and sanders sparred with the heavy scent of spent sawdust, hair tonic, and tobacco. Why, Pawpaw had the place packed so tight, I don't reckon those walls could've collapsed if they'd wanted to.

My momma's most favorite childhood possessions, aside from her short barrel pistol, were those tools of calculation. From a metal compass and on down to the shabbiest of tattered tape measures and splintered wooden rulers. Oh, how she loved that shed and and most everything in it.

"If you're gonna fix something, fix it right," Pawpaw insisted, sometimes adding with a sideways look, "And if you're gonna shoot something, shoot it dead," just for effect.

Pawpaw hadn't taught her much else as, for reasons beyond even my reckonings, he'd left most instructing to Memaw Veta Sue. Still, he did his best to impress upon little Vidalia Lee the value of precise figuring and that only the poorest of carpenters blames his tools.

For a fellow who placed such stock in preparation, one might suppose Pawpaw would've done a better job priming her in other ways of the world. I reckon he just got distracted by his own personal qualms and quagmires.

AT THE TIME OF MEMAW and Pawpaw's marriage of convenience, Veta Sue was but sixteen years old and seven months pregnant. Clyde Royce Kandal, impotent since the Tuscaloosa Disaster of '38, knew full well the child was not his.

Injured in the mining accident, trapped in a coal pit with twelve others, Clyde Royce had been rescued from deep in the foothills of Alabama and thought to be one of the lucky ones to escape alive and intact. But he wasn't intact, not for practical purposes anyways, as he'd never ever be a manly man again, nor sire a child, due to the nature of injury to his dingle.

Now, I don't expect I need explain what kind of blow that is to a man's assuredness. Especially to one untested, otherwise sturdy, and somewhat attractive.

The lovely young Veta Sue's predicament presented him a chance at a normalcy. My great grandma LuLa Belle Dixon jumped on the opportunity, offering this prospective relation a three-for-one. Not only would he take responsibility for Memaw and the baby who wasn't his, but for LuLa Belle as well.

Soon thereafter my Vidalia was born unto this dynasty of misfits, and for a short while they appeared one happy family. Memaw Veta Sue and Pawpaw Clyde Royce shared a bed during those years, but it was not a marriage bed. Not in any traditional sense.

By the time little Vidalia got to be just about three years old, Veta Sue, though not yet showing, found herself with another biscuit already buttered and warming in her oven. Before long, LuLa Belle, a first generation descendant of mountain people known for their uncanny sense of presentiment, picked up on the change in her daughter's aura.

True to her form, LuLa Belle ripped into Memaw. "I smell a rat in here, Veta Sue. A fat, smelly little rat." Under a grave duress, which only a mama bound to a self-serving and dishonorable intent can inflict, the young Veta Sue choked out a tearful confession.

She had tried to stay away from him, truly she did. Yes, Veta Sue had succumbed, again, but only just the once. "I was weak and lonely for a man's touch," she sobbed. "It won't never ever happen again. This time I swear on my immortal soul. You'll help me, won't you, Ma?"

Unnoticed, Clyde Royce hovered just beyond reach, stunned to silence, held fast only by the grace of shame.

LuLa spied him cowering in the shadow of that mighty two-hundred-year-old oak. She grabbed her daughter by her white, quavering shoulders and thrust her into his darkened silhouette. Veta Sue dropped to her knees, tears streaming down her cheeks, as she looked back over one shoulder. LuLa nodded, encouraging her to prostrate herself further.

"I'm sorry, I done you wrong, Clyde Royce." The young adulteress spoke in shattered tones. "I swear, I won't never see him again. You're my husband. I 'preciate all you done. All you do. Please," Veta Sue went on, "please, tell me how I can make this all up to you?"

Although he believed her, that it was just the once, Clyde Royce remained upended by the supposed mockery.

"A deal's a deal," he countered. "I don't want to hear no more about your cuttin' the fool. I won't be back for nary a fortnight, Veta Sue, for I intend to leave you to your figuring. As to what you got in there?" he said, raising his chin in the direction of her belly. "Why, it best be gone. One way, or any other."

Veta Sue looked on open-mouthed, clutching her midsection, pleading with her eyes.

"A deal's a deal," LuLa repeated, swiping one hand against the other. Memaw Veta Sue slunk to the floor, her pale, slender arms wrapped tight around her gravid middle.

"Now then, Clyde Royce. Ain't no sense gettin' worked up over nonesuch," LuLa chimed in. "The girl knows what needs be done. By gum it, she'll get it done."

Though Memaw Veta Sue had never loved Pawpaw as a woman is meant to love her husband, she had, up until that towering and enduring moment, respected him for all he'd done for her and her little Vidalia Lee.

LuLa wasn't about to give up on any of this nor that, especially not the soft security she'd wormed her way into. Her daughter needed to put an end to this pregnancy. One way, or any other.

After Pawpaw left them, LuLa picked up where she had left off.

"You know you got no druthers here, Veta Sue," LuLa Belle Dixon proclaimed, with a quick snort. "Not a one."

MEANWHILE MEMAW VETA SUE'S ILLICIT suitor near buckled under the weight of their dilemma. It had hurt her to bear witness to his lack of fortitude.

"I love you, Veta Sue," he'd murmured, "with all my heart. I have always loved you. And I always will, for whatever that is worth. I will help you," he'd told her, but his voice seemed overfilled only on his own account. "Veta Sue, I have a wife and a reputation. A family name to uphold. You knew all of this. I'm sorry, my dear. We have no choice this time."

All that aside, and by any other indicators, he was a good man. A pillar of the community, if that makes any kind of sense.

VETA SUE WIPED THE TEARS from her cheeks with the back of her hand and smoothed her skirt. "You'll come with me, won't you, Ma?" she asked, unmoving.

"I'll carry you as far's there, but no further," LuLa replied, her eyes blank. "Go get your stuff. That baby ain't gonna up 'n disappear on its own."

LuLa walked with her then still-pregnant daughter, all the while carrying on about the weather and such. When the two reached the fork in the road, LuLa pointed toward the dirt path beyond where the branches parted. "No more lollygaggin' Veta Sue. G'wone now. And tell him to be quick about it."

After a time, Memaw Veta Sue returned to the cabin. Bloodied. Broken. Emptied. The deed for which there is no undoing had been done.

"Good God, Veta Sue," my great granny LuLa clucked at the sight of her daughter. "You look like you been in a fight with the devil and the devil done won. Best warsh up 'fore you scare the buzzards."

CHAPTER TWELVE

MY VIDALIA HAD BEEN SITTING alone in the stands minding her own fourteen-year-old self as usual, just as she'd been taught.

It was on the evening of that first home game of the season, back before they'd even met, that Jamerson Booth "JB" Jackson made note of the lonely but expectant nature of this queer duck. Although it was, even then and even there, against the law to take a child and make her your sweetheart, that is exactly what he'd intended.

His legs, long, lean, and muscular, straddled the half-wall. "This one here's just about ready to be plucked," he chuckled to himself.

JB Jackson knew the type. His swelter would soothe her like a hot water bottle on too tight a muscle, and she'd melt nice 'n easy into his illicit well. This here Little Miss Lonely Heart from No Place Special would cause him no problems. Not now. Not ever.

The solitary figure in section 6, row F, may've had her dreams and expectations, but she didn't have near a pinch of the wherewithall needed in a situation such as this.

I wish I'd been around then to help her think him through better.

ON BREAK FROM HIS MAINTENANCE duties during the halftime, JB brought the awkward freshman an icy-cold Coca Cola. With it, he offered up some inane but friendly conversation.

"Sure's hot," he said. Like a wind gauge, he was figuring just how much he needed adjust his rate of speed.

"Mm-hmm," my Vidalia murmured. She maintained a steady focus on the bench below, keeping her hands crammed into their respective pockets.

"Injun summer, I 'spect," he prodded, placing the sweaty container on the split, grayed plank.

"Mm-hmm." Her head tilted to one side, but still, she did not dare to look him in the eye.

"Peanuts?" he asked, pouring half the Lancer's packet into his own bottle.

"Huh?"

"Peanuts. D'ya want some?"

"Oh. No. No thank you, sir."

"Well then," he said, with a wink. "You enjoy that there Co-Cola. I best be getting back to work—"

"Okay then. Thank you," she responded meekly, her eyes now riveted on a scrappy fire ant as it darted across the worn wooden slab.

"Okay." Smirking, JB shook his head. "Bye, then."

Left again to her own company, my Vidalia's right shoulder raised itself to meet her cheek. She gnawed at one corner of her lower lip. Her blue eyes, hooded by an unruly fringe of auburn bangs, studied the empty row of bleachers from whence he'd appeared.

She took a deep breath and peeked around and behind herself before peeling back the thin wrapper from the white-and-red drinking straw. She shook her head, tsk-tsking at the sight of her own bitten-down nails, then smoothed and folded that paper sleeve and slid it into the chest pocket of her overall jumper, tapping it gently to reassure herself she had not imagined the encounter, and exhaled. Inserting the straw into the bottle of the caramel colored liquid, my Vidalia took one last look around before taking a first sip.

JB leered from behind the bleachers, entertained by the gravity of her every move.

Later that evening she made her way through the crowd, her head down, oblivious to that otherworld where teens in boisterous groupings came together for a bit of post-game revelry before their curfews took hold. My Vidalia did not have a curfew. She'd never needed one.

At 8:57 p.m. JB clocked out after scribbling 10 p.m. onto his timecard and rolled up the sleeves of his tee shirt to be sure his young prey wouldn't miss his tanned, toned biceps. He licked his palm and slicked back his lips outlining the black hole that was this girl's mouth. "I, uh, we don't talk no more."

"Well, now," the clerk went on, with an air of I-told-ya-so. "Ain't that a pity. You and her was alwes thick 's thieves—"

"And you," my Vidalia'd murmured under her breath, "always was a busybody."

"What'd you say, Vida Lee?" the gal asked, one penciled eyebrow now arched much higher than the other.

"Hmm? Oh, nothing. Willa Jean, can you just ring me up? I gotta git—"

"Oh, my. Of course I can do that," snapped the pink-painted lips.

My Vidalia half-smiled and said good-bye, figuring in her head just how much longer of a walk it might be to the Five & Dime across town.

Shortly after the murder of Sunny's older brother, in the middle of that last night in September of 1951 and with no fair warning, Misses Rosie O'Connell Beauregard had uprooted herself and her daughter, Marigold Sun.

My Vidalia and her Sunny never did have a chance for a proper good-bye. For the longest time, from the right tender age of eleven, she had expected Sunny back any day now.

Those two little magnolias had been as much of one another's childhoods as they had been of their own. But such a loss, unforeseen, is not one easily reconciled—most especially for those left behind. And most especially now, when a true friend who knew-it-all would've been just about the best present the universe could offer a lonesome, bewildered adolescent.

THE UNEXPECTED BURSTS OF ATTENTION and out-of-the-blue flirtations from others of the male species, while both pleasing and perplexing to my Vidalia in her new state of full flower, only angered JB. Meanwhile, back at the Kandal cottage, the night air, thick with its own suspicions and unspoken denials, was but a small price to suffer for my Vidalia's new transcendence. This newfound confidence of sorts.

But JB didn't much see it that way. Protecting his own insecurities, he twisted her innocent delights into a noose around her neck, doing all he could to steer her backward, to wonder over her own worth.

My Vidalia attempted to regress. Oh, yes she did. But try as she might, that genie would not, could not, be stuffed back into that bottle.

Not one to be brushed aside—even though that was not her intent toward him—JB trailed her. Why, he once even followed her into the Girl's Room and kicked in the stall door while she was peeing. He'd skulk in the stairwells and lurk behind the partitions. When he thought no one was looking, he'd grab at her, pulling her into him, even as she scurried to and from her classes.

"No time for me no more?" he'd snarl.

"JB, now, you know better 'n that. I'll meet you behind the bleachers after last class. Like always—"

"Says who?"

"Aw, c'mon JB. If I don't make my classes, I cain't keep up my grades. You want me to graduate, don't you?"

"Hell. G'wone then," he said, shooing her off with a flick of his finger.

He watched as she danced backwards down the hall. With the one hand she caught her classroom door just about to shut, with the other she threw him a kiss.

Static filled what air was left between them as a buzzer signaled the start of the new period. JB stood there like a hard plastic, bobble-headed toy. "G'wone then, darlin'," he grumbled. "You keep up them grades. Ain't gone do you no good. No good a'tall."

CHAPTER THIRTEEN

ON THE FIFTEENTH OF FEBRUARY, 1954, a square, shiny box of cherry cordials, and one lone, day-old long-stemmed rose sat perched atop my Vidalia's shared locker.

"For Vidalia Lee Kandal, From a Admirer," the card read.

"Well, hell me." JB reached up, knocking the carefully beribboned treasures to the ground.

Crimson petals spurted like blood. Gooey confections, bite-sized bits of sweet, dark truths, escaped pleated vessels. JB mashed each hand-dipped chocolate into the black-and-gray checkered linoleum with the steel toe of a grass-stained work boot.

As my Vidalia bent in retrieval JB lifted his knee, catching her nose hard. He then snatched the single stem, tore off what remained of the bloom, and squeezed her hand tight around it. Thorns pierced her palm and dug into the pads of her fingers.

"I swear to Jesus, JB," she'd winced. "I don't know who left 'em. I thought they was from you—"

JB twisted her other arm behind her back and yanked upward. "Goddammit-all, girl. Either you're the dumbest jackass alive or you think I am. Well, then. I'll tell you what. It's now or never time, darlin'. A man needs proof. And this time I mean it." With this bit of foreplay, my daddy-to-be had exacted her promise.

She didn't know better than to buy into his ultimatum. After all, his constant state of agitation was her fault. Who the hell did she think she was making him wait on her? What kind of stupid fool did she take him for? And so, even in the absence of any safety net, as her slack rope bridge dangled loose above a murky unknown, my Vidalia went ahead and sidestepped her bindings.

While she did her best to allow him to believe she enjoyed it too, she had never imagined lovemaking would be so physical. Or so quick. All along she'd supposed something, well, different. Something slow and kind. Something sentimental.

BACK AT THE KANDAL CABIN later that evening my Vidalia struggled to explain away her facial swelling and the visible scratches and brush burns on her hands, arms, nose, and cheeks.

"Yes, Maw. If that locker door'd been a snake it woulda bit me. Yet I walked smack into it. I don't know what I was thinking—"

"Sooner or later I expect you'll get your head down out them clouds, child," Memaw Veta Sue declared, giving her daughter the eye.

Memaw added, her voice lightening just the slightest bit, "You walk around with your eyes closed, Vidalia Lee, and you won't never see a thing the world's trying to show to you."

THOSE INTIMATE ENCOUNTERS MY VIDALIA had finally granted JB provided little immunity from his wrath. But she'd not given herself over lightly. There was no turning back now. Nowhere for spoilt goods to look for salvation but to the spoiler.

JB's devotions, though questionable, filled up in her some of those spaces most in need of filling.

In blurred hindsight she reckoned she probably did make things hard for him, just like he said. Though she didn't really understand how, as she most surely hadn't meant to.

She expected she'd just need to try harder. To be more easy to get along with. To not talk so much. To not look at him in ways he didn't want to be looked at. How come she had to be so peapickin' disagreeable, anyways? Why, he had no choice but to knock the sense back into her now and again. He loved her too much to let her act the fool was all.

But try as she might to please him, their lovemaking usually always left him wagging his head. "Pull up them drawers, hussy. I'm done," he'd command loud enough for the couple three trucks down the lane to hear. Why, on the night I was conceived, he'd called my Vidalia a whore of the worst kind.

"Now why'd you have to go and say that, JB?" she'd whispered, glassy eyed.

"Why? *Why?* You disrespected me. That's why," he hissed, just like the yellow-bellied snake that he was.

She tilted her head to one side, still puzzled.

"I seen you with that retard the other day," he went on, in explanation. *"'H-h-hello there, Vidalia. You're looking real lovely t-t-today.'* Jesus H. Christ, Vida Lee! That boy don't even talk right."

"But JB, that ain't no reason to dislike a person. He cain't help how he talks. It ain't his fault. You know who his daddy is, don't you?"

"What're you sayin' now? That I don't know who my daddy is?"

"No, JB. I'm not sayin' nothing of the sort. It's just that, well, I understand why he stammers so. I feel kinda sorry for him, that's all. And he ain't a retard, neither—"

JB jabbed at her midsection with a balled fist. My Vidalia doubled over but held her tears.

"There you go again, goddammit," he'd sputtered. "When you talk stupid like that, it just sets me off. That's all."

⁌⁍

HOW COULD MY VIDALIA HAVE known about this or that? She'd watched closely as Memaw Veta Sue carried out her role without investment, and Pawpaw Clyde Royce, while providing a roof over their heads and food for their table, rarely spoke above an utterance. But never ever had he laid an angry hand to either of them.

CHAPTER FOURTEEN

Plain and simple, Memaw Veta Sue had turned her back on my Vidalia since long before her wedding day. Pawpaw Clyde Royce followed suit, for the most part, obliging his need for some semblance of peace in his own home. Sure, he did this and that behind Memaw's back, but truth be told, he had, as well, neglected my Vidalia in her time of need.

Those early years passed, as years do. How Gamma Gert and her ways aided in Momma's eventual salvation isn't easy to explain, not even for me.

It was there in the back bedroom of Purgatory's farmhouse beyond dried shocks of oats, rickety gates, rusted threshers, and overgrown corn fields, Gamma lobbied, pretty much single-handedly for my momma's redemption.

Since my presentment, as much as she was able, my Vidalia, my momma, had come to terms with both the restrictions imposed by my nature and those parameters within which I needed to operate. For the most part she no longer acknowledged our reality to others, she just plodded on to where she needed to get to next. Meanwhile, Gamma Gert, our unlikely nurturer for more reasons than meet the eye, rested assured that one of these days her boy was "gone turn hisself around and surprise near ever'body."

"Well then," Gamma'd go on, "Don't you worry about the horse gone blind, Vida Lee." Neither Momma nor I had any idea what that meant, but as it seemed a favorite of Gamma's sayings, out of a respect for her and her generosities, we never did question it.

With time, my momma managed most day-to-day chores on her own: personal hygiene, laundry, some housekeeping, cooking, and many other such natural events. And when Gamma Gert suggested some kinds of things just aren't meant for public display, Momma took it to heart. Oh, she and I still communicated back and forth, but only anymore in private and so that no one else might see or hear. There were times of late, she might even go on ahead to certain places without me.

I knew this was all part of the process and I didn't much mind her taking leave of me for a spell now and then. In a way, it was a kind of relief. But still, she fretted over our times apart. I reckon she might've been afraid I'd up and disappear during her brief absences. I wished she'd understood I wasn't going to do that. Not while she still needed me.

And she never spoke of me to others anymore either, suspecting it might be easier on those folk around her to believe she reckoned whatever it was they reckoned.

"Well now. How you doin' these days, Vida Lee?"

"Why, I'm finer than a peacock's feathers. Thank you for asking, ma'am. And how are *you* doin' these days?" Pretty soon, most folks accepted whatever it was she put out there for their consideration.

Most, that is, except Gamma Gert's no-nonsense posse who overall remained leery and disbelieving. Even so, those Wild Women of God reassured, "Don't you fret none, Vida Lee," and, "You got years of plenty ahead of you, dear child."

Of course, time to time, Momma lost her footing, especially when one or the other of her next, new pregnancies came undone. But I was usually always there to break her fall from grace. Either that, or Gamma Gert would drop everything else and reach deep down into her big bag of excuses, managing to get her hands on a good enough one, every single time.

ALONG WITH MOMMA'S RESURRECTION OF sorts, came a condition of an uncertain capacity. "Disassociative behavior," was what Doc had pegged it. "Seems our Vidalia has begun examining her sorrow as an observer rather than a participant." As if she'd been fretting over some person other than her own self.

"Why, at first, the poor girl, she didn't know what to do," Momma'd explained to him during one visit. "But by and by, she filled the sink, sure to test the water first with her elbow. That tiny body was so cold," she hushed, shaking her head. "And after she warshed it good 'n clean, the girl wrapped it in the little pink blanket she'd knitted using unraveled hand-me-downs and leftover scraps of yarns.

"She laid the tiny package into a carved oak box. It was a small box—just two feet long by one foot wide, and only eight inches deep—but it was sturdy.

"Then the girl set the crate to rest on a mound of red dirt under a sorely stooped willow. A posy of fresh cut forget-me-nots sat aside a newly dug hole of the exact width and height, there, just beyond the cemetery gate. Wasn't no stone, yet. She'd save up for that, by and by."

Unbeknownst to anyone else, especially Memaw Veta Sue, Pawpaw Clyde Royce had purchased the necessary materials for the small pine box. By moonlight, and with the greatest of care, he'd assembled the miniature casket, planing and sanding each wooden surface until it was as smooth as sea glass. Dovetailed corners intersected without contest, as fingers clasped in prayer. And he made sure the cover closed just right but not too tight over its base.

CHAPTER FIFTEEN

ONE WHOLE HALF DECADE HAD passed since my coming and by then, Momma had more than properly revised her actions. On a regular basis she displayed a demeanor cautious and relegated as we went about our business like any other mother and spirit child.

For all outward appearances, "Our Vidalia has made significant progress," Doctor Feldman liked to boast.

"Doc's got more degrees than a thermometer," Gamma Gert countered to herself. "But he ain't got a whole lot of sense if he thinks he can put out the fires of hell with a squirt gun."

AFTER MOMMA'S FEIGNED RENEWAL, THREE misguided pregnancies had made fair enough effort. As it turned out, not one of them had grit enough to secure a stronghold in light of JB's ongoing and volatile protests.

"Dang, woman," he'd scold her. "What makes you think you c'take care of a child anyways? You cain't take right proper care of your own self, much less a baby."

I wished I could've put him in his place. I wished I could've told him, "Oh yes she can too. And if you just stay clean away from her, then it won't be no issue!" But of course, I couldn't do that.

"I been trying. I been trying real hard, JB." Momma stared down at the floor, avoiding his glare.

"Shee-it," he said, tugging hard on one earlobe.

"I'll do better. I promise—"

"Just how simple are you, girl? What part of no d'you not get, Vida Lee?"

"Please, JB, please hear me out. I reckon maybe if I—"

"Lookit here, dummy," he said, his lips pursed. "If God wanted you to have a kid, don't you think you'd have at least one by now?"

We had learned all about rhetorical questions in those grammar books Miss Dandy loaned Momma back before our eviction. She knew enough not to answer.

JB's nostrils widened. He dipped his head, making his neck all but disappear, and locked eyes with hers. A raging bull undoing his shirt buttons.

As he loomed in, her eyes probed his face. *But for what?* I wondered. Some faded ideal of possibility? Or respite? Hadn't her hero impaled himself one time too many already on the pitchfork of his own misdoings? Once again, she groped for support where there was none. I could have explained this to her, but again, that was not the nature of my mission.

"What the hell," he scoffed, his fist poised midair.

"Please—" she begged, her one arm raised as if blocking a blinding light.

Fragrant and plump, pea-sized beads pooled on her forehead.

JB unbuckled his belt, unsnapped his waistband, and unzipped his Levis using only one hand. The other, fist unfurled, rested heavy on her bruised shoulder. Before long, gravity took over and his drawers ended up bunched around his ankles. He smirked, looking down at himself and back at her face as he forced his way into her.

Momma tried not to, but she cried out anyways.

"Dammit, girl. Shut the fuck up. Y'already got people thinking I'm married to a crazy." Framed by the door whose job it was to separate Gamma Gert's pantry from their back bedroom, he banged away at her.

One. Two. Three. *Four.*

"I don't mean t—" she whimpered. A dented can of tomatoes tumbled off a shelf and hit the floor slats with a *p-p-ping*, rolling itself out of harm's way and into the farmhouse's kitchen until it hit the leg of Gamma Gert's pie safe.

"I got my rights!" he said in a voice higher-pitched, while carrying out his mode of husbandly license.

"I know. I'm sorry, JB, but—" Momma faltered under his weight like a rag doll whose neck couldn't support her own head.

Five. *Six.*

Momma's face, wedged between his sweaty chest and her own bruised right shoulder, dropped its gaze to the floorboards below. Rushing haphazard amid hot flesh and bodily fluids a backlog of tears broke free, dissolving the remnants of any lines by now so badly blurred.

"Oh Lord. Dear God. No. Please. Not again," she whimpered. Spent, Momma stared down at the fresh crimson-brown clots spotting the knotty planks below.

⟵⟶

AS FAR AS I COULD reckon, it wasn't a bad thing for her to have such strong wants. But like her childhood friend Sunny Beauregard had tried explaining to her, over and over again, wantin' ain't gettin'—which was exactly what Momma was coming around to realize, slowly but surely. And for as bitter a pill such a loss is to abide, and even though her stability did wander some during this period, she never, not once, neglected me.

Nourished by her generosity, comforted by her kindness, and cradled in her boundless love, my spirit thrived. I looked forward to the day she might do the same for her own self.

"I love you, Cieli Mae. You know how much I love you, child?" Momma whispered, looking like she might be about to cry all over again. "It's just that you always seem to know more than you're sayin'. To know so much more than me. And well, that just ain't how it's s'pposed to be is all."

"Oh, Momma. Maybe you don't yet know what all you do know? Maybe you just need listen closer to your own spirit?"

Some things are how they're supposed to be. But, some things take time.

CHAPTER SIXTEEN

THOSE EARLY PREGNANCIES HAD TOOK root all right, but they'd come undone soon into their growing seasons. And for as quick and as hard as each of those dreams came unraveled Gamma Gert stood fast, gathering up the loosed threads.

According to Gamma, "Folk alwes do worst by them they love most. Hell. There's even a song about it!" And while she'd go about tending to Momma and tidying up after another one of her boy's ragings, she'd perform her version of a sing-along, dancing around her Victrola, and swiping away at her own tears as the forty-five spun 'round and 'round, getting caught here and there, or skidding some over the velvet tones of its crooners where the grooves had been so sorely worn down.

"Now then, baby girl," Momma asked of me during a private moment following one of Gamma's indulgences. "Does that make any kind of sense? That folk do worst by them they love most?"

"Well, now. Does it?" I replied. "I mean, does it make any kind of sense to you?"

"I reckon, Cieli Mae, there's times—not always mind you—but there's times a person will hurt another person just cause, well, just cause they suppose somethin'."

Rather than express an opinion to which I was not entitled, or make some point for which she was not ready, I posed another question.

"What d'you mean by that, Momma?"

"Like, a man supposes he cain't never get enough."

"Enough for what?"

"To fill the empty," Momma said.

"The what?"

"The empty." Momma had lowered her voice to barely a whisper though there was no one in sight.

"The what?" I asked again.

"The empty," she said, loud and clear.

I wasn't sure where she was headed with this, so I let her have a minute to settle herself. To think it through.

"And so," she continued after a few seconds, "he puts a lid on it."

"On the empty?"

"On the empty."

"But why would a person do that?"

"'Cause, he's afraid."

"Afraid of what?"

"I'm not sure of what, exactly," she said, still contemplating. "Of the empty, I reckon. And maybe so's what little he's already got tucked inside there don't get out."

"Now, Momma. S'that make any kind of sense to you?" I posed.

"Folk don't always make sense, Cieli Mae. Sometimes it seems a person cain't be hurt by nothing, then in the end turns out he's more fragile than a pane of glass that ain't been tempered."

But—and I'm not saying it's right, mind you—I suspect Momma's cockamamie theory might explain how a person would act in such a way, on purpose. And I reckon that person   even understand how acting in such a way would bring   what he's most scared of.

TIME TO TIME, GAMMA GERT'S Wild Women of God arranged outings into downtown Atlanta where they'd hunt and gather up some of the harder to find home goods, and other canning and knitting supplies.

Those women also enjoyed events such as parades, church services, street fairs, and when the timing was right, listening in on the Peachtree Women's Auxiliary monthly meetings. Why, every so often, those loose-lipped prayer warriors even managed to take in a concert or a picture show at the Loew's Grand Theatre.

The Wild Women always tried to include Momma in their junkets, facilitating, in their own way, a less bumpy reentry for her into a world progressed without her input.

By the time a measure of *what is* grabbed a stronger hold of her, so did a pregnancy finally allowed to reach fruition.

"Well, glory be! There's two!" Gamma Gert had yelped as the second head presented. It was a good thing Doc Feldman had quick reflexes on this, my Vidalia's first real live birth. It didn't hurt any that Nurse Lana Joy had insisted on assisting even though Sundays were her only days off.

Momma was just about halfway between twenty and twenty-one years of age when she'd safely birthed our first set of twins, packed tight and wound around one another like one long, soft pretzel braid. Pawpaw Clyde Royce, and even the querulous Memaw Veta Sue had joined forces with Gamma Gert and Doc Feldman and his nurse, Lana Joy, to ensure those critters' favorable passage.

Thank the Lord for small favors, during such time, JB was nowhere to be found.

"Today, we been doubly blessed," Momma hushed to me after the others had dispersed. "Look at them babies, all pink and prickly. All soft and warm. Listen to them holler, Cieli Mae. I declare, I ain't never seen nor heard such a wonder."

Awed and wearied, she smiled that smile I hadn't seen for some time, and it soothed my spirit like nothing else in this world. "Oh, yes. I see them boys, Momma. And I hear them," I whispered back.

"I wish they could see and hear you too, baby girl," she'd said, teary-eyed.

"I know you do, Momma."

Near three days later, JB resurfaced smelling of rot-gut and piss. Momma had just placed those pink, naked babies gently side-by-side into a cleared-out dresser drawer, freshly plumped with straw and an old blanket, and newly lined with one of Gamma Gert's worn cotton housedresses.

"Where you been, JB?"

"Goddammit Vida Lee. Where I been ain't none o' your business!"

"I birthed you a son while you were gone. Two, in fact. Two strong, healthy boys. Come see."

"Christ, woman!" JB yelled. "I'm giving you fair warning this time so don't say I didn't. I got more on my mind than you and your damn babies. Now, make yourself useful and get me somethin' to drink."

"Maybe you done had enough to drink," Momma suggested, her hands twisting around each other like loose ribbons in a drawer. "Please, JB, the babies been waiting on meeting their daddy," she said, her voice rising, gaining a strength.

Now, it wasn't like Momma to push her luck in this way. But then again, ever since the live births, something strong and otherworldly had taken ahold of her, and it wasn't me, nor any of my doing. Why, she just wasn't her old self anymore. Like somehow, all of a sudden, she had forgot to be as scared.

"That's enough, woman!" JB snarled. "I ain't in no mood—"

"But them's your sons."

Holding onto his own left arm, he looked at her like the top of his head was about to come off. "Jesus H. Christ. You just don't know when to shuddup do you?"

"But JB—"

I guess he'd had enough cause he hauled off and smacked her so hard, she hit the wall and bounced back before he struck her again.

"Momma? What're you doing!" I whisper-shouted. "Don't you think it best if you just leave him be?" She didn't hear me for the ringing in her ears.

Oh, it was not as bad a beating as it was with me, and not nearly as bad as just before each of those three past misbirths, but it was bad enough to loosen a few of Doc's fine stitches.

Still, somehow, she'd managed to hold onto her sureness, and full of her own hopes, to convince JB she understood how hard this all must be on him. And that she knew just what he was going through, worrying over how he was gonna provide for them all in the best ways possible, and how this kind of thing weighs heavy on a man's spirit. That she was sorry for pestering after him so. And that she'd leave him be so he could do his figuring in peace. And maybe after a nice nap, he might want to take a look at his new sons. But if he still wasn't yet ready, well, she reckoned, that'd be okay too. All good things take their own course, she'd said. In the meantime she figured it might be best if she got them babies fed before starting in on his supper.

It was not my place to suggest she should be doing anything

otherwise, so I trained my thoughts on some back-wondering over how any being in their right mind could think it was all right to hurt the ones they were supposed to love best.

"Better me than them," she whispered to me over JB's snorts and snores as she lifted her bruised chin in the direction of the twins.

While he rested his curdled, surly old self, Gamma returned home from her prayer meeting. She placed her Bible in its rightful station atop the icebox and made mental note of Momma at the sink peeling potatoes, the new bruise below her lower lip, and the babies in their drawer at her feet. That their kitchen table was still on its side with only two of the three aluminum kitchen chairs righted was not lost on Gamma Gert.

"My boy's home?" she chirped. Another one of those rhetorical questions.

Momma nodded and Gamma disappeared behind the damaged wooden door panel that separated the two rooms.

Several minutes later Gamma reappeared with JB in tow.

"Lookit here," he said, waggling a finger at Momma. "You know I wouldn't never hurt you without no good reason, Vida Lee." Gamma Gert's stare just about bore a hole in his skull. "You know how sorry I am, don't you?" he said to Momma, sending a so-there look in his mama's direction.

I didn't understand how it was that Momma'd had the fortitude to bring those two screaming rascals, twisted and kicking, into this world, but she'd not yet found the strength to not believe in him.

Gamma Gert didn't help matters any, what with her prompts and her own hefty sides of excuses always at the ready, "You cain't sew buttons on ice cream, Vida Lee. No more 'n you can blame a pig with a docked tail for being ornery. Blame the dang moonshine runners. Blame them whores down at Picayune's. Hell. Blame that worthless sumbitch done left me 'n my baby on the side of the road!"

Gamma protested too much. I reckon she must have been trying just as hard to convince her own self as any other.

CHAPTER SEVENTEEN

THAT THERE WAS ONE PRIME wrongdoer and the root of most all our problems was an open secret. JB's sins, considerable and always by design.

Momma had reckoned against reality how our first set of twins might grant her a fresh start. A chance to get things right.

In many ways I reckon the double birth made good sense. After all, a roller coaster ride with its peaks and valleys, dips and spills, is more easily suffered when there's a partner strapped in alongside. Some other being to lean upon. To hang onto. A brace. Most times, a life companion seems a good thing.

Over those nine months prior to Jamerson and Booth's emergence, JB had gained some padding around his middle and lost a slice of his swagger, along with a bit of his hair. And then, seeing how this particular incubation was pretty near a done deal, in his own way, he needed to be sure Momma still knew who was boss. "Best be a boy in there Vida Lee," he'd threatened. "The little shit will take my name and wear it proud."

At the mention of a given name, she had started in gnawing at her fingernails. "Oh my stars. But what if?" she'd whispered to Gamma, setting aside her on the front porch swing.

Gamma shook her head, "You cain't take ever'thing so personal, Vidalia."

"But, what if this baby turns out a girl?" Momma'd worried aloud, dropping her gaze to her belly.

"Now, Vida Lee. Don't be pickin' nits at a time like this," Gamma Gert had said back, eyeing her daughter-in-law sideways. Gamma's mouth made a hard line, but her tone came across more protective than mean-spirited.

"Maybe Gamma's right this time, Momma?" I'd offered into her other ear.

My momma smiled a soft smile, then. Nodding, she closed her eyes and began rubbing her tummy. One long, lone tear streaked her cheek. On that day she taught me something I didn't already know: There's such a thing as happy tears. Why, in all my days, I'd never even suspected such.

Anyways and like I said, the first set of twins took us by pleasant surprise. For as excited as we all were though for those two healthy beanpoles, we'd have been just as happy with one. For a while JB bumbled about, even more confounded than usual. "Now what?" he shouted. "There's two of 'em? I only got one name, for chrissake."

After three weeks and five days, prompted by Gamma, he came up with a solution all on his own. That those two firstborn, nameless cubs would just have to share their glorious birthright.

The family of four, plus Gamma, burst into the Willin Town Hall to amend the birth certificates formerly titling the twins Jackson Boy Number One and Jackson Boy Number Two.

From the get-go, the eldest, Jamerson—Baby James, as Momma and I called him in private—came across as spit smart. Instinctive, impulsive, and outgoing. He'd be reading the big words on the cover of a cereal box before he turned five.

Booth had met the light of day bearing just as many smarts but with a more reserved and observant nature. Baby James laid a claim to the leadership position, having emerged a full thirty seconds sooner, but truth be told, Booth—our little Bootie—would be the one who'd keep them both out of trouble.

Although my first pair of brothers was named after their daddy, the juxtaposition ended there. Baby James and Bootie always were, both of them, their momma's boys. Sweet-natured and even-tempered with pale, speckled skin that blushed in the sun. Their hair, though a faded yellow like their daddy's, had come in all wild and wispy, like hers. And although both sets of eyes started out a deep, deep cocoa bronze, by the fifth day they'd turned.

"Well now, this is highly unusual," Doc commented. "In my experience most babies' eyes start out blue, then darken as time goes by."

"It's a miracle," Momma declared, looking down at her now blue-eyed babes.

⁓

NOT LONG AFTER BIRTHING THOSE first two, Momma found herself, once again, in a family way. Gamma Gert skittered around, beside herself with joy. And though not near enough time had passed for Doc Feldman's liking, he'd intimated things looked promising as far as another "full-term gestational period."

Now tired all the time, JB bore no interest beyond his one basic requirement, "I'm naming this one after my pa." Believe you me, only The Good Lord Above might understand the reasoning behind that dictum, and maybe not even Him.

JB knew all about how his daddy had left him and Gertrude Kaye. And so did most everybody in town.

Just another one of those open secrets.

"That there was to 'a been my honeymoon," Gamma began. "Clayton Booth even gave me a *ci*-gar box tied with string for a marriage present. Made me swear to Jesus I woudn't open it til after we got to where we was gone. You wanna know what was inside that *ci*-gar box? One photograph of his own self gussied up and grinnin' like a frog. And two hundret and fifty-nine one dollar bills all wrapped up in a yellow rubber band like a roll of toilet tissue. And a note scratched out on a old matchbook cover: 'For the kid.' Now, don't that just beat all? My only wedding gift, and it wasn't even for me."

There, in Purgatory's snug farmhouse kitchen, smelling of liquor and lavendar, Gamma spilled her heart over a cup of corn whiskey to anyone who'd set a spell. A crackled oilcloth hid samples of JB's earliest handiwork. The unnatural dings and dents had been forced upon that poor tabletop with his bare knuckles. A section of blackened wood and blistered paint—remnants of the night Gamma forgot to remind her nine-year-old son she might'nt be home in time to make him supper—sat aside the many scuffs and scars he'd carved into the wood with his regulation army knife.

"I hadn't never been nowhere 'cept Purgatory, and even though I was still tore up from the birthin'," she'd go on, "I was tickled fancy just being took on a trip to somewhere else. But no sense crying over spilt milk now then, is there?" Gamma sighed collecting herself. "Cain't unring a bell what's been rung."

Out of sight, wedged between a dumpster and an alligator fence behind the mechanic's garage, baby JB nursed hungrily at his young momma's teat. Meanwhile, Clayton B. Jackson topped off the gas tank of his truck and hightailed it out from that Sinclair filling station, leaving those two haplessly bound souls behind.

Momma and I suspected Gamma's story wasn't near as bad as it might've been had Clayton Booth Jackson stayed put, but out of respect for Gamma, we kept that conjecture to ourselves. This was Gamma's story. All she wanted was for someone to hear it. No more, no less. In an equal blend of sympathy and support, Momma tsk-tsked over the sorrowful nature of the predicament as put forth.

It near broke her heart to consider any blameless child to be named for the likes of that no-count.

"But there don't seem nothing I can do about it," she'd whispered to me. "I reckon I ain't got no choice?" Now, I expected this was just another variation on that rhetorical theme. One more of those kinds of questions folks ask when they're feeling unsure but not because they want an answer. And although I knew my place, I have to say, figuratively speaking of course, my tongue was getting mighty sore from being bit down upon so hard and so often.

Still unemployed, JB had otherwise been on his own brand of blue-ribbon behavior through Momma's second, and final, pregnancy of plenty. I reckon it had something to do with knowing all eyes from Willin County to Coggins—including those of Memaw Veta Sue, Pawpaw Clyde Royce, Doc Feldman, and Sheriff Truith—were set upon him.

Even Gamma Gert noticed now how her boy had grown a complacency, wearying mighty easy these days. Nevertheless, when called upon, he could still pass a mighty first lick.

"I 'spect there's weather on the way. A real duck drowder," Gamma mentioned upon her return from the grocery.

"What the—" JB grumbled. More and more of late he reminded me of one of those scale insects we'd come to read about who wouldn't move from their feeding spot, so their legs just withered away. He'd found his post on the old couch and wasn't about to give it up.

"Sky's all clabbered up. And my thumb aches like a sumbitch," Gamma persisted.

"Hmmpf," JB mumbled, unimpressed. He turned, rolling onto his other side.

"Why, it might be nice if you'd haul yourself upright. Take them babies outdoors some," Gamma suggested, as if the idea had, just now, smacked her upside her head.

"Mind your business, Ma."

"You been lookin' kinda pale is all, son. Gray, awmost. And 'sides, this here thumb—"

"Ma!"

"Ain't never wrong—"

"Goddammit!" JB yelled so loud he woke both Baby James and Bootie, who in turn started in on their own screaming match.

"Praise Jesus," Gamma cried out. "The color just come back to your face!"

"For chrissake. A body cain't get no rest 'round here. Leave me be! And while you're at it, take that damn thumb of yours and shove it up your ass."

⟿

COME THE BIRTH DATE OF our second set of twins, JB had been nowhere in sight. When he finally heard the news, you'd have thought it was him in labor those thirty-seven hours.

"What the hell," he growled, slowly lifting his head from the bar counter. He'd been coming out of one stupor and was well on his way to another.

Brimley Curtis-Mahoney slapped JB on the back and almost knocked him from his perch atop the tipsy Pourhouse barstool. Pat Picayune, on a break from his duties as proprietor of Picayune's Pub, just down the road a piece, bought a round of suds for all.

"I reckon I best get the bitch spayed 'fore she goes and gets herself knocked up again," JB said, preening boldly, like the drunken peacock he was.

Lacking in even basic creativity, he was, once again, stumped. After all, by now he'd used up his own supply of role models. The only other male relative he knew of was Gamma's pa, Grady Bo—and JB was damned sure he wasn't naming one of his after him.

CHAPTER EIGHTEEN

ALL TOLD, FOUR BABY BOYS had managed soft landings just months beyond Momma's twenty-third birthday.

"I know folks wonder about me, Cieli Mae," she whispered, contemplating with awe, our second set of twins. My momma hunched over the blanketed drawer now, once again, chock-full of baby boy. She let out a sigh, "And rightly so, I guess."

"Shucks," I said back, slipping a forcefulness into my words. "You know you're stronger than them all think you are. You know that, don't you?"

Now, it wasn't like I had told her anything or was trying to put new thoughts into her head. That would've been against the rules.

Straightening herself to full height, Momma looked around that back room, taking in the stacks of cloth diapers and other hand-me-downs which she herself had scrubbed, mended, and folded. The piles sat neatly atop of her and JB's quilt-covered pallet. One stormy night, after a few nips of corn whiskey, during another of her boy's extended absences, Gamma Gert up and stripped the coverlet from her own bed in order to cozy things up for her long-suffering daughter-in-law. Those baby items had been an extra kindness, courtesy of the Wild Women.

Momma placed her hands on her slightly broadened but still slim hips. She smiled back at me, nodding. "Well now, baby girl. I expect I do know that."

As I been saying, that there was just another one of those things of which she, from time to time, needed to be reminded.

Between us, with all circumstances considered and accounted for, she did fine.

When she forgot her good sense, I refreshed her memory. That's all.

I don't mind saying right here and right now, it was hard to fathom just how she brought about what all she did for the boys in her near-perpetual state of dog-tiredness.

Wanting to provide Gamma a kind of a break, my momma had taken to managing a portion of the household. Aside from her being laid low time to time, by a bad case of the vapors and suffering one of her spells, Momma did it all with grace and gumption. I watched in amazement as she flitted to and fro with a flexible determination. Her might and quiet durability being outdone only by her sense of good will toward all.

I, on the other hand, did not possess that same let-bygones-be trait and found it near impossible to make light of a situation such as ours. Oh, I had known all about this 'n that in plenty of time, and maybe I'd picked my Vidalia for just those reasons, but irregardless and all things heeded, I found my spirit unable to seek out humor or to believe in others as easily as she did.

To her credit, our little colony ran about as smoothly as could've been expected. Except, that is, when she came undone. Upended, by one of her spells.

Between our four babies' non-schedules and JB's helter-skeltered husbandly visits, Momma did not get to sleep much or with any regularity. That all led to those times where her reasoning clouded up and her sensibilities teetered between the there and then, and the here and now.

During those times she might forget where she placed the babies. Or that they needed tending. Or that supper ought be started if Gamma was out at prayer group. Things such as that. But it was all right because I was always on hand to bring Momma back on course.

And they passed, as spells are wont to do.

If she dared be asleep when JB staggered in, he'd squeal and poke at her. "Whay-ell. What we got here?" Oaring her with a broom, he'd tip her to one side as if she were an opossum needing to be awakened for a fight. Sometimes he used the broomcorn grass end, but most times the hard wooden stick handle was his prod of choice. Not an easy sight to bear witness to, even with all I knew. To my shame, there were times even I turned away.

Still, when she needed it most, Momma'd kept her command.

With nothing other than her own sense of mastery, she'd won us *The Wonderful World of Insects* at the Twenty-Third Annual Welcome Elementary School Fair. It was our first brand-new reader ever.

"Oh, Momma. Lookie there," I had suggested with a shy slyness. "Just look at that booth. Look at all them fancy books!" When she bent down to adjust the buckle on her shoe, I added, "I wonder if you could win us one?"

She looked quick from the dartboard to the prize shelves and back again to the dartboard, her eyes beaming like the headlights on a spanking-new Cadillac. Grabbing up her red pleather change purse, a birthday gift from Gamma Gert, she fished out a lone dime from amongst fuzz, buttons, and safety pins, and handed that coin over to Tildie Ann Partridge Jones, a former classmate.

Tildie Ann scrunched up her face as if she smelled burnt catfish, accepting the coin with pinched fingers. Those two had never been friends.

Momma tossed off Tildie's appraisal as a quirk of one who'd never worn a hand-me-down, considered her mark but briefly, and fired the rubber-tipped dart gun, hitting her target smack in the middle of the bull's eye.

Given a clear shot, my momma never missed her intention.

She was the first contestant that afternoon to land dead center. Near everybody on hand, except Tildie Ann of course, stopped what they were doing to whoop and whistle. With her eyes brighter than the light from a naked bulb and her full lips turned up in a big smile, Momma's cheeks pinked. She'd never appeared more pretty or righteous.

A fierce longing surged within. I fought hard against my urge to yell into the crowd, "That's my momma!" but I don't rightly know why because even if I had, no one would have heard me.

Awarded her choice of anything at all on that top shelf, and—even though she would have liked the shiny, new aluminum washboard, as ours was a bit rusted and sorely misshapen having been run over "on accident" by JB's back tires—with her fingers now trembling, she pointed to it. The big book with the hard, shiny cover and the golden trim:

The Wonderful World of Insects.

Within its slick pages we'd come to learn how each and every insect, each and every one of those pesky little critters, though considered beyond lowly in most circles, had their own worth and capabilities. Why, even the ordinary ant, Momma read aloud that evening, has the ability to carry effects heavier than itself. And some ants have wings. But for some reason, those females lose theirs after mating.

"Every last one of God's creatures has a story needs telling," Momma said. "With the most of us just wandering 'round, day after day, searching for some soul kind enough to listen."

"WE SHALL ASSUME," DOCTOR LEWIS Feldman had begun during another one of our unscheduled emergency calls to his office. Under pretense the good doc turned to inspect his library, adjusting his spectacles and rearranging those few volumes out of alphabetical order.

White metal cabinets lined three of his office walls. Along the fourth, a portly rolltop desk reigned supreme, flanked on either side by rich mahogany built-ins. The floor-to-ceiling shelving supported hundreds of medical books and one lone picture frame whose photograph had been long since removed.

A pungent bouquet of rubbing alcohol, pine-scented Lysol, and Vicks VapoRub seasoned the air as a timed metronome imposed a mild tempo. Atop his work surface, amid periodicals and prescription pads, a Bayer aspirin bottle, caught by surprise, lay on its side. Its contents had spilled from their glass container and rolled across the tabletop to an untimely demise, accidentally crushed into the fibers of the carpeted floor beneath his desk.

"As I was saying," he continued, having thoughtfully regrouped. "We shall assume the abundance of disproportionate demands, and the lack of proper tools needed to deal with such, have facilitated a disconnect. This detachment might manifest in a variety of ways."

In his final analysis, Doc declared Momma's most recent spells due to a form of nervous exhaustion.

He did not reference the puce-colored bruise on her temple. Or the purple one on her forearm. He did not mention JB either, not by name, anyways. "The children," he noted with a tentative display of satisfaction, "show no signs of neglect and for the most part are progressing well ahead of the norm."

The doctor hereby granted Momma what she wanted at the expense of what she needed. I wondered, *Did he really reckon this the way to do no harm?*

OFTEN DURING THOSE GROWING YEARS, Doc house-called upon Purgatory, always pretending he was passing by on his way to or from somewhere else.

"Why, hello, Gert. How are we doing, today?" he'd ask politely. "I was just—"

"Why, bless your fool heart, Doc," Gamma'd respond with a wink. "I'm fair to middlin'. And the boys? Them boys're just about as happy as hogs in sunshine. C'mon in and have a look-see. Can I bring you a cup o' coffee? It's already blowed 'n saucered."

MOST TIMES, AS ON THE very day of Momma's more recent spells, we'd all just show up on the doctor's front stoop at Number Two Hospital Way. Nevertheless, and as always, Nurse Lana Joy welcomed us as if we'd arrived but the teensiest bit early for a scheduled, long-standing appointment.

Since before the twins, and whenever Momma found herself newly pregnant or beaten down—as she usually always was at least one of those two—at the very sight of her, Doc's facial muscles tightened into hard aches. He wasted no time grabbing up whatever medical publication lay within reach and started flipping pages. He'd pace the room in circles around my momma, my Vidalia , supposing interest in anything but her. This mode of the jitters allowed his eyes a chance to look away without actually turning his back on her.

But here's the thing I learned about pacing in circles: No matter where you stop, the center is always the same.

Some times it took longer than other times, but eventually the good doctor's bedside manner prevailed. He would set Momma's splints or stitch her back up, and then he would kindly reassure. Because that's what she wanted. And because, at the time, that was all he had to give her.

ONCE THE BOYS ENTERED OUR world and his, Doc Feldman no longer needed fake his distraction. After tending to Momma first, he'd check them all out as well. Four little throats and four little noses and four little sets of eyes and ears. After pronouncing one after the other of them, "A fine specimen!" he'd go on, "These four are the handsomest, healthiest, smartest youngsters I've seen in a long while." Then, oddly and excitedly, he would summon Lana Joy.

"Nurse, would you mind helping Misses Jackson gather her tribe? And please don't forget those few items we put aside for her and the boys."

Well now, that angel of mercy loaded our buggy up to its hilt! In addition to my brothers, there were vitamin pills and analgesics for Momma, a fresh bottle of either iodine or mercurochrome, and one dozen St. Joseph's baby aspirins in a small, mustard-yellow envelope marked In Case of Fever. Oh, and always there'd be a peck of clean bandages prebundled in crisp, white paper wraps.

Along with the bushel's worth of first-aid supplies, there would always be at least one large carton of powdered milk, a box of sugar or oatmeal raisin cookies, canned meats, cheeses, and a valerian root. Fresh okra, a green tomato, a few peaches or plums, and whatever other goodies might've been sitting around in the Doc's candy dish, cupboards, or refrigerator, capped off our booty.

I wondered how Doc ever had anything to eat or whether he got any sleep for himself if he fretted over all of his patients the way he did over us.

We'd been making our way through air as thick as sorghum syrup, and over dry red dirt and parched pokeweed, and on to Gamma Gert's. "Why do you 'spose Doc does all that? For us, I mean?" I asked.

"Well, now." Momma stopped pushing the overstuffed cart, granting herself but one moment before releasing her grip. With the back of her left hand, she brushed one sticky copper-colored tendril, then another, from her damp forehead. Next, using the bib of her smock, she wiped both palms dry and reattached herself to the buggy's handle.

"I reckon he's just tryin' to do what's right, but that don't mean he is," she said, shaking her head. "Ain't nothing always right, Cieli Mae."

I did my personal best to agree without seeming confused.

Momma didn't talk much after that. Not to me and not to the boys. Her mind was turning something over, and I wondered if it might have been Doctor Feldman's previous offer. I hoped so. He wanted to help her but she needed to tell him the truth about what'd happened, even from way back then on the eve of my deliverance.

If only that new, fretful neighbor had come forth. If only she or Miss Pickett Dandy had named JB the missing link. Sheriff Truith would've had to take him in. Would've had to make him stay away.

As it was, the only true witnesses had feared for their own safety. After all, I reckoned it wasn't *their* job to look out for Momma's best interests, now was it.

WITHIN MINUTES OF ONE OF our more hasty departures, with Momma put back together almost good as new, the compassionate team at Number Two Hospital Way folded themselves back into their own more familiar patterns. Nurse Lana Joy busied herself out front while Doc Feldman purged his desk, trying to clear his head of those raggedy ends our visits often left loosened. Even the soft ticking in the background scorched his ears in rebuke.

I understood how he might reason that, all along, he'd only been giving Momma what she wanted. That he supposed it in her best interest to have other renderings put forth. When all was said that could be said, maybe he and I weren't so different in our constraints after all.

No matter how brazen, loud, or ugly a truth might be, even up close, a person with her ears plugged and both eyes squeezed shut can't salute it.

Doc Feldman, long accustomed to the guarding of secrets, was well versed in the art of face-saving and proved a reliable and most trustworthy co-conspirator. Truth be told, he seemed grateful to my Vidalia for allowing him the dubious honor.

Nurse Lana Joy finished tidying the greeting area and headed for the

Office & Examining Room. Disinfectant in hand, she did a quick knock-knock. She turned the glass knob slowly and poked her head inside. A deflated white coat slouched over the desktop, its head resting upon crisscrossed arms, spent and bent, like a used safety match still stuck to its cardboard folder.

The refilled spray bottle slipped from her grip landing with a soft *spfft.* "Gracious light!" she gasped, her gaze flitting around the room. "Doc . . . Doctor Feldman? Are you all right?"

The figure inhaled deeply, and the white coat swelled back to life.

"I'm fine," he'd said, wearing a dazed look. "I just needed a moment to collect myself."

"I'm sorry to've intruded," Lana Joy apologized, stooping to grab up the spray bottle. "I was only trying to—"

The doctor waved her off, "No need for you to be sorry, my dear."

"Those boys look good 'n hardy," she offered.

"Yes. The boys look well," he accepted.

"Doc? Is there anything I can—"

"Why, yes. Yes, there is," he'd said, thrumming his long fingers against the desktop. "Please go home, Lana Joy." His words landed harder than he'd meant them to.

Now, this made no sense to her. Aside from the Jackson clan's unplanned visit, it'd been quiet, especially for a Monday. Doc liked to use such slow times following up on those patients with telephones and gathering the addresses of those without. He'd make a few house calls on his way home. During any other lull, he would've expected Lana Joy to be catching up on bills or updating and deciphering his prescription logs and surgical notes.

"You sure? I'd just as soon stay awhile and get some more work done—" she responded, her hands fluttering nervously.

"I'm sure, nurse. You go on. I need to think."

CHAPTER NINETEEN

OF COURSE, JB HAD LONG since made good on his threat. He'd dubbed the first one of that second set of twins Clayton, after his pa. Then, insisting he couldn't care less one way or the other, he allowed Momma to name the runt of the litter.

Elijah. Our own little prophet.

Eli moved more slowly than the others, but gosh darnit if he wasn't as sweet-natured and adorable as all three of his brothers put together. He had this magical way of weaving his short and otherwise awkward fingers through Momma's hair without ever pulling a strand to hurt her. Looking into his eyes she found not her own cloudy shade of cornflower, nor James or Bootie's more dusty variations, but one clearer and brighter, mirroring all about him. Two happiness pools reflecting tenfold whatsoever glimmers of light might be cast his way. His laugh, like Momma's, made my insides smile. His cries puddled in my heart.

Clayton Junior, on the other hand, with his very own determined set of steely blues, demonstrated an iron grip and a will to match. From when they both started to crawl, time and again, Clayton left Eli behind but never for long. Little Clayt always came back for his mate.

FROM THE START, THERE WAS nothing Momma wouldn't do for those boys, often using her best efforts at tomfoolery to make light of our plight for their benefit.

"Now don't y'all be playing with matches near this laundry pile," she'd chide. "I don't want to end up with cinders instead of childrens. I got enough sweeping up to do 'round here as it is!"

Her lightheartedness in the midst of our ongoing crises was lost on me. Though somehow, and with a regularity, she managed to spur our boys into hysterics, providing a necessary, if queer, relief. I suspect for her it was like the loosening of a too-tight screwcap from atop her head.

As she made her way, Momma tried stirring in those ingredients lacking in her own upbringing. Memaw Veta Sue, always so filled with empathy for only her own self, had no kindness to add to any other's mix. Not even her own child's. All those years Momma was just trying to make up to her own children all she'd needed but never got.

Pawpaw's attempts, though well-intended, had served up as more garnish than staple. The void forced Momma's wants forward, leading me to a kind of understanding as to how Jamerson Booth Jackson may have seemed, at one time, a passable alternative.

It'd been well after the little Penny Rae Ledbetter incident but just before my folks' nuptials of necessity, the necessary portion being how JB'd have been back in jail without such a ceremony, that he'd lost his post at the high school.

For the most part that firing was a direct result of "the inappropriate nature of his relationship with a minor student." This time, my Vidalia. Little did she know back then, that maintenance job was to have been the only steady employment JB would keep up during all their years together.

On a regular basis he'd proclaim himself too good for farmwork. Even while he, his wife, and his children, had been living, almost comfortably, under Gamma Gert's roof.

His stance had left Gamma bearing sole responsibility for not only his highness but them all. Even under circumstances such as this, Gamma Gert would not do or say anything to upend her son's superiority complex.

Gamma'd long since overturned the example set by her mama, the infamous songbird, Jolene Palmer Picoult Jebbitt Lambert Poole, by sacrificing her own peace of mind, and whatever else, for the sake of her unkind and unthankful offspring.

I reckon my poor Gamma had made her points a whit too convincingly.

"Let the old biddy take care of her damned dried-up self for a change," JB'd tell Momma. As if he'd ever lifted a finger to do anything more than cause Gamma harm or distress.

When my great granddaddy left out of Purgatory, deeding Gamma the homestead, I expect he knew right well what would happen.

Though uneducated in any formal sense, Grady Bo Jebbitt was a wise man. He knew what and when to give out, and what and when to hold back. The bulk of Purgatory got sold off at auction shortly after the births of Clayt and Eli.

Gamma Gert held onto the tiny farmhouse, but it would have made for too-tight quarters if we'd taken her up on her offer of permanent shelter there.

JB said it was all her fault for losing the farm, that she couldn't hold onto nothing, and that she ought to just move on out to make room enough for us all. And she'd have done it, too, she said so, but Momma wouldn't hear of such a thing and made Gamma take back her offer.

Momma then snuck out behind JB's back, proposing a deal to one of the local landlords. On her end, she promised she and her husband would look after things, tending to odd jobs on and around the premises of the train track apartment for a reduction on rent. JB pitched a hissy fit. When the time came, he did help some with the move, but that was all she was getting out of him.

"That sonsabitch should be payin' us to live here!" he yelled, greeting her at the door. "It's hot as hell in this place. Damn trains passing through all hours of the day and night. Fuckitall. I'm gone out. It's like trying to sleep in the middle of a god-damned war zone."

Momma had just returned from cutting the lawn and weeding the flower bed for Mister Marley, the landlord. She peeled off her threadbare garden gloves and tossed them into the sink.

"At least we don't need worry none about disturbing the peace," she mumbled after JB. My giggles surprised both myself and Momma.

"Well, what do you know," she said, smiling. "My baby girl has a sense of humor after all."

It was only Momma's pleasant nature and willingness to barter herself that had allowed us to remain in the forsaken shake 'n bake for as many months.

She loved it there. Especially the mismatched ruffled valences in the windows. She didn't even care that they'd been left behind by squatters.

"Nothing says Home Sweet Home like curtains in a window," Momma liked to say. And she didn't mind patching up the holes in the walls, either. Or the missing doors to the bathroom and the bedroom. Or the indoor toilet that wouldn't come unstained no matter how hard she scrubbed. Why, that john wouldn't flush at all without having a bucket of water tossed into it.

In spite of the noise, the heat, and the trembles, Momma had truly appreciated that apartment and especially the washer hooked up in the basement only just two floors down.

But charity based on pity has its limits, and with watery eyes, our Mister Marley gave us the boot. His new wife insisted he find some tenants willing and able to pay at least a portion of their rent in cash.

After spending several sleepless nights in the bed of JB's truck while he was out on the town, we relocated to a shoulda-been-condemned rental at the rear of Tribesmen's Trailer Park.

Determined to make the best of any hand dealt her, Momma took just as kindly to this next situation. With no help whatsoever, she moved what little we had from the F-1 into that rundown mobile home.

There was no welcoming committee as Momma set about unloading her children, her tools, and her other meager belongings, but there were no protests either. Our new neighborhood already housed almost as many broken homes as broken people.

CHAPTER TWENTY

TIME TO TIME AND QUITE on accident, JB might land some type gainful employment. But he always made sure any overseer understood it was all to be on a trial basis.

As if it was his call.

With Jamerson Booth Jackson on-site, be it a mill or a mine, employee morale would hit new all-time lows. This state of despair and uncertainty amongst the rank and file eventually led the foremen to conclude, irregardless of JB's strength or potential, he wasn't worth the trouble.

Some folk, I reckoned, are quicker to figure that kind of thing.

At the end of those days or, sometimes, weeks, JB'd collected a pink slip along with his pay. But that didn't near stop him from tossing what little he'd made into the coffers of the moonshine runners who lived behind Picayune's or the prostitutes who lived above, when those gals weren't selling their favors to higher bidders.

JB returned to us with little or nothing to show other than a mound of grimy duds steeped in cheapjack whiskey and other less mentionable fluids. If laundry could walk on its own as folks sometimes say, his would've tripped over itself and drowned. Or died of the asphyxiation.

"I made that money and I'll spend it any god-damned way I wanna."

Some kinds of men might see the error of their ways. Some men might try and do better, if only for the sake of their families. JB wasn't either of those kinds.

Momma didn't seem to mind much most of what he did or said

anymore. What bothered her was hearing the hunger rumbling in her babies' stomachs.

"JB," she pleaded. "Cain't you just go back there and apologize? We need some money to put on our due bills. You know, just so they might maybe let me have something on account—"

"Jesus H. Christ!"

"I'm sorry, JB. Truly I am. But we got next to nothing in the cupboards. Them boys, they need their milk an' such. You want your sons to grow up big an' strong like their daddy. Don't you?"

It tore at my heart to hear her grovel so, but not near as much as listening to those little-boy tummies grumbling in the dark quiet of each night.

JB didn't believe in milk. He believed in White Lightening and Sugar Top. Tiger Water and Fire Spit. Near Beer and Buckeye Bark Whiskey.

"It's about time you started figuring some things for your own self!" he yelled. And that all she did was nag, nag, nag. And wasn't this just a fine how-d'you-do to come home to, after being paid but one thin dime for a dollar's worth of work.

And that was why soothing his own aches and scratching his own itches had to come first over her and her four little snot-nosed pains in the ass.

"Okay, then," Momma said, softening her voice, shrinking her presence. "Maybe just this once we should borrow a little something out from what you got hid in your pa's ci-gar box and use it for the boys?"

She knew right well JB had been siphoning funds for his own wants, digging up and reburying that box as if it were some mystical relic or rare artifact, as his own selfish needs moved him.

"My pa left that to me," he snarled through clenched teeth.

"Yes, JB. I know that. But don't you think Clayton Sr. might've wanted to help out his own grandbabies?"

"It's mine, not theirs. You look at that box sideways, Vida Lee, I'll kill you. Sure's I'm standing here."

"Now settle down. I don't need nothing for myself. Heck, JB, I don't even get hungry no more," she offered. "But this all just ain't fair to our childrens."

"It just ain't fair," he mocked. "For chrissake. I'm the one owed here.

I didn't drop you and them li'l bastards on the side of some road like my pa did, now did I? No, I did not. Shit, girl. Give a man some credit. That money's mine. I earned it fair 'n square."

But there were four little mouths needing feeding right there, right then. And ever since we had moved out from Gamma Gert's farmhouse seven months prior, we'd been pretty much on our own. JB would just take off from that dilapidated trailer knowing we didn't have two nickels to rub together. And that half a loaf of bread, two potatoes, and a few slivers of scrapple weren't going to last long.

A FEW YEARS BACK, SOMETIME after our first but before the second set of twins, while Gamma was off on a planned overnight with her Wild Women, JB had tread too heavily on Momma's last nerve.

"I got to warsh some clothes in the scrub pot out back, JB. Can you stay put and watch over the twins for me in case they wake up?"

Almost done in the yard she started hearing too-loud, too-happy voices and a misplaced kind of gurgle-giggling.

She came inside but two minutes later to find JB, Bootie, and Baby James on the floor, all three leaning up against the kitchen wall. One twin propped against the other. An open, empty jar of Pine Top on the floor in front of them.

"Now, don't throw a hissy fit, Vida Lee," JB slurred. "They woke up—"

"You fed my babies lickker?"

"I's just havin' some fun—"

"You fed my babies lickker?" she asked again, this time more challenge than query.

"Well, 'scuse me, Missss Prissss," he said, wearing a lopsided sneer-grin. With his back still against the wall, he slid himself to upright, leaving the tiny, pickled pair to fend for themselves.

"I'm gone out but I'll be back," he said, moving as quickly as his current state allowed, one hand on the latch and one foot out the door. "Maybe by then you'll be in a better mood."

At that point Momma's ears were so red I don't think she heard, nor cared about, what all he was saying.

"Momma. I believe—" I started whispering to her.

"Hush, Cieli Mae. I need to think." Momma took out the brown bottle of ipecac and gave one spoonful to each of the boys followed by a steady stream of drinking water from the sink. Soon enough they'd both puked up their insides into the rusty bucket. Momma started crying but shook off the feeling, just in time, before losing herself to it.

Within the hour she'd had the boys both cleaned out and cleaned up. She swiped at her eyes and willed herself to quit trembling as she dragged a stool over to the icebox and stepped up onto the seat. From the overhead cupboard, she grabbed her childhood prayer book. The boys and I watched as she pulled out a brittle envelope from between the book's opalescent pages where it'd been stashed.

Momma stuffed the yellowed mailer into her pocket and crammed the carpetbag full, scooped up James and Bootie, and hurried me along. Off we all went under the cover of night hitching a ride to the bus depot in Big Creek with our old landlord who'd just happened to be passing by. Mister Marley gave a nod and bless his heart, he did not ask one question of her beyond *where to?*

"Where we gone, Momma?" I asked once we'd arrived at the station.

"To visit Aunt Patsy and Cousin Arlis in Tuscaloosa," Momma whispered back, almost excited. Long ago she'd committed to memory the barely legible address scrawled onto the wrapper, but that hadn't stopped her from saving it.

I reckon in the back of her mind she might've been thinking about Pawpaw Clyde Royce and his brother making it out alive from that mine collapse—the one that left Pawpaw with the bad injury. His older brother, Cousin Arlis's daddy, hadn't been so lucky.

Pawpaw and Memaw had been married for close to five years when our mailman delivered that paper wrapper with an Alabama return. It was addressed to Pawpaw, but Memaw Veta Sue had opened it anyways. The enclosed note read:

Deer Clyde Royce,
    Thank u for riting me and asking after us all. Glad u are well. We are not. Ur brother has died from his njrees. Little Arlis crys all the time.

Pleesz help us.
   Sined,
   Ur grateful inlaw Patsy

Memaw ripped the letter into tiny pieces and crumpled its holder on the spot. Tight-fisted and in a hurry, she ran it to the trash heap out back and shoved the remains beneath a pile of Pawpaw's old newspapers—those ones she wasn't supposed to know about.

Just as soon as Memaw went back inside, my Vidalia snatched the wrapper out from the pile. She just wanted the stamp was all, but instead she saved the entire wrapper and kept it all these years pressed within the pages of her prayer book.

"But how we gone buy tickets?" I asked.

"Well now, baby girl," she whispered. "You know how Doc sometimes pays me for pressing even though he don't need to, what with all he does for us? I been saving it up. And well, I was just about to take it out and go to market but something told me not to."

It was true. Lately when we'd visited Doc, when Momma was just about fine, while he was checking the boys over, she'd sneak off and iron up a few shirts for him as long as Nurse Lana Joy said it was all right. And even though Momma didn't expect such, Doctor Feldman insisted she take payment. Whether or not she willingly accepted depended mainly on our most current situation.

Momma and I shared a seat on the bus, as did James and Bootie. We were running away! I wasn't sure whatall Momma was hoping. That maybe JB wouldn't notice we were gone? That maybe he wouldn't even care?

Oh, he'd caught sight of Momma, Baby James, and Bootie—one sorry looking trio—waiting by the side of the road. But, he didn't try to stop them. Not then.

After we'd boarded, he coaxed our destination, the return address on the envelope she'd mistakenly left behind, from the unwitting station agent who'd sold Momma our tickets.

First double-checking to be sure his Winchester was still under the front seat, JB followed with us unawares. Pawpaw would've said he was allowing Momma just enough rope to hang her own self.

There he was. Puffed up like a proud peacock on Aunt Patsy and Cousin Arlis's front stoop as we trudged down the narrow, twisty path to their lean-to. They'd all been waiting on us.

Momma, ever so pale to begin with and after our long journey all the more so, lost what little color she'd had left. Even her freckles seemed to disappear at the sight of him. Her mouth hung wide. In slow motion her arms went limp, and she almost let go of both twins. "Momma! Hold on!" I shouted, snapping her back to the there and then.

Besides warning them of our coming visit JB also explained to Cousin Arlis and Aunt Patsy about Momma's spells, and how she was just having another one.

"It ain't been easy, most 'specially now with the babies," he'd said, hanging his head and shaking it briskly, looking down at his boots. "She'll be fine, though. Soon's I get 'em all home where they belong. And get my sweet gal back on her physics. Don't you worry none."

Aunt Patsy nodded.

"You're a good man, JB," she'd said. "Them's lucky to have you." She patted JB's hand and left the men to their porch sitting while they waited on us.

Noting JB's twitchy trigger finger, Cousin Arlis picked at the bare spot on his otherwise whiskered chin, not sure what to think now as he'd heard little good about this here in-law from Clyde Royce's side of the family. But JB had outdone himself to win this one over. Why, he'd even brought along a box of snuff for Cousin Arlis and a posy for Aunt Patsy as props.

As we got closer Arlis jumped up, on instinct alone, inserting himself between us and JB.

"I don't reckon to know nothin much—" Arlis began.

"You're right about that, cuz," JB'd said, assuming a ready position. "Now, I'd appreciate it if you'd get out of my way."

"Don't hurt him none, JB," Momma said, clutching one baby boy under each arm. "Please. I'll do whatever you say." She'd always had a soft spot for Arlis, her only known cousin, though the two hadn't seen one another but once when they were both toddlers themselves.

Aunt Patsy poked her head out the shanty's front window, "Arlis Abraham Kandal, don't you be actin' the fool!" she yelled. "You're gone get your head blowed off! We don't owe them folk nothin'. Nothin' a'tall. Why, hear tell, she ain't even blood—"

If Cousin Arlis had been a bigger man, or even a slightly smarter one, or if he'd had a shotgun within easy reach instead of a banjo, Momma might've stood a chance. As it was, Arlis was no match for either his ma or JB.

After some consideration Arlis stepped aside. JB latched onto Momma's elbow, pinching the tender skin just above it, leading her and the boys, lambs to slaughter, back to his truck.

In the cab Momma sat in silence just waiting on her punishment as babies James and Bootie, tucked in at her sides, slept on.

When my Vidalia was growing up, instead of "Give us this day our daily bread" before each meal, the soft-spoken Clyde Royce Kandal cited biblical quotes such as this one, burnt into a wooden plaque and still hanging over his and Memaw's kitchen window: "Wives, submit yourselves unto your husband, as unto the Lord" –Ephesians 5:22.

After a heated discussion with her best friend in elementary school, Marigold Sun Beauregard, Momma challenged Pawpaw as to the accuracy of his source. "Look it up," he'd said, aiming his index finger at the lectern across the room.

There it was. On a page as thin as an onion's skin.

But my Vidalia later wondered if Pawpaw had left off the rest on purpose, and why? Those parts about loving your wife as much as your own self? And how come Memaw Veta Sue hadn't ever brought that all up? Could it have been she just didn't care?

Having to swallow such garbage so early on, I suspect, left my Vidalia more susceptible to whatever leavings got offered to her down the road.

BY AND BY, I'D COME to wonder whether JB's hurtful ways might be considered normal in any world and fell into the habit of observing other daddies.

At church. In the market. Even at the Laundromat.

None seemed to come and go or act out in the ways he did.

On the best of days he might show up with a half-full bag of groceries and a dollar or two. He saw this as a good thing and reason enough for Momma to want to spend all of a night whooping it up with him. She'd built a partition to shield me and the boys—by then aged six and almost three—from such grown-up activities.

As much a wizard with wood scraps as with a pistol, Momma had scavenged a mess of two-by-fours from the local dump. She'd sanded down the warped slats and decoupaged over any worn spots with magazine cutouts. My momma had what folks liked to call an eye for detail, so that screen was not totally unattractive.

By then, JB didn't much like the way James and Bootie looked at him when he got to carrying on. Still, he wasn't beyond issuing her a few "love taps." Just his way of seeing to it she stayed awake and in a good enough mood for him to enjoy her.

I especially didn't like how he'd yank her toward him or knock her out of his way, depending on the urgency of his wants or the level of his orneriness.

Momma didn't seem to mind it all as much as she should've, except for when, time to time, he tried his nonsense with the boys.

CHAPTER TWENTY-ONE

"UH-OH, JAMES," BOOTIE WHISPERED TO his six-year-old twin. "Now you done it."

"Shuddup!" James grimmaced with one side of his mouth. A raspy growl crept up his throat and escaped out the other side.

Halfway between a tease and a threat Bootie hissed, hopping from one foot to the other. "I'ma tell, James! I'ma tell on you!"

"I'ma tell on my own self," James said, narrowing his eyes, marching toward the trailer. "MOMMA!"

Momma looked up and out the kitchen window. "What is it? What's wrong?" she whisper-shouted. She'd warned them to stay close and out of trouble while she put the babies down for their naps. "Y'all need talk softer. I just got them babies to sleep."

"Lookit what James done!" Toes tapping, Bootie pointed to the rickety structure sprouting from our side-neighbor's overgrowth.

"Bootie. I tole you, shuddup," James said, tiny nostrils flared, miniature fists clenched at his sides.

"Oh my stars." Momma looked far right. JB had left the F-1 under the next door neighbor's carport while in search of a tire to replace the one he'd tore up last night.

Momma's fingers rubbed circles onto her temples as here came JB, a tire under one arm and a near-empty jug attached to the end of the other.

"What the hell!" he shouted, taking in the fear registered on Momma's face. His sneer ricocheted from one twin to the other.

"You little god-damned sonsabitches," he slurred, slamming the tire to the ground. At first that tire seemed to want to bounce back to him but reconsidered right quick and rolled over and played dead.

JB tipped back his head as if he meant to catch a raindrop on his nose, lifted the jug way high, and drew one long, last pull into his mouth. Once his fuzzy tongue met the stale hollow, he chucked the chipped earthenware vessel directly at the two of them. He then grabbed hold of his stomach and doubled over letting go a loud belch which, under other conditions, might've inspired the boys to a raucous laughter.

He then straightened, swiped at his chin with the back of his hand, and fixed his sights on his namesakes.

"But, I din' do nothin'!" James cried out, tossing his head side to side, his curls bouncing in a kind of affirmation. Bootie rushed forward, arms spread, defending his mate like a pint-sized human shield.

Momma barreled toward them all clutching her rolling pin in her right hand. After a thunk to the back of his head, JB went down. The boys looked on, brows raised, eyes wide, mouths agape.

"What'd you do, Baby James?" Momma whispered. Unnerved but exhilarated, she lowered herself to a single-kneed kneel next to him like a death row inmate seeking a pardon.

"First off, Momma, I ain't no baby no more. I just turnt six. Remember?"

"You're right. I'm sorry, James, but—"

"It's awright. Just don't call me a baby no more. Okay?"

"Okay. Now then. What'd you do?" she asked again. Poor Momma. She was trying as hard as any mama could to hide her horror so as not to frighten the boys further.

James took one deep breath. Bootie, his scrawny arms still outstretched in protection of his tattletale sibling stepped aside. "I let the air out of them other tires so's when he comed back," James mumbled, lifting his tiny chin in JB's direction, "he'd right quick need to go 'way again."

By this time, Clayt and Eli's cries inside had progressed from harmless wimpering to more noxious wails, drawing us back indoors. All of us, that is, except for JB.

James and Bootie knew better than to add more to the story. They'd banished themselves to the back room, laid down on their pallet, and serenaded the littler ones until they all dropped off. For the first time in a forever, a peaceful quietude reigned over our kingdom, as four little dreamboats sailed away, adrift in a sea of innocence.

When JB came to, near three hours later, Momma greeted him with an ice pack and a cool drink. She'd refilled those other tires and even replaced the shredded wheel with that newer one. Lucky for her, seeing his truck ready, willing, and now able to go, JB didn't bother to recollect what all had gotten him so riled in the first place.

"What the hell," he said, wincing as his fingertips moved gingerly over the bulbous lump on the back of his head.

Wearing a pinched face, Momma looked down at her grease-stained hands and knees and her soiled apron. "I reckon there's no sense to denying it, JB. It was all my fault. I'm sorry. I was trying to 'flate them other tires to surprise you, and on accident, I unflated them. But all four's fixed now."

"I got no time for your nonsense, Vida Lee," he spit out, wiping the clay-dust off his hands and onto the front of his shirt.

"And, also, JB, I didn't no more mean to break my rolling pin over your head, than you meant to throw that bottle at the twins," she went on, but backpedaled swiftly once JB grabbed her by the scruff. "It was a accident, JB," she said, "I *said* I didn't mean it."

If I tell it right, I have to say I'd thought of it all as less of an accident and more of a finest moment.

"I got somewhere I need be," JB grumbled. "Else y'all wouldn't know what hit you." He stripped off his soiled tee shirt, dropped it to the ground as if he had a dozen new ones in the bottom drawer, and slipped a Cloroxed-clean one over his head. "You never were the sharpest tool in the shed, girl."

As the rattle of the F-1's loose muffler faded into the distance, and that blue driver-side door hung onto its mostly red body for dear life, a sense of relief took hold of us both.

Before too long, James and Bootie awoke. Knowing better than to do otherwise, they went about their business, digging through old issues of *The National Geographic.* As slick and as tempting as a fresh corncob boiled and buttered, each satiny cover hinted at some other world of possibility, with near every page providing flush and velvety images of faraway places for dreaming upon.

Along with a bounty of treats and vitamins, our Doctor Feldman, ever mindful of the boys' growing intellect and curiosity, had begun adding a tightly bound stack of magazines to our spoils.

Bootie, with motor skills finer than a frog's hairs, was well ahead of the fray. He took his time tearing out photos of castles and pasting them to odd scraps of colored construction paper. With a long, bent nail he poked three holes along one edge of each page and stitched them all together with an old shoelace. Bootie beamed as he presented Momma the catalogue and informed her of his plans.

"You pick the one you like best, Momma. I'ma buy it for you someday, and then you and me and James and Eli and Clayt will live there. Together. And we'll all be safe," he said. "Gamma Gert and Doc can come too. Oh, and Nurse Lana. And if Memaw and Pawpaw want, they can come too." Bootie especially liked those images showing moats and drawbridges. "But when the bad folk come, we'll quick yank up the bridge. And they'll be a whole mess of gators in our moat to keep our emmies out!"

James, in the true spirit of one-upmanship, ripped out whole pages of tropical islands, presenting them with equal enthusiasm.

"Someday I'ma build you a whole island Momma! Ain't nobody can get onto it unless *I* say so! I'll keep lookout from my tree house. And we won't have to pick nothin', neither. Them coconuts and bananas'll just drop to our feet, and we won't never be hungry no more. How 'bout that, Momma? Would you like that?"

"Well, now. That'd be nice," she said, as if he'd just asked if he could pick her a wildflower.

James pestered after her to name what kind of housing she'd prefer and he'd build it for her on her island with his very own hands. "Don't you know," he told her, looking over his shoulder to be sure his twin was paying attention, "I a'ready started c'llectin' the sticks and stones I'ma use."

Sibling rivalry at its best.

Momma'd been teaching me some new nursery rhymes, including the one about what little boys are made of. Truth to tell, I was right tired of snakes 'n snails and puppy dog tails. And though she had not yet confided in me, she once again had The Look about her.

"Dear Lord, Heavenly Father," I prayed. "Might this one be a sister, instead? Please? I mean, only if it's not too much trouble on You."

"All babies are gifts from God, Cieli Mae," Momma whispered, countering my prayerful request. "We'll be thankful for any kind we get to keep."

"But Momma—"

"Ain't no buts about it, baby girl."

"I s'pose you're right," was all I could say back to her.

It's just that my brothers, well, they never usually slept at the same times. Oh, one might quiet down some and then another. But by the time the last drifted off, the first, the second, and usually the third, had already awakened and found their way into some new manner of monkey business.

"It's just what little boys do, baby girl," Momma cooed, bent down on one knee, scraping colored wax off the wall. James had drawn a bouquet for Momma using a candle.

"But there weren't no crayons left," his good-enough reason.

CHAPTER TWENTY-TWO

WITH NO WORKING TELEPHONE TO ring ahead we'd set off on foot from Tribesmen's for another unscheduled visit to Number Two Hospital Way, relying solely on Doc Feldman's solicitous nature and Nurse Lana Joy's creative planning.

For as much as Momma fashioned things were not as they were, even to Doc, time after time after time, the evidence contradicted her claims. More and more of late those certain truths upended his constitution and wreaked havoc on his otherwise organized thought processes.

On that particular morning especially, I'd wished I could've packed Momma into that buggy along with Clayt, Eli, and Bootie. As for James, he preferred hanging onto one side or the other.

"Not much further, Momma," I coaxed. "We're in the short rows now."

Her floral-print housedress dripped, translucent with sweat, though she was moving only about as fast as pond water. Even with me and James cheering her on.

"I'm sorry," she'd said. "I cain't do this today, sugar."

"Cain't?"

"Well, maybe I'm just not sure this is a good idea. The doc don't seem real happy seeing me in this condition no more."

"Is that what you truly think, Momma? Or do you think Doc'd much rather see you any way, than not?" I posed, knowing full well what her answers would be. "If you wanna slow your pace some, you oughta. Don't matter how long it takes, 's long as we get to where we're going to. It's not like we have an appointment."

Momma's weariness, an ongoing problem, was even more an issue when she was newly pregnant. Putting one foot in front of the other would've been a challenge for her even without having to push that carriage full of boy.

Upon our arrival, right quick, Nurse Lana Joy ushered us all inside and pulled out the treat jar for the boys. "No ironing for you today, young lady!" she teased Momma, plopping her down in front of the electric fan and offering up a short, stout, stool for her swelled feet, along with an ice-cold sweet tea. "Won't be long," she assured. Doc was just finishing up with old Mister Sorenson's impetigo.

Only a few minutes passed before hearing Lana Joy's familiar refrain, "Vida Lee, sweetie, the doctor will see you now."

Once within the inner sanctum of Doc's Office & Examining Room, Momma studied her own puffed ankles while the doctor studied the rest of her.

"Comes with the territory, young lady," he said. Poor Doc was having a much harder time than usual masking his disapproval. An outsider might say he appeared less than pleased and more than offended.

"Vidalia. Child. We discussed this very matter not that long ago. I thought you understood. This," he said, gesturing with his hands, "is not a viable option. Not now. Not for you. You have four beautiful boys, Vida Lee," he sighed. "I just don't understand."

The good doctor feared for her wellbeing as if she was his own. The mysterious falling out between Doc Feldman and Memaw a few years after she'd hitched herself to Pawpaw had not dampened Doc's concern for any of them. Not for Memaw Veta Sue, nor, more noticeably still, for my momma.

For some time now he'd questioned her ability to withstand another pregnancy, but his suggestions of different forms of birth control had fallen on plugged ears.

He'd told Momma all about a new medication approved for other purposes but being considered by the medical community as a means of planned parenting under certain circumstances.

Not yet sanctioned for the likes of what he had in mind Doc would've prescribed them for her anyway, even at risk to his own medical license. All she needed to do was agree to take one every day, excepting on her special days of each month.

"Lemme think on it some, Doc," she said. "But I'm pretty sure JB ain't gonna like the idea."

Not much in favor of babies, JB was even less in favor of any form of contraception fearing it might in some way interfere with his manly pleasures. Not even The Rhythm. "God-damned voo-doo," he called it.

Doc assured Momma there was no reason for her husband to be involved in the decision. This was *her* body they were talking about. Confirming this ninth pregnancy in almost as many years, the doctor gave all four boys the up-down as if they'd had anything to do with her condition or any kind of say in the matter.

Years back Doc Feldman had playfully teased, "My dear child. Sweet, sweet, Vidalia. You may be the most fertile female this side of the Mason-Dixon!" But on this day he wasn't in that kind of mood.

On this torrid Tuesday afternoon he appeared powerless and disheartened as he added anemia to her chart of previous diagnoses. That, he said, might explain why she always black and blue'd for no reason at all. Oh, there were plenty of reasons, but she insisted he let it go at that. As usual, the good doctor would've rather climbed a tree to tell her what she wanted him to say than to stand there on firm ground telling her what she needed to hear.

With the official portion of her visit completed, Momma hummed as she set about to gather up her things while the metronome ticked and an electric fan blew almost cool breezes her way. Why, she even managed a smile at the sounds of her boys' giggles wafting in from the wait room. Nurse Lana Joy had kept those young rascals amused with stories and songs while plying them with fresh strawberries, shortbread cookies, and boxes of Jujyfruits.

We left that day with Momma's pride relatively intact, one dozen eggs, one king-size loaf of Wonder Bread, a half bushel of apples, a supply of daily vitamin pills for all of them, and a twine-bound stack of magazines which had been sitting there in the corner, just waiting on us.

A few days following that last check-in with the doc, JB paid us a surprise visit. During that husbandly call he did something more scary and much awfuller than anything ever, in any times past.

CHAPTER TWENTY-THREE

Almost home from our trip to Number Two Hospital Way, and with the boys in need of a stretch, we had stopped at a thickly wooded play area just up the road a piece from our trailer.

Before sunup that very next morning, our boys, every last one of them, had been taken by a forceful affliction. If one wasn't screaming from the stomach pains, another was. If Momma wasn't stripping one of soiled clothing, she was bathing another in tepid water hoping to bring down his temperature. This cycle ran steady for upwards of three days.

As our boys circled the drain, Momma's sensibilities made steady decline. Dirty laundry stockpiled. We couldn't go out, not even to the Laundromat. Momma would not, could not, leave her babies for any stretch. She hadn't any coins to put in those wash machines anyways.

Momma hand-scrubbed as many soiled pieces as were needed, using the old rub board over the wash pot out back. Not knowing when there might be money enough for a new bar, she managed that small chunk of Fels-Naptha down to its last sliver. In the process, she'd scraped her knuckles near raw.

During the third hour of the third day, our pint-sized patients, one and all, fell into a kind of restfulness. Momma kissed each one on the forehead using her lips as a thermometer.

"Cieli Mae," she'd said, a few minutes later, taking a break from peeling taters. "I cut away the green parts and the spuds are ready for boiling." Her face now looked more worn than worried. "But first I think I need lie down a spell."

Momma scooped up the spent peels and dropped them into the aluminum pail just below the sink and then slid the whetstone to the back of the counter. She rinsed the short fillet knife, leaving it in the basin for cleaning later. Wiping her hands on a soggy dishtowel, she let out a soft sigh, untied the damp apron from around her waist, and hung both rags on the hooked nail.

"But, baby girl, if one of 'em makes even a slightest move, you'll wake me," she warned. As weak as they had to be by now, she still didn't trust those little rascals.

While Momma might've let me watch over the boys during other times, she'd never allow such when they were doing poorly. "That's my job," she'd say with certitude.

Even so, I had decided it was my job to see to it that Momma got herself some rest. This whole dang mess was all my fault. I knew it was, though she insisted it wasn't.

We'd stayed too long at the play park, amongst the rag-tag McClurgh triplets, because of me. Momma wanted to leave right away but their throaty, unbridled laughter had lifted my spirit.

Unbathed and unkempt, with matted hair and runny noses, the trio's barks and wheezes, coughs and croaks, grated unchecked against one another's. But I was oh so desperate for the sounds and company of any young beings, other than my brothers, and Momma knew it.

Finally free of their buggy the twins had run about, frolicking wildly in tainted clay dust while sharing their treats willy-nilly with that shameless, unholy trinity.

The McClurgh's hearty virus had hitched a ride and spread through my brothers like the wildfire, turning our little men inside out.

USUALLY ALWAYS, I WAS GOOD about keeping watch while Momma slept but this time I'd allowed myself a distraction. All was quiet and our patients appeared to be resting peacefully, and I was getting bored. Without considering any consequences I'd trained my concentrations on the billowy cloud formations, noting how lucky they were, as one after another drifted by us and on to other places.

The eerie *click-click-clunk* of a locked door forced open without benefit of a key rousted me back to my worldly charges.

"Hell me!" JB yelled as he tripped over the toppled chair Momma had wedged under the doorknob for just in case.

His glazed eyes scanned the scenario, and his hands moved herky-jerky. "Well, now," he snickered. "Lookit this here shit hole." A low whistle passed through his pale, parched lips.

"Please!" I tried to interject. "The boys been sick and it's all my fault. Don't be mad at her. She's plum wore out, JB. Just let her be. Please?"

But it was too little and too late. My pleas went unheard by him, who needed to hear them most.

The boys stirred. Some of their color had returned along with a good dose of their gumption. They wasted no time getting back to their usual little-boy nonsense. Teases turned into tickles and pokes into pinches. Elijah's cries set off a chain reaction.

The commotion set JB to flinching as strange and uneven noises rose in his throat. Under twitching lids, his pupils had doubled in size.

"Wake up, whorebitch," he yelled in Momma's face. Up until that very moment she'd been fast asleep. How he could wake her, after what all she'd been through, was beyond any sense of reasoning. "Now!" he commanded. "Get them babies-s-s quiet! I cain't think!" His arms flapped and his eyes darted crazily. A crusty backhand soared. The boys screamed in chorus as Momma tried to raise herself from her semi-comatose state.

"Vida Lee! Shut them up!" he yelled, grabbing onto the table for steadying.

JB hollowed his cheeks. He stripped off his belt, folded the strap in half, and snapped it twice. "I mean business!"

"NO!" I yelled. "Don't you dare!"

Disoriented, he stumbled forward. The metal buckle seared through the thick air, landing with a clank up against the unplugged Hoover at the opposite end of the room.

His face a burning beet, he yanked Momma upright using her ponytail as a lever. Momma reached up one hand and held tight to her crown. Her head and neck followed his pull, trying to keep themselves attached to her shoulders. Purposing a distorted smile in my direction she shooed me, with her free hand, toward the boys.

"Hush now please, Jamerson," she said in her calm voice. "You're gonna get us kicked out this place too—"

"*Me?*" he called down from his high horse.

"I swear on all that's good, JB. I know it don't look it, but I been working my fingers to the bone. The boys been sick. So very, very sick—"

"Well now. Shut my mouth," he said, looking at her, still holding her up like a magician pulling a rabbit from his hat. "Let me just take a gander at them tired fingers of yours. Damn," he said in an oddly repentant dismount as he let go her hair. "I'm sorry, sugar."

JB came around from behind, encircling her gently and bending her forward from the waist, her arms now splayed on the tabletop in front of her. Her skin tightened as he reinforced her left arm with his, bracing her hand with his, holding her flattened palm firmly in place. Next, he overturned that same hand forcing her fingers wide with his own like he was fixing to trace its outline, all the while nuzzling her neck, whispering sweet nothings.

From this position, slowly and purposefully, his lips meadered along her shoulder, down her upper arm, then her forearm, and onto her hand. Tenderly, repeatedly, he kissed Momma's scraped knuckles. Then, with his right hand, and in one slick motion, he reached over her, grabbed up the short sharpened knife from out of the sink, and whacked off the top of her pinky finger.

Momma shrieked, one quick shriek.

"Whoa," he said. "Jesus H. Christ."

My spirit froze in time. Even the boys remained frightfully unmoving.

Momma's blood came up fast. JB paled and handed over the dank dishrag left hanging from the crooked nail at the end of the counter.

"Now then," he said. "I reckon we got ourselfs a little less of them tired fingers to worry about."

JB shook his head as he stuck the severed snip of Momma's flesh into his pocket. "I told you I meant business, girl. Look what you made me do now. Shee-it! I need some air." And with Momma bleeding like a stuck pig and the boys screaming and hollering, he turned on his heels and left.

"Momma!" I whisper-squealed.

"Hush, Cieli Mae. Go."

I caught up with JB, trailing him from behind, just close enough to see him pull that tiny chunk of her from his pocket, pinch it between the pads of his own thumb and forefinger, and flick it over a pen fence and into the water bowl of Matty and Tatty Burleson's guard dog. I snuck up on those chainlinks and peered through. There it was. The little snip of Momma's pinky, afloat in Bitsy's water bowl.

And here came Bitsy. And she looked thirsty.

Upon my return I found Momma seated cross-legged on the kitchen floor. Her eyes were still red as a turtle's and her cheeks still slick, but she'd already mixed a rinse of salt water, cleansed her injury, applied a salve left over from a previous visit with Doc, and fashioned a tourniquet of sorts from pieces of gauze and duct tape.

The boys had positioned Momma in a heap in a corner, out of harm's way, with James taking his shot as her watchman. Her sad, wrapped hand rested high atop his head to slow blood loss.

They'd taken turns, directed by Bootie, with each twin waiting on the chance to help some, using themselves as props to keep her injured fist above her heart as Doc Feldman had once shown them all.

"I'm sorry, Momma. That he done that to you. What're you gonna do now?" I murmured.

"It's gone?" she asked. I reckon she'd hoped that somehow I'd have brought it back. And that somehow, someway, she'd be able to make herself whole again.

Momma looked over at the four faces, forlorn. "Shoot," was all she said.

Motioning sideways with her head, she directed me to observe our Bootie as he tried to keep Eli and Clayt quiet, and Baby James, doing his best impression of stoic, holding back his tears.

"Quit scowling, y'all," Momma said with a forced lightness. "Little fingers ain't good for much anyways." Momma winked at the twin sets.

James forced a giggle. It was his duty as man of the house to assist in the keeping up of morale. Soon Bootie managed a chuckle, followed by Clayt and Eli. I reckon I was supposed to laugh too. I didn't though. I tried, but I just couldn't.

"Everything's gonna be fine from here on. I promise y'all that." Looking worse off than the underside of a turnip, there she went, again, comforting us.

JB FINALLY MADE HIS WAY back late that following evening, just as if nothing had happened. Hugging a brown-bagged jar under one arm tight to his chest, he stumbled past us and headed for the big pallet, stopping to take a piss. It took some time before his stream found its mark, thrumming hard against the sides of Momma's tin scrub pail.

Once settled in, he called out to her from behind her jury-rigged divider. "Hey there, Vida Lee. Put them boys down for the night now and c'mon back here. I got somethin' for you."

James and Bootie popped their heads out from under the sheet-draped kitchen table. James spoke first, "Don't you go, Momma."

"Please, Momma. Don't you go," echoed Bootie. "Please—"

"Get over here, woman," JB called from that back room where his shadow plumped. "Unless you want me t'give them boys a taste of your medicine."

Momma turned to the boys, her gaze faraway and unnatural. "I won't be long, boys. Y'all be good now. And tuck in those little ones for me."

CHAPTER TWENTY-FOUR

THAT NEXT MORNING MOMMA LIMPED into the kitchen looking like what gets left in the skillet after you fry an egg and take out all the good parts.

JB entered the room whistling, bloodshot eyes fixed fast. "Don't you be s'prised none if I don't come back," he hissed to her. "Not for a long, long time."

I, for one, was getting tired of his empty promises.

She never raised her gaze to meet his but asked, once again, if she might have just a few dollars to get some supplies at the grocery.

JB rubbed his chin as if he was thinking on it.

"Well, now," he said, shaking his head. "I'm afraid I cain't help you there none."

"But what about your daddy's money, JB? What about—"

"I'm warning you for the last time, girl. You touch my *ci*-gar box, I'll kill you. You don't wanna make me kill you now, do you?"

"As Jesus Christ is my Lord and Saviour, I don't even know where you got that damned thing hid," she muttered, absentmindedly folding and refolding the dishrag she'd just used to wipe up an old spill.

"You know what, Vida Lee? You 'n me were married under false pretenses."

"What?"

"You heard me. False pretenses." JB cracked his knuckles.

"I don't know what you mean by that," she said, genuine in her bewilderment.

"I mean, I thought you were special. Hell. Them whores down at Picyunes are more special'n you. Hell, my big toe's more special'n you."

"Hush now, JB. You don't mean that." Her voice sounded dead.

How could he say such things to her? "Godblessit!" I wanted to shout at him, "She has more special in the tip of her little finger—that one you cut off—than you have in your whole stupid self!" Why, Momma had more special in her than the nasty in his mouth, than the mean in his hands. And that's saying something.

Now that I am older and more learned in the ways of this world, I am even more amazed by her compassion toward him. Just how did she manage to hold onto her own special blend of grace and grit in the face of his ill will? And how was it she could command such a strength and yet be unaware of her own true force? And why, for as far as he went out of his way to be cruel, had she always gone further out of her's to avoid hurting him?

I knew where he'd stashed that dang *ci*-gar box, but he didn't. I saw him last week out back, digging around in the dirt like a dog, tearing up the grasses and any other growing thing in his path. He had come home skunked the previous week, and not that he'd near remember, buried that box in the southwest corner of our lot. I decided then and there, rules or no rules, I aimed to take her to it the minute after he left.

"Oh for chrissake, woman!" JB yelled. He made his way to the sink and twisted the cold faucet to full on. He bent his head and positioned it, openmouthed, under the basin spigot where he gulped down at least two quarts of the cool liquid.

He then swiped his lips with the back of his hand before spitting any backwash into the sink. "You an' them boys ain't nothing but deadweight around my neck. D'you know that?"

Momma looked up at him and nodded.

For the first time, in that one peculiar moment, I questioned which of them truly was the more senseless of the two.

On his way out JB stopped for one last look. He'd washed up some, shaved, combed his hair, and even splashed English Leather under his armpits. Head cocked to one side, he grinned in appreciation at his own reflection.

Momma, still in her threadbare dressing gown, shivered in the 101 degree heat.

Ripping the already cracked looking glass from its wall hook, he flung the mirror her way. She flinched but her feet stayed put. It was like Momma's reflexes had taken their leave of her, along with the last of her good sense.

"Might wanna take a peek at your own self once in a blue moon, girl," he advised. "Lookit you. Why, you oughta kiss the ground I walk in on." JB then adjusted his John Deere cap so the visor faced sideways, relit the stub of a smashed Marlboro, and slammed the splintered door behind him.

Favoring her one side, Momma hobbled like a two-legged sadness to back behind that homemade partition. There she settled herself down on the floor with both arms wrapped around her middle, rocking back and forth for the longest time. She'd done this now and then, but never without at least one of our babies in her hold.

"Momma?" I whispered, unsure what I was meant to do or say.

"Not now, Cieli Mae," she muttered. Her voice had stalled in neutral.

She wore a look of despair the likes of which I'd not seen on her before. Not even when, after our trip to visit Cousin Arlis's place, JB'd told her if she ever ran away again, he'd find her and cut off her feet with a rusted sawtoothed knife. And any of them little bastards she took with her? Why, he'd saw off their feet too. But he did not intend on them bleeding to death or anything of that sort.

"Hell no," he'd said, chuckling at his own cleverness.

JB promised to wrap them all up so that the end of their legs where he had sawed off their little feet would heal into stumps, just like Momma's pinky. They all would, he said, "never be able to run no more." Never. Not ever. And that any folk seeing them would gasp out loud and walk away, shaking their heads. "Oh my," they might say. "Look at that poor woman. She ain't got no feet. And all them pretty babies. They ain't got no feet neither. Tsk, tsk. Must be somethin' runs in the family."

Some might even laugh at them, a little circus of feetless people trying to make their way around in this world as best as they could.

"Momma," I'd wondered aloud, soon after that threat of short-leggin' had been leveled against them all. "D'ya reckon you and the boys ought sleep in your boots from here on?" It wasn't that I was advising her. I was just putting out a piece of what had been on her mind, which truth be told, wasn't that what I was there for?

"JB's just talking nonsense," she sighed in rebuttal. "He don't mean nothin' by it."

I don't know how it happened that my spirit did not reach out and grab her's and give it a good shake.

"Why," she went on, "even Pawpaw Clyde Royce used to say what he might do whenever he got riled. But deep down, sugar, all daddies love their childrens."

"Is that so, Momma?"

"Cieli Mae, I'd never let anything bad happen to our boys. You know that, don't you? Now, don't you fret no more."

Maybe I was not so wise in all the ways of this world but I knew one thing for sure. Whatever it was JB felt for his children, it was not love.

And our baby, the one that just took root? Why, Momma hadn't even told nobody about her yet. Now it was too late.

My little sister-to-be, our new baby, the one I'd prayed for in secret every night after Momma cut out the lights? She was gone from this world. I knew it. Momma did too.

Though I'd already chosen a name, and though I felt for Momma in her heartache, it was of some comfort to know baby Alexia rested at peace in a better place. A safer place than here.

⌒

AFTER WAITING NEAR AN HOUR'S time I reckoned I had let Momma be for long enough. I peeked back in on her and there she sat, right where I'd left her, perched on that soiled pallet in her badly sullied dressing gown, arms crossed, fingers clenched, rocking no one.

Not until that very moment though, did I notice the new smudges of clay dirt stretched across one cheek and on the backs of her hands, knees, and elbows, nor the gilt-edged pressed-cardboard box at her feet. JB's cigar box. His inheritance. Why, my spirit just about drowned in sickening waves of compunction over that instant in which I'd doubted her.

The boys howled on as they hadn't yet been fed so I snuck away once more to leave her to her figuring. It was the least I could do.

Before a body could say "Jack's your uncle," those little rascals were into the leftover mashed potatoes Momma had thinned with water. Though not directly taken with the texture, they did quiet down some once they'd figured, and rightly so, that it was more agreeable to finger paint with the runny starch than to eat it.

Once past, when they cried hard with the hunger, I prayed over an empty bowl for help. After all, God's Son had fed a large crowd lickety-split, just by multiplying a few loaves of bread and whatever fishes were on hand. Well, now. Those folk ended up with enough and then some. As there were only four little boys at my table, the way I saw it, I wasn't even asking all that much.

There was nothing in that bowl to be multiplied, but I prayed He might use just His imagination this time. That one or two loaves of bread would do just fine for now. Our boys were not much fond of fish anyways.

"Please. Pleease, Sweet Jesus," I implored. "My little brothers are so awful hungry. I don't know what else to do. Please put some food in this bowl right now, and I will never ask You for another favor ever. I swear to you, oh Heavenly—"

Suddenly, I came aware of what I'd just avowed. And to whom.

I knew it was sinful to put forth false promises, especially since, probably, I might be calling up another favor in the near future. Right quick, I tacked on, "Still, maybe someday I might, but I promise I will hold off for as long as I can. Amen."

While nothing did appear in my makeshift miracle bread bowl, within five minutes Misses Ruby Pearl Banks, the dark-brown church lady in red Keds, those high-topped kind, came by with a basketful of breads, muffins, and buns left over from the Jeremiah Baptist's morning bake sale.

Like my momma says, "Prayers don't always get done in the way we expect, but somehow or another, in due time, they get done."

MOMMA HAD FINALLY STOPPED HER swaying. She'd changed out of that God-forsaken dressing gown, bathed and dressed, and cleaned, salved, and rebandaged her finger wound. She'd even smutched some Vaseline petroleum jelly on her lips and dabbed a pinch of rouge onto her cheeks for good measure.

She just about floated into our kitchen in that pretty flowered skirt, her limp near gone. The high ruffled neck of her blue-green blouse set off the deep auburn glint of her hair and the ivory tone of her skin, while its sheer, tinted sleeves served well enough to camouflage any fresh bruises.

Just about six months prior, Momma'd picked up this outfit and a pretty pair of pumps at the Goodwill Store. She'd meant to wear the getup for her hostessing job interview down at the Bubba's Burgers & Brews Road House. But when JB heard about it all, he took those shoes and snapped the heel off the one. Then he set the other on fire.

All gussied up, now, with her hair tied back in a ribbon and the pink ballet slippers passed off to her by one of Gamma Gert's Wild Women, Momma looked mighty fine, in spite of the swell under her left eye and the leftover hitch in her giddyap.

Today, she seemed clever as well, and I could not help but tell her as much.

"You look smart today, Momma. Very, very smart."

"Why, thank you, Cieli Mae," she said, unblinking. "I feel smart. Very, very smart."

Momma's rosy cheeriness was welcome though a touch bizarre in light of our most recent household pandemonium.

"Okay, then. We're all going into town today!" Momma exclaimed. With her own a'twinkle she looked me square in the eye. Purposely drawing on more lilt than drawl, she whispered, "Lookit here, Cieli Mae, I'ma need you to look after the boys while I make small talk with some womenfolk. Is that awright, sugar? Can you do that for me?"

Enveloped in her goodness, I just did not understand how anyone could want to hurt her.

Oh, Momma. My precious momma. There isn't anything I wouldn't do for you. Don't you know that?

She must have read my thoughts just then because she laughed a quick laugh, smiled an overdone smile. "Oh, my baby girl," she said, tilting her head to one side. "What ever would I do without you?"

I was sad at that thought for just one moment. I'd wondered the same thing from time to time, and it frightened me some. But then I snapped my spirit back into its rightful place, and we finished getting ready for our day's outing.

CHAPTER TWENTY-FIVE

It WAS NOT EASY MANEUVERING that shaky carriage with all four boys jammed into it, and over such pocked terrain.

That stroller was meant only for two but for as much as our little guys had stretched out longwise, none, aside from Eli, took up more in breadth than a bag o' bones.

Most folks know it's easier to shoot a fly with a slingshot than to keep little boys on the straight and narrow, especially when it comes to the out-of-doors. We just did not have time to chase after bunnies or stop to ponder over anthills today so despite the boy's earsplitting objections, the carriage it was.

I ran up a'ways and backwards facing them, making funny noises and silly faces and doing the dumb stuff little boys find amusing. I'd wanted to believe I had something to do with the suds of happiness flowing from that rig, the smiles bursting like fireworks, but I knew better.

NOT LONG AGO, MOMMA HAD come upon that baby buggy by way of Sister Anna and the Church of the Twelve Apostles' Child Swap held in the parish hall. This event attracted more of a crowd than their weekly masses and bingo nights combined.

It'd been awhile since those flyers had gone up all over town, posted in shoppes' front doors, taped to poles, and tied around tree trunks with brown twine.

The brand-new Catholic church, just built between a copse of ironweed and scruff pines in neighboring downtown Surprise, offered free Catechism classes for natural-born Catholics and heathens alike. The flyers read: SUNDAY SCHOOL! Transportation available! Cookies and milk after each session! And then there were the ones proclaiming: CHILD SWAP! Come see our selection of heavenly, gently used products at prices too good for this world!

The twins pestered after Momma nonstop until she marched us all into the parish hall and signed them up for Sunday school after inquiring as to the actual meaning behind the term, *Child Swap.* She breathed a sigh of relief upon learning any trading had to do only with a child's belongings and not the actual child.

Momma found the teacher-nuns the most evenly tempered and kindly species she'd encountered in her lifetime. They seemed to've taken an extra-special liking to her and the boys as well.

It was hard to figure how those women remained cool and saintly under so many layers. The boys half-teased, half-questioned, "Why're them ladies wearin' them funny getups, Momma? Why're they dressed like pa-anguins?" Momma hushed them up, right quick. Having had only limited exposure to Roman Catholics and their ways, she wasn't sure whether those merciful sisters would be amused or take offense. Surely, she didn't want us labeled a family of heretics from the get-go.

The class roster for religious instruction in their age group was still wide open, and our boys, never baptized into any denomination, were wholeheartedly encouraged to partake. The Church of the Twelve Apostles hadn't yet made its way into mainstream thinking in these parts. At Sunday Mass and even Friday Night Bingo, attendance was light at best. Most local souls had already been otherwise spoken for, and unlike at Gamma Gert's River of Hope Springs Eternal Church and Pool Hall, gambling was restricted here, which, I reckon, explained a lot of the absenteeism.

Clear-eyed and full of faith and conviction, these Sisters of Endless Mercy looked after near everything having anything to do with Twelve Apostles. Everything from the Sunday School to the Friday Night Bingo to the Child Swap.

They were not, as we later learned, allowed to officiate a mass or listen to a confession. Or drink the altar wines. When Bootie asked

Momma, "Why not?" Momma answered, "Well now. I 'spect it is because underneath those robes, they are women."

I reckon that made sense enough to her at the time, but the boys seemed confused by the notion.

Pint-sized Sister Anna had designated herself our own personal welcoming committee after being assigned as our boys' Sunday school instructor by the Mother Superior.

During their first ever Catechism class, James nudged his twin with an elbow, almost toppling Bootie from his desk chair. "Where do babies go, Sister Anna, I mean, them that die 'fore they're born?" he asked. An earlier coin toss between the two brothers had determined which of them would pose their burning question. A heavy silence descended upon the class of cut-ups. The otherwise rowdy five-, six-, seven-, and eight-year-old boys, staid and wide-eyed.

Sister Anna shaped her mouth to speak but no words came forth. It appeared her Cupid-shaped lips were ready, but her thoughts were not. Fingering the wooden beads of the rosary hanging from her thick, woolen belt, she bowed her head and quickly paced the front of the classroom. From one side to the other. Her short black veil trailing after her like a flag on a breeze.

Making rounds, Mother Superior stopped in the open doorway. With an unearthly calm she nodded once at Sister Anna, halting the frantic runaway in her tracks. The supervisor smiled and nodded once more. She then took two steps back into the dimly lit hallway, and floated on to the next classroom.

Sister Anna raised both hands to prayer level, looking, for that moment, like a miniature version of one of those saintly statues in her church. Then, with her palms pressed firmly together, she touched the tips of her fingers to her lips. Caressing my brothers' faces with her dewey eyes, she spoke tenderly, "Those tiny souls who don't make it through to this world? Well, we're told they go to a place called Limbo—

"Limbo? What's a Limbo?" asked Bootie.

"Well," Sister Anna continued. "Limbo is, hmm. Limbo is a holding cell. A wait room for unbaptized babies' souls," she explained with a false authority. Concerned, the teaching novice tilted her head to the one side perplexed by what had come out of her own mouth. Noting the sadness and confusion inflicted by that which had never made sense to her in the first place, she let out a sigh. "But I've always believed they go straight to heaven . . ."

"See there, James? I tole ya so! Them babies go straight to heaven just like Momma says!" Bootie shouted into James's ear.

"I guess," was all James could muster at that moment.

Sister Anna nodded sagely, holding tight to her rosary beads for support. Under her breath she quickly said three Hail Marys and one Our Father—hoping they might hold her over until her next confession—before finishing her thought, "As there is no chance for any sin, not even a venial, to sneak in and tarnish their immortal souls."

Then, with a missionary's conviction, she moved on to the intended lesson, putting forth the fable of The Milk Bottles, according to the holy grail of every Catholic Sunday School since then, *The Baltimore Catechism*.

Between its flimsy cardboard covers, the greatest mysteries of humankind had been solved using a simple question-and-answer format. Basic pen and ink drawings defined the tried and truest ideals of the faith, starting with the Immortal Soul as akin to one of three milk bottles.

The first, and obvious vessel of choice, embodies purity in its whiteness. The second, like a Holstein-in-a-carafe, represents the mildly sullied soul of a venial sinner. And last, but not least, full to its brim with mortal sins, a decanter of black bile, the jug of the damned.

I listened, resting assured there were no dark blobs oozing their way through our little baby Alexia's soul. Although, time and again, I wondered about my own. As an eyewitness to malice with intent to harm, I, unlike Momma, willingly hated the perpetrator, even knowing hate is the most mortal of all sins. Could it be possible my momma was made of better, stronger stuff than I?

As detailed, I imagined the silky unstained soul of the beautiful baby Alexia arriving at those pearly gates and being promptly admitted with not even a timeout for our little angel. Many of our other siblings, notified of her early arrival, would rush to her welcome.

I smiled, grateful to little Sister Anna for shedding her own special light on a subject of such concern.

As for the Child Swap involving outgrown and gently used belongings, I questioned the term gently used. Why, anyone who knows children knows they do not use things all that gently. At least, not the ones I'd come to figure up.

But I must declare, personal experiences aside, that double-wide stroller was in good condition. Like new, almost. Gamma Gert liked to say it didn't owe us a penny, and that was for sure, as we'd gotten it for free.

Her eyes dancing, Sister Anna had called Momma aside after one Sunday service. "Come with me, Misses Jackson," Sister Anna whispered with a wink. "There is something I'd like to show you."

The baby buggy had been dropped off anonymously. Sister Anna told Momma she could think of no household more needy or deserving, and she wanted to offer it to us before the doors of the swap officially opened that Friday afternoon.

We didn't have anything worth trading, but the Mercies, as we'd come to call those godly women, especially that little Sister Anna, were good about understanding all that. Those nuns always seemed so overjoyed to see us, a household in such need, that we showed up with a regularity just about as much for their sakes as for our own.

There weren't a whole lot of honest-to-goodness Roman Catholics down around here, and some folk, truth be told, were afraid of them. Our boys attended their Sunday school mostly because of the sisters. And because it was free. Momma believed some form of religious education a good idea, so long as it wasn't anything too radical. I reckon she may have been taken aback some had she done a more thorough job investigating Catholicism.

The Church of the Twelve Apostles was also the easiest to get to from Tribesmen's. Some of the times Momma just couldn't bring our boys there, such as when JB showed up unexpected. On those occassions Sister Anna, as promised, drove the rickety mustard-colored station wagon to carry them up, along with any other stray, heathen trailer children in need of ministering.

The nuns always provided for their charges a lesson and a lunch. More often than not, even if we weren't there with them, the twins returned home with what the sisters claimed were leftovers, wrapped carefully, in waxed paper, or tin foil, and brown-boxed.

As Momma had a way of bringing out the best in all kinds of people, not a day went by anymore without some church person asking after us.

It got to be that most Sundays our trailer stoop might've been mistook as a drop-off center for the Salvation Army or some other such organization of do-gooders.

Time to time, our late day Sunday suppers turned into ecumenical smorgasbords featuring any combination of baked goods from the Baptists, fried chicken from the Methodists, tuna and potato chip casseroles from the Lutherans, or the spaghetti and fried pork chop dinners brought home from the Catholic's Sunday school.

"We need be mindful of our many blessings. Now and always. Amen," Momma said before any meal regardless of the bounty, or any lack thereof.

"Amen!" The boys shouted in unison, especially on their days of plenty. Praise the Lord and please pass the ammunition.

AS MOMMA TRAIPSED ON, JOSTLING her way through leathery clay dirt and craggy, pebbled earth, wheels turned, boys giggled, and the kindly brown, high-top-wearing church lady, Misses Ruby Pearl Banks, called after us, "Where you bringin' all them chirrens on this fine day? Where you all headed to?"

Beneath a wide-brimmed bonnet, Ruby Pearl rested the back of one hand on a shimmering forehead, further blocking the sun's rays from her dark chocolate eyes. She knelt on one padded knee and leaned an elbow on the other, aside a flower bed of her own design. Three tires painted a bright fuchsia sat side by side, daring her to add more color to the already overly perky parade of plantings.

"Why, I do believe we're headed straight to the poor house," Momma replied, unblinking.

Using the handle of her shovel as a brace, Ruby Pearl uprighted herself right quick. There she stood apart from her digger, head cocked at a questioning angle, hands on her hips, and her full mouth agape.

"Oh my gracious light!" Momma gushed. I could feel her exaggerated drawl coming on. "I was just making a li'l ole joke, Misses Banks. Now, now. How purty is all this! Lookit here! Don't you have the greenest thumb? Why, I 'spect you could coax flowers from those rocks over yonder."

Ruby Pearl wagged her head and let out a low whistle. I reckoned she was thinking how this here white woman had one mixed-up sense of whimsy.

"I thank you Misses Jackson fo' respecting my garden," Ruby Pearl said, composure regained. "So where is you all off to then, on this fine day?"

"Why, we're headed into town!" Momma's lips pressed out a smile, and a new kind of glimmer shone in her wide eyes. "My JB got hisself some day work at the pine gum distillery down in Valdosta. He'll be gone one week. Or two. Or more. In any case I 'spect I better stock up some. Cain't never tell what the weather's gonna be, what with tornado season upon us and what all else's been going on just outside Willin."

Having piqued Ruby Pearl's interest, Momma tossed a devil-may-care look into the dank atmosphere.

"Huhn. Seem them chirrens might be happier here with me, than in that there contraption while you run them errands," offered Ruby Pearl. "Cody don't mind. Woun't bother me none, neither."

James, Bootie, Clayt, and Eli shrieked with glee. Sweaty little-boy limbs careened in a jumbled but precise choreography, the way little-boy limbs do. Around and through one another they stretched and strained, grabbing at the dense air with sticky fingers and reaching out for Cody. The mindful border collie zigzagged this way and that around his captive audience cautious but joyful in his own anticipation.

I was convinced. Momma was not.

"I'd be happy fo' the company! Ol' Ruby got no one to cook fo' no mo'." Ruby Pearl slipped her still-gloved hands into her deep apron pockets. "Lordy. What happened to yo' hand Misses Jackson? That's a mighty big bandage you got—"

"My hand?" My momma took a step back. "Oh, I was peeling taters is all. Silly ole me. My eyes weren't paying enough attention to what my fingers were doing."

I could tell by the way Momma started picking at herself, she needed to change the subject, and quick, before Ruby Pearl went and asked any more of those kinds of questions. "If only I could be sure the boys wouldn't be too much trouble—"

"No ma'am, Misses Jackson. I got biscuits 'n blackberry jam fo' them boys to snack on. Fresh churned butter. I'll fry up some ham. Fact is, I was just about ready to boil up some black-eyed peas and collard greens."

The scale had tipped. The boys grinned, holding their collective breath.

I made a mental note to ask later whether those were little white lies or boldfaced ones my momma and her overdone drawl had been spinning for poor Ruby Pearl.

"Well now," Momma said, her brow furrowed deep in consideration. "I reckon leaving my boys with you might be a good thang. For my sake, as well as theirs. As long as you're sure you're up to it, that is. I am still worried over the escaped prisoner. Why, I just don't know what all is to be thought. Hearing that lunatic madman is still on the loose sticks in my craw something awful," she paused, letting her words settle.

Once again, Ruby Pearl appeared dumbfounded.

"Oh my stars, Misses Banks, you ain't heard—" Momma raised her unbandaged right hand to her lips, as if she were trying to halt the flow of her words.

With the backside of one orange gloved hand, Ruby Pearl pushed back the brim of her straw sunbonnet. Holding steady the garden rake with the other, she leaned forward. Her round eyes had narrowed into slits, and her glistening face was now stamped with a giant question mark.

"You ain't heard nothing about the breakout at the federal prison?" Momma gasp-asked gently, testing the waters. "My JB, he learned about it from a fella at the filling station just the other day."

Ruby Pearl shook her head, her countenance wide open to concerns my momma seemed all too happy to feed.

"Mister Jackson says I must keep my gun loaded. And within arms reach. At all times. Until he gets back. From Valdosta. He hated to leave us at a time like this—just as he always hates to leave us—but a man cain't cut off his nose none just to spite his face, as Gertrude Kaye might say. Not when there's good money to be made. Not when he's got this many mouths to feed. Ain't that right, Misses Banks?"

Momma rushed on in what seemed, to me at least, a monologue of some predesign. "It ain't like that penitentiary's next door. But it ain't that far neither."

"You sho' about all this, Misses Jackson?" Ruby Pearl asked, still in a state of puzzlement.

"Why, I'm as sure of all this as I am that my husband loves me and these here babies."

"Well. Hmmph." Ruby Pearl puckered her dry lips, pulled off her gloves, wiped her sweaty palms on the skirt of her garden apron, and scratched at her forehead. "I wonder how come I ain't heard nothin'." I suspect she might've been thinking other thoughts, but that was all she'd said.

Momma squirmed, causing her halo to teeter as Ruby Pearl studied her closer. "Misses Banks," she responded, just like if she was saying grace before a meal. "I swear to you on my childrens, there's a bad man on the loose. That's the solemn truth—"

"I promise you, Misses Jackson, I won't let them boys out my sight. And it don't look like my Cody will neither." Ruby Pearl took a breath. "But you got to do what you think best, chile." It was her way of handing over what she suspected Momma needed.

I wondered how come some folk know how to give to others and some, well, they just don't.

"Hmm," Momma said, her sigh full of focus. "Well, now. The sooner I get done, the sooner I can get us all back home and under lock 'n key. And yes, Misses Banks, I do believe if they had their druthers, my little ragamuffins druther be running 'round in your fine yard with Cody here than doing errands with me. But what can I do to return the favor? Might I pick up something for you?"

"I got my Bowie knife. But I don't s'pose it'd hurt none to have a extra round for my handgun. I'd surely 'ppreciate, if it's awright with you—" Ruby Pearl puffed up in an air of conditioned servitude while she actually meant nothing of the sort.

"Oh heavens to Betsy! But of course, ma'am. Well now, lookit there, you'n me, we both got .38s! I know exactly what you need, and I will be most pleased to do that one little thing for you. It will be my treat. You been so kind, always bringing goodies and whatnot from your church bake sales those times my JB was, um, between jobs. Plus and all, I got more 'n enough fretting to do over this here brood. I most surely don't need to be worrying over you waking up dead."

"Why, thank you, Missy, but Ruby Pearl Banks aw'wes pays her own way." Ruby Pearl reached down the front of her dress into her bosom and pulled out a mess of neatly folded dollar bills leaving me to wonder what other treasures she might've had stashed in there. "You take this," she said, forcing the cash into my momma's hand. "Don't you fret none about these here babies. They in good hands."

"Thank you kindly," Momma said, that air of servitude had switched to the other foot soldier. "And may God bless you, Misses Banks."

"God done bless me, Missy. Don't you worry none 'bout that."

Momma turned to the boys. "All y'all be good for Misses Banks, y'hear?"

And off we went. Momma and me. Just the two of us. Cream and Sugar.

I was not at all sure where this journey was taking her, but she was not going it alone. Not this time.

CHAPTER TWENTY-SIX

WE'D GONE ONLY BUT ONE quarter mile when Momma came to a halt. She looked at me. She looked away. Then she looked at me again.

"There was a right nice side to JB at one time. You know that, don't you, Cieli Mae?" she asked.

I wondered what toll the heat had exacted on her brain already and so early into our sojourn. I've seen him up, down, sideways, and even inside out, and I can't say I ever noticed a nice side.

"I'm not sure what you mean," I said back. That was the best I could do.

"When we first met, he had a most pleasant, honeyed measure about him. And the other girls, how they swooned over him. That's how good lookin' he was. And he was nice to me. Back then, he was oh so very nice to me." Momma strained to keep her voice even.

"I 'spect lots of girls in your place mighta done the same's you, Momma," I offered.

"He called me a 'pretty little thing.' Plain ole me with my coveralls and scraggly hair and bit-down nails." She looked at her hands, one wrapped, one chapped, and started twisting them like strands of hemp into cording. "Sad ole me who didn't need a curfew because I didn't have no friends. Homey ole me. Why, I hadn't never even had a beau before him. He said he loved me. That he wanted to take care of me."

"And you believed him." I was not one bit doubtful.

"And I believed him. Even though a little voice inside of me, oh now, nevermind," she'd whispered.

"You were young and trustful then, Momma. Just waiting on a body to come along who might deserve your best."

"Still and all, that little voice grew louder and louder until I could hear it clear. But by then it was too late. I loved him already."

"You didn't know no better then."

"I didn't know no better then," Momma whispered, scrunching her eyes shut to keep any tears from tumbling out.

"Hear tell, there's such a thing as a 'late bloomer'. Maybe you're just one of them. Do you know better now, Momma?"

My momma didn't answer but just stared ahead like she needed to think on it some. Then she looked up. Noting the sky was starting to turn, we got back on our way.

THAT DAY TRIP MAY HAVE SEEMED uneventful by most folk's measures, but for us there was nothing regular about it. This time there was a course of action in Momma's head. And a whole mess of dollar bills in her pouch.

She had always gone out of her way to impress upon me and the boys the value of having a plan. "You need to measure twice if you expect to cut but once," she told us, same as Pawpaw Clyde Royce had told her. Sometimes the words changed but the message stayed fixed.

Before hitting the aisles with an empty shop cart, Momma sawed a good chunk off of our long-overdue due bill. "I wish it could be more, Miss Martha," she said, meaning it. Momma and I both knew it could've been more if only JB hadn't been so dang selfish. Why, over those years and little by little, he'd siphoned off a hefty portion from his legacy ci-gar box, all in satisfaction of his own piggish wants.

"Oh, now you hush child. This here's a fine start. A real fine start. I knew you'd make good as soon as you was able, Vida Lee. What happened, hon, some rich relative drop dead?"

"Uhmm. Well, truth be told, it was something like that," Momma said back.

Word spread faster than the McClurgh virus. Shop folk stared at her, but not out of pity. Not this time.

Maybe it was her new way of walking with her shoulders tossed back, her steps assured. Maybe it was the new twinkle in her eyes and the smile, true and genuine, pulling at her lips. Or maybe it was just the good soldiers in her purse.

Whatever it was, it took them all by happy surprise.

After paying down our standing obligations as much as she was able, Momma collected the envelope full of S&H Green Stamps which Misses Parson's oldest daughter had been holding onto for us. As Gamma Gert liked to say, even a blind pig finds an acorn once in a while.

"I knew you'd make good, Vida Lee. And lookit what I been saving up for you. Lookit here. Now you can get something special, something y'all been hankerin' after."

Now I already knew how, for the most part at least, my momma could bring out the best in some others, but that Martha Parsons, well, even on her own she was a right fine human being.

All fired up and bubbling over on the inside, my momma still managed to keep her balance on the outside. She didn't dare to let on that Martha had had more faith in her than she'd had in her own self.

"Why Miss Martha, I thank you kindly for taking such good care of my account. Aren't you just the smartest business woman? Why, yes, you are."

WE'D KEPT THE EMPTY FREE Green Stamp booklets and a free S&H Green Stamp catalogue for as long as I could remember, stashed safe and sound under Momma and JB's straw mattress.

It would be my duty to keep a sharp eye out while Momma sorted, licked, and fastened those tiny green trading stamps onto the proper pages, in their rightful spaces, according to face value. I'd compliment her on her exactitude, and I would hide any amusement as her tongue turned greener and greener with each passing lick.

On some summer nights when the air in the trailer got so thick and heavy it made it tiresome to breathe, with the one small electric fan blowing on the boys, my momma dragged the smaller pallet onto the backyard grasses. With not a care in this world, we'd study that S&H catalogue. The Ultra Modern Chrome Toaster with its temperature-control knobs looked to be something we might need, but Momma had her heart set on a new cast iron skillet.

A few years back JB borrowed her fry pan, even though she'd begged him not to. That seasoned skillet had been passed on from Great Granny LuLa to Memaw Veta Sue to her, and Momma'd had a mind to, maybe someday, pass it on to one of her own. That fry pan was the one thing she'd wanted to hold on to from the past. JB knew all about that, but he went and ruined it anyway. He went and used her prized skillet to drain the oil from his pal's old fire-engine red '51 White truck, dang him.

STROLLING THOSE AISLES WITH A newfound sense of wonderment, my momma filled our market cart with two king-sized loaves of Wonder bread, a pint-size jar of Duke's, one pound of orange cheese, two green apples, a box of Fruit Loops, one brand-new bar of Fels-Naptha, a can of Comet cleanser, a sixty-four-ounce bottle of Mr. Clean, and other such housekeeping necessities, plus a six-pack of Coca Cola, one box of candy cigarettes for the boys to share, and some sticks of Blackjack chewing gum.

Schoolgirl giddy, she unfolded and counted out each bill one at a time, one after the other, and we paid for our loot on the spot. Why, she even got change back. That transaction completed, Momma rezipped her red pleather pouch and snapped her purse shut with a near haughty air.

"Lookit here, Cieli Mae," she whispered to me as we exited the establishment. "I paid for it all and didn't even need sign for nothing this time. So what do you think of that?"

"I think it's good, Momma," I hushed back. "I think it's how it oughta be."

ALMOST TO OUR NEXT STOP, our buggy bulging with earthly delights, it occurred to me that my momma most surely did have, at her beck and call, a stockpile of smarts. And that she might be just about ready to use it.

But had she just come upon it? Or had she always had it but supposed, for reasons beyond reason, to keep it hidden? Or had she finally just made up her mind?

Doc Feldman explained two things over and over, time and again. I reckoned he hoped at least a one might take root during his lifetime:

"The more difficult the practice, Vidalia Lee, the more valuable the lesson," and "Once you decide, my dear, all else will follow."

For mostly all of her life my momma had wanted to do the right things. Misled by those misled before her, she just never knew for sure what those right things were. But now, well, maybe she did.

BEFORE LONG, MOMMA PARKED OUR buggy in the shade of a giant scrub oak. She took in one big breath and stepped up onto the paved sidewalk, closer to a strange storefront.

Her eyes glistened but her voice smiled as she read the sign, *Sunny Knight's Heavenly Hair: The Higher the Tresses, the Closer to You Know Who.*

Momma took two steps back as her playful grin turned down. Like a frightened turtle, she recalled her delight back into its protective shell. The unbandaged fingers of her left hand clutched at her purse strings, the other hand held tight to nothing at all.

Entering the shop to a tinny jingle-jangle of silver bells tacked above the sun-weathered doorframe Momma introduced herself to the owner, as if such was needed.

Marigold Sun Beauregard Knight stood at attention. With golden locks piled high atop her head and lacquered stiff, she looked like a keeper waiting on her honey bees. "Well, shut my mouth!" Sunny exclaimed, unmoving, hands on hips. "Lookit you, Vidalia Lee Kandal. Get over here sugah and give your Sunny a great big hug!"

Many years past, Sunny and my momma had been one another's best halves, and now, there they stood, at arms length. Two separate balls of yarn all knotted up inside themselves. A tightrope stretched taut above the chasm between the two. Momma didn't move even one muscle. And truth be told, for a good while there, neither did Sunny.

I guess I had always reckoned on something other than a stalemate when those two finally re-met.

EIGHT-YEAR-OLD MARIGOLD SUN BEAUREGARD had rushed into my Vidalia's life as if they were meant to be.

Just outside the gate of the Willin County Fairgrounds, Momma had eyed the pint-sized golden girl struggling to control her pink cotton candy on a stick.

"Hey!" Sunny yelled. "You there. Matchstick girl with the burnt hair. Quit your gawkin' and gimme a hand here 'fore this all gets blowed away!"

My Vidalia looked around. She saw tall girls. Skinny girls. Tall, skinny girls. But not one other coppery redhead. "Me?" she mouthed. Hopeful in her confusion she pointed back at her own self.

The petite goddess dressed in pink, as if to match her treat, rolled her eyes and waved the sugary puff, "What're you waitin' on girl? A engraved invitation?" Sunny huffed. "Come help me eat this right quick."

From that moment on those two coached, cajoled, and abetted one another, in, around, and through, much of girlhood's joys, sorrows, and confusions, pinky swearing to stand by one another, "Forevermore. And always, too."

Unlike Momma, Sunny had found the strength to stand fast and firm, no matter what strong winds gusted at her back and even after the sudden death of her only brother.

In those stormy days following the Beauregard's abrupt departure, my Vidalia's confusions swirled in her head like a tornado. Reckoning how her own challenges paled by comparison and though she'd understood the leaving was not of Sunny's own doing, she blamed her still. Instead of taking comfort in her friend's fortitude, my momma, my Vidalia, turned resentful, which piled onto her loss a sense of shame.

"We reckon we know ourselfs from the inside out, Cieli Mae," she'd told me while the boys slept on in the next room. "Then one day a light shines on us from someplace unexpected, and it casts a different kind of shadow. A deeper darkness that falls behind us. That follows us. One we don't want to accept but cain't near deny."

Prior to the untimely killing of their young Wildy Jax, the Beauregard's had been regularly practicing, almost fully sacramented, Roman Catholics.

As I have mentioned, Catholics, especially those of the Roman variety, were a curiosity in these parts. But then again, Mama Rosie O'Connell Beauregard was a transplanted Yankee, so I expect that justified the family's strange leanings.

ONE AFTERNOON DURING A SCHOOL picnic, my Vidalia and her Sunny snuck away from the pack. Running along the dirt path and up a small hill, they played I-Spy until Momma stopped short.

"I hate Maw Veta," she wailed. Her bare feet kicked up a dust of red clay as a waterfall streamed steady down her cheeks.

"Hush now, Vida Lee. You don't hate your mama!"

"Oh, yes I do!" she'd cried out between sniffles. "She never braids my hair no more. Never makes me new clothes no more. She don't even talk to me or Paw 'cept to scold. All she does is cry. All the time. I hate her. I do."

For as quick as those words burst from her mouth, she wanted to take them back. Sunny would never ever let her get away with such imaginings.

"Don't you know Vidalia Lee, H-A-T-E does to the soul what M-U-R-D-E-R does to the body!" Thus began Sunny's sermon on the mound. "And 'sides, Veta Sue didn't never offer you up to the lickker patrol to keep her own self out of trouble, and she didn't never leave you alone at night while she went off whoring and such. And that makes her a better ma than the one she had. And that means, at least she's tryin'."

Momma reckoned she might as well settle in. No telling when this would all end, nor where it might stop along the way.

"Do I hate my two-timing sonofabitch daddy for what he done? For leaving me, Mama, and Wildy Jax to fend for ourselfs while he run off with that tramp secatary of his? No. I don't hate him. I pray for him is what I do. Even tho I 'spect he's already been damned to the fires of hell. And rightly so.

"You listen here now, Vidalia Lee. Hate is a sin from which there ain't no coming back. Not unless you are truly contrite. Even then, there ain't no guarantees. We best pray quick," Sunny commanded, "'fore them words get wrote down in a ledger somewheres."

The two little magnolias then dropped to their skinned knees faster than a twenty-pound bag of flour from a second-story window.

"Dear Lord, forgive this child sinner!" Saint Sunny implored, leading the litany, holding Momma's hands in a vise-grip. "For she is truly sorry beyond any measure. She just ain't in her proper mind, is all. Must be the heat." The duo finalized the plea with several rousing rounds of amens.

While cocksure she'd end up in heaven, Sunny feared visiting rights might not extend to those less godly.

"Wouldn't it be a crying shame, Vida Lee, if we couldn't visit during eternity? That's a looong time, in case you didn't know."

More than once, Sunny had saved Momma from herself. And vice versa.

Back then, the raising of their respective retaining walls had not yet begun. Life, thus far, hadn't provided enough of the raw materials necessary for such construction.

For as quick and as deep as this world took its scoops out of them, Momma and Sunny kept on filling each other back up—like those tender grains, finer than gravel but coarser than silt, that keep pouring back into a hole dug in dry sand.

"We knew more about each other than anybody's got a right to," Momma recollected to me with a sigh. "But even that didn't stop us from lovin' each other to pieces."

⌣⟶

AFTER ROBBING THE COLD TURKEY Package store at gunpoint Wildy Jax Beauregard and his getaway car got T-boned by Povis Alley Roswell's pick-up.

Povis, the son of Mayor Tremont Roswell, had been driving along those backroads blindfolded on a dare when he smashed into Sunny's brother's Chevy Bel Air convertible. No charges were allowed to stick against the mayor's son. The fool walked away without as much as a stitch.

After that miscarriage of justice Sunny and her mama didn't practice much of anything and surely not religion. They had no use for Willin County or any citizen of it. The grieving mother and her remaining child left town in the middle of one night, destination unknown.

Unawares, my Vidalia had wandered idly, skipping along as if nothing had changed. She'd stopped for Sunny on her way to school the following morning, as usual, and saw the For Sale sign in the Beauregard's front yard.

The two had not seen nor heard from one another since. Not until Momma visited the beauty shop Sunny had come upon by way of a right dandy divorce settlement.

THAT AFTERNOON IN THE HAIR salon, before long, bygones went the way they were meant to, and the distance between Sunny and Momma diminished to a hairsbreadth. Poised and ready, Momma jumped into the margin feetfirst.

"Vidalia, honey? What all happened to your finger?" Sunny asked, even though Momma had done her best to keep that wounded hand tucked away and out of Sunny's line of vision.

"Oh, you know me. I was chopping up some rhubarb for a pie and one of the babies started screamin' and well," Momma faked a laugh, held up her injury, and braved on. "But Sunny, dear friend, there is something important I need be sure y'all know about. For your own good, I mean."

The fable of the escaped lunatic prisoner took on a stronger flavor with this retelling, silencing even Sunny who had rarely come upon a yarn she couldn't outspin.

The new-and-improved beauty parlor version included sheets tied end to end and strung from the jail cell window, with the mad escapee shimmying down a jagged stone wall leaving behind not only a pint of fresh blood, but near a pound of shredded skin.

"An' even that there didn't slow him down none!" Momma exclaimed, her eyes blazing wild.

Thanks to his superhuman strength and size, that savage put down thirteen armed prison guards with only his own two bare hands before clearing the sky-high barbed-wire-topped fence and making a mad dash to freedom.

Momma lowered her voice. Her furtive glances about implied she did not mean to be overheard by those curious patrons nearby, while her loudly exaggerated hushed tones suggested otherwise.

"And us women? Especially us with childrens for whom there ain't nothing we wouldn't do to keep safe from harm." On that note she muted her wary words further, causing those down the assembly line of ash blondes, from beehives to bobs, to strain and swivel in their chairs.

"Why, my husband? He liked to'a died! He could not even speak of what all that monster had done to them women, to their babies, 'cept to say it was too awful to talk about!"

Momma's words got sucked up into the roots of Sunny's regulars faster than those coats of semi-permanent hair coloring.

With the clientele now fluttering about like chickens in a henhouse with a randy rooster on the loose, and more *Well, I never's* and *I declare's* mucking the air than Aqua Net hairspray, Momma cautioned again that Sunny not concern the whole town but to just be on her guard. "Who knows if it's all true, anyways?"

Wandering from a righteous path of absolutes, knowing that Momma had something else up her sleeve besides her bruised arm, I wondered how many, if any, of this world's quandaries could be resolved with a simple yes or no.

Is a crime a sin? A sin a crime?

Are there different degrees of premeditation? Of self-defense?

Is premeditated self-defense a crime? Or a sin?

If so, why? And if not, why not?

"I 'spect it is what it is, and it takes, well now, it takes what it takes," Sunny replied. "Be safe, Vida Lee—no more pies for you. Least not 'til you're all healed up. And don't be a stranger no more! Come on in sometime soon. Let me try 'n do something with that mop o' yours. Maybe give you a little height. Gently, Sunny's red fingertips swept Momma's frizzled and overgrown bangs to one side. Then, leaning in conspiringly, she shushed into Momma's ear, "Why, girlfriend, bless your little white cotton socks, you know I won't charge you no more'n my best employee."

My momma smiled until the dimples on both sides of her mouth deepened. With her purse draped over her wrist, her good hand held fast to the loosened cut-glass doorknob. "Well now. You be careful too."

"Just come back soon. I been missing you, Vidalia Lee. Truly, I have."

A jumble of keepsakes danced around in Momma's head making her dizzy. Oh, Sunny, Full of Light. "I've missed you too," Momma said. If only Sunny had known how very, very much.

Momma switched her bag to her injured side, squeezed shut her left eye and drew her right elbow in, close to her side. With her right thumb crooked upward, she aimed her index finger straight ahead. "POW," she mouthed.

Sunny mirrored the familiar stance, puckering her lips, as if readying to douse a candle on a birthday cake. She blew out, directing a stream of air downward toward her own upturned index finger. "POW," she mouthed back.

Years ago, behind Jeb Maijer's filling station, regularly and unchaperoned, the duo had honed their skills with BB guns and clay targets. Calamity Jane and Annie Oakley in training.

Even JB was made aware of Momma's history of prowess as a champion skeet-shooter from the time she was knee high to a Georgia little grass frog. Pawpaw Clyde Royce had seen to it that this ill-begot in-law knew at least that much of her pedigree.

Finally, Momma and I departed Heavenly Hair and headed toward Gookin's Ammo & Gun Shop where we picked up a box of bullets for Ruby Pearl and one for ourselves.

"Just in case," my momma said to me, by way of explanation.

Mister Gookin had looked surprised to see Momma standing there at his front counter, and rightly so. It'd been a while. Nonetheless, and not because she'd grown any less fond of Mister Gookin, she had meant to make quick work of this segment of our adventure. Looking down at her naked wrist imagining a watch, she chirped, "Oh my heavens, don't time just fly. Why I do declare I could stand here chatting with you til the sun goes down Mister Gookin, but it's clouding up out there and I best be on my way and let you tend to your other customers." Mister Gookin looked around, confusion painting his face. Other than him and Momma and me, the shop was empty.

Munitions secured, our army of two marched on.

The air swelled with a murkiness common in these parts come late August but too early still, as we'd not yet hit mid-July.

Momma unbuttoned and folded down her ruffled collar. With my spirit up alongside of hers, we simmered in the juices of the day's adventures thus far. Our carriage moved at a steady pace over the gouged terrain.

"Momma, I wonder," I began. But just then a hummingbird paused midair, smack in the middle of a batch of wild honeysuckle. Its wings fluttered wildly while its body remained stationary. Just another one of this world's curiosities.

"What? What is it, Cieli Mae? What's wrong?" she asked, saucer-eyed. Plump beads of sweat made their ways from her frizz halo, bursting onto her forehead, while the thick air lunged at her throat.

Be out with it quick, I told myself. I hadn't meant to upset her. My mission was to ease her struggles, not add to them. But still I wondered why it was that everytime she started in on the story of the brutal escapee she'd tuck her good hand behind her back, its fingers discreetly crossed.

"Are you scairt?" I began again.

"What d'you mean, Cieli Mae?"

"Are you scairt of the bad man?"

"Oh. Surely I was. I surely was scared of him. But I reckon, I ain't no more."

And so it was, and we let it be. Just like a bygone.

CHAPTER TWENTY-SEVEN

THE SKY WAS JUST ABOUT ready to pop by the time we returned to Ruby Pearl's place. It was half past four o'clock.

We'd never been inside a colored person's home before, but not out of any conviction to that end—we'd just never been invited.

So excited by the possibility, I near jumped out of my spirit. *Please, Misses Banks. Please, ask us in.* Why, her carport twinkled red, green, and blue with Christmas lights even now. A magical, sparkling curiosity in the awkward heaviness of this summer.

Time to time, Momma and Ruby Pearl had passed each other's places on their ways to here or there. They'd howdy do'd and how are you'd, but never once had they engaged in any conversation beyond the day's forecast, or Misses Bysa's chickens. And nary a one of us had ever set foot inside the other's dwelling.

As our own current rental trailer was nothing much, even as far as that particular species of housing, my momma's indifference was the result of a more practical embarrassment than anything convoluted.

THIS PAST DECEMBER TWENTY-FOURTH THERE was a knock-knocking.

"Momma?" I'd hushed to her. "D'you hear that? Why, I believe there might be someone rapping at our door."

The boys had just quieted down some but it was still noisy, what with the howling winds and JB's debauched rampaging.

"Well, now. Wouldn't that be a nice surprise?" she whispered back to me, forcing a smile. "But I do believe it's too early in the day for a visit from Santa Claus, Cieli Mae!"

Cursing a blue streak, JB stumbled his way to the back room. Momma took one deep breath and unlatched the side door, twisting the handle ever so quietly.

There on our tiny porch sat a brightly beribboned sea-grass basket, big enough to hold at least one set of our twins if need be. Chock-full of breads, biscuits, muffins, and two calico-smocked mason jars, that hamper sat proud and pretty just as if it belonged there. To find an assortment of staples left by some churchgoing do-gooder was not all that unusual. But this was different. This was not an offering made out of guilt or sympathy as those do not wear bows. This was a present.

"Well, I declare," Momma said, peering over her shoulder and on down the lane. "Chocolate gravy and elderberry jam!" She looked to the left and then to the right. "It's that guardian angel again, I s'pose." With a shrug and the faintest of smiles, Mona Lisa gathered up our bounty.

That time I was quick enough and managed to catch a fleeting glimpse of Ruby Pearl Banks scampering down the path, her shawl pulled tight over her head against swirls of snow and buckets of hail.

And there I went, lickety-split, hoping to catch up with her.

Ruby Pearl moved mighty fast for a woman of her age and measure. I didn't rightly know how I'd go about doing so, but I wanted to thank her. I wanted to invite her in out of the ice and howling winds. "Please stop!" I implored. She didn't hear me of course. But then, as my spirit came up next to hers, something, something like a *sh-h-hush,* passed between us. From her to me. From me to her. Ruby Pearl stopped in her tracks.

She looked around, carefully, slowly, before her curious scowl turned inward. "You best take hold of yo'self, Ruby. Ain't nobody there. Ain't nobody else fool 'nuff be out in this here mess on Christmas Eve."

Tugging her wrap closer up around her, she scurried on, head down. "Just passing through. Don't expect to be akst in fo' no visit neither," she murmured, her breath making puff after puff in the air. "All chirrens deserves treats come Christmas morning. Don't matter who they daddy be."

As sturdy as she was kind, a wise solemnity radiated from her. A steady brilliance remained in those dark, cocoa-bean eyes, still and indestructible, despite the troubles she had known in her lifetime. "White or no," she murmured, shaking her head and waving a mittened hand over her heart. "I don't like that man none. Don't like him none a'tall."

Ruby Pearl hurried though the park, climbed into her truck, and popped the clutch. She eased her way slowly down the paved road back to her house. Number Five Sherman Oaks. One hurricane lamp burned bright in each front window. "Never know," she believed with all her Ruby-heart, "when some po' lost soul might come on by, stumblin' in the dark, just tryin' to find his way home."

The property and everything on it, including the large stone house and the clapboard servants quarters to its rear, had been bequeathed to her by her former employer. Ruby Pearl had cared for Madame Lafayette for eighteen long years, fiercely tending to both the homestead and the elderly woman through countless infirmities and lonely sorrows as if they were natural-born kin.

There were no other negro homeowners in this paved section of Willin County, and the legacy caused quite a stir amongst the townspeople at one time but became old news fast enough. We—most of us anyways, aside from the Fugate and the Battle families—settled comfortably into Ruby Pearl's being amongst us, irregardless of what all else was going on in that other world outside of ours.

Why, this September past, just two months before our beloved JFK ended up shot in the head, four little colored girls got blown up when a bomb exploded in their church. In their church.

Momma and I had just reached Speight's TV & Radio as the terrible, awful news story broke in black and white. Even though it was a Sunday, seven Philco televisions on storefront display choked on the horror of it. The bleak vision of man-unkind.

We watched in trepidation as a crumpled, sobbing mother was helped into a car. Then my momma stepped over to the curb and spewed bile, as, I reckoned afterwards, there was not much else in her stomach.

It was white men planted that bomb. The explosion had been planned. Plotted. Premeditated.

"Sweet blessed Jesus. Mary, Mother of God," Momma wept. "On this day I am shamed by the color of my skin."

The Innocents: Addie, Carole, Cynthia, and Denise.

It was the image of eleven-year-old Denise McNair that reached out and grabbed hold of my spirit. Shy but knowing, in her stylish hat and coat, she clutched at that white freckle-faced Chatty Cathy doll as if her life depended on it.

If only we'd known. Momma would have carried those little girls home with us, forbidding any of them to attend their Sunday school.

"I'd a told them it was not a good day for church in Alabama," Momma sniffled, brushing tears from her dirt-stained cheeks with the backs of her hands. "Why, if I needed to, I'd tell one big lie after another to keep them babies safe."

And she would have too. As I have figured by now, not even a bold-faced lie is wrong if it's told for a right enough reason.

In my heart's mind, alongside the images of my waylaid siblings, I carried the portraits of those most precious child martyrs.

Each evening before Momma put out the lights, I called up the images of the dark-skinned angels from their four press photographs. Gray, grainy, and full of grace.

We'd bless ours who'd gone on before us, and I'd tack on an additional *good night, sleep tight* for Addie, Carole, Cynthia, and Denise.

I expect they are all comfortable and safe. Now. That they laugh and play together, as a natural course of events, as all God's children are meant to. That they love one another without qualms, and look out for each other equally, with no one ever bothered, or thinking anything should be otherwise.

To this very day, my spirit bears a bottomless hurt for the families and friends of those four little girls.

I pondered over Ruby Pearl's loneliness, what with none of her people around in these parts anymore. I prayed she'd not hold it against us that our skin was the same color as the hellions who had blown up the Sixteenth Street Baptist Church. After all, we didn't even know the louts.

By the time, two months later, when our beloved Mister President got shot in the head and died, my momma just didn't have any tears left in her.

"I wonder how much bad news a world can make," Momma posed with a sigh.

"As much as it can hold, I reckon," I said back.

A FIRST GROWL OF THUNDER struck as we reached the top step of Ruby Pearl's front porch. Through carefully parted red, blue, and yellow striped window dressings, I studied the boys, snug and satisfied, in that tidy kitchen.

A multicolored foot mat proclaimed, Welcome All Ye Who Enter.

Ruby Pearl bustled to the door wiping her hands on her red and white polka-dotted apron, shaking her head from side to side, trying in vain to contain a grin.

"Whoo-hoo, Missy. Them boys is full o' beans—"

"Oh, Misses Banks, I am so sorry. I do hope they were bein' haved for you?"

"No need to 'pologize. Me and Cody had the time of our lifes!"

Overcome with the curiosity herself, Momma peered quizzically over Ruby Pearl's head, past the foyer, taking in the pristine cheeriness of this place with its lively curtains and the yellow, green, and orange kitchen with the black-and-white floor.

"Mmmm, something smells mighty good in there," Momma said, still craning her neck. "Well now. Just lookit how you have thangs all purtied up in there!"

Apparently Momma and I had already come to a silent agreement, that we'd very much like to come live here and not ever go back to our own spurned tinderbox. Between the boys, the sickness, and other more sordid comings and goings of late, that trailer was just about beyond any kind of human redemption, no matter how much scrubbing and painting and mending took place.

Unsure of what situation she was in, Ruby Pearl looked torn. Would she offend us more by asking us, or by not asking us, to come on inside?

"I can have those chirrens ready for you in less than two shakes, Miss Vidalia—"

Well now. I was not leaving. Not yet. I refused to let voices of ignorance dictate who I could visit with or befriend.

Momma and I admired Misses Ruby Pearl Banks, and I decided, if it pleased her, it'd be nice for us all to spend more time together. I would not grant weight to other folk's thoughts about predicaments such as this, nor take offense over what Ruby Pearl held against JB. Most likely she was correct in her supposings.

And besides, I felt the call to rest my spirit in the calm of this place. Even if only as an intermission.

Momma and Ruby Pearl made their own version of small talk in the doorway, dancing in a square around the issue until I could take it no more.

"Don't you reckon Misses Banks might like us to come in and sit for a spell," I said aloud, expecting my momma was the only one to hear. Ruby Pearl tilted her head my way. Momma near swallowed her tongue.

She and Ruby Pearl looked at one another, dumbfounded.

Ruby Pearl was the first to speak. "What you say, Missy?"

"Did I say something, Misses Banks?" Momma squeaked, caught off her guard.

Ruby Pearl gave Momma a look of grave concern. "Missy Vidalia. Might be nice if you come inside and set a spell. You bin out in the heat all day. And it sho' look like this here's gone be one o' them gulley washers."

Do-si-do.

I passed lightly over Ye Who Enter, eased carefully by Momma and Ruby Pearl, absorbing a new welcomeness.

"Well now, Misses Banks," Momma gushed, her face flushed as if it'd been dipped in a vat of tomato juice. "I do declare. There just ain't nothing as pleasing to the weary eye as a crisp curtain at a open window." Ruby Pearl looked about scratching her head and wondering what just happened here.

ONCE UPON A TIME, BACK before Clayt and Eli's coming, Momma'd hung some delicately flowered lace curtains in the window above our kitchen sink.

"Well now. Lookit what we got here, Cieli Mae," Momma'd said, spotting those fragile discards in a heap by the side of Glen Echo Valley Road.

She'd carried home the two abandoned veils, tender but tenacious, frail and yellowed-with-age, as one might a pair of stray kitties. Then, carefully, one at a time, she kneaded them clean on the washboard out back.

With a respect due to tribal elders, she had pinned each gauzy fabric strip to the clothesline, and we watched in awe as they floated, uncertain but unsullied, on the warm breezes.

Momma'd pressed and mended the intricate panels as needed, before checking on the kudzu shoots she had previously plucked and stored to dry. It'd been two weeks now. Earlier that afternoon she had gathered up and crumbled their parched leaves almost to a powder and scooped the fine fragments into a clean white sock, leaving them to steep in her quart cook pan of boiled water.

Standing on tiptoe, Momma opened the cupboard and reached behind the empty metal sugar canister. She pulled out a clump of blue tissue and placed the fluffy wad ever so gently onto the kitchen tabletop. Then, and not without some ceremony, she peeled back layer after layer of the thin, soft paper, like a parson saying a prayer of gratitude.

Doc Feldman had gifted Momma the delicately painted rose-covered cup and saucer as a get-well token after one of our more urgent visits to his office. The tea set had belonged to his mother. This cup and saucer were all that remained of that prized collection.

After pausing to exhale, Momma stole one more glance at her gentle window covers and readied herself to pour the carefully prepared libation from her cook pot into the china vessel.

It was at that exact moment that JB straggled in. "Wha'cha doin' there, Vida Lee?"

I guess there was just something about seeing her at peace that set him off.

"Just admiring my new curtains," she mumbled.

"Y'ain't got nothing better to do than gush over rags?" he slurred.

"I like lookin' at them, JB. I reckon it seems silly hanging them from a broom handle but still, don't they look like angel's wings? How they flutter and all?" she said. "And 'sides, it's—"

"Jesus H. Christ. Enough already!" JB stopped his pacing. Teeth bared and nostrils flared, he leveled a long, icy glare before turning to yank the makeshift rod off the wall and snap it into two halves over his right knee. With a splintered end he came down hard on the table and smashed the cup and saucer to pieces, planting his muddied boots atop the crushed roses. "There y'go. Now you got something better to do with them angel wings."

After Momma'd cleaned his boots and tidied up the rest of the mess, JB came up behind her. "I'm sorry, Vidalia Lee. You just bring out something in me. I—"

Momma jerked back her elbows and spun around right quick. Her eyes unable to hide her hurt, her anger.

"I 'pologized, didn't I?" JB said, one foot pointing toward the door. "Fuck it all. I'm gone out. And oh yeah. Happy birthday, whorebitch."

WITH MINDFUL ATTENTION, MOMMA AND Ruby Pearl guided our strollerful up the front steps and onto the newly screened porch. As if on cue, the sky opened up and heavy rains pounded the old tin roof like rapid gunfire. "Well now," Ruby Pearl said. "How 'bout I fix us some elderberry tea?"

First she was welcomed to come on inside and now Momma'd been invited to take tea. And she didn't even have to worry none about JB stumbling in. I could not believe our good fortune on this very day. *Thank you, Lord Jesus!*

As the weighted thundershower pelted the housetop with a fury, we spent a most memorable late afternoon cozied up in Ruby Pearl's kitchen. She brought out photograph albums of her own children and of her dearly departed husband, Ruben. I looked forward to meeting up with Mister Banks one day. He sounded like a fine man. A fine man, indeed.

"The good dies young, missy. Umm-hmm," Ruby Pearl murmured. "An' the bad? Well sometime it seem there ain't no rightly way to get rid o' them." Her words gently sidestepping a trail better left untrod for the time being.

"Amen," Momma said as she, Ruby Pearl, and I nodded in a harmonious unanimity.

In the next room, the boys carried out their duties. This was the first time I'd ever seen all four wait on their own turns without some kind of commotioning. First Bootie, then James, then Clayt, and finally Eli. Ruby Pearl had taught them all how to brush Cody's fur. Nice 'n tender like.

Bootie, James, and Clayt needed showing, over and over again, the proper way to stroke gently without getting the bristles all tangled in the sheepdog's long shiny coat. But little Eli was a natural. Cody didn't need nip at him, not a once.

THE BANKS FAMILY PORTRAIT INCLUDED one husband, one wife, and three small children not far apart in age, one boy, two girls. Above those precious little beings, Ruben and a slightly less robust version of Ruby Pearl gazed into one another's eyes. It was easy enough to see they'd given up more of themselves to each other than they'd ever willingly take away.

Well now, I reckoned. So that's what *in love* looks like.

RUBY PEARL MADE NO MENTION of her boy but did tell us of her daughters, now grown. Their schooling and other interests had long since taken them away from these parts.

"We watch out fo' our chirrens from the day they born. We tell them 'don't do this' and 'don't do that.' But we don't never know what done took until they leave us."

"I 'spect so, Misses Banks."

"My Ruben, he made me promise to push them far away from here. An' I done that. I done that." It was almost as if Misses Banks's lips didn't quite know what to do as she fumbled a tainted smile. "Oh, I gets plenty lonesome. But things 'round here just ain't good enough fo' my babies. My girls, they doin' fine where they at now. My Melinda, she aw'wes akst'n me to move in up north. With her and her husband. To Philadelphia. Got themselfs a big house with a basement, a attic, two indoor bathrooms, an' a lilac bush in the side yard. My Melinda, she know how I love them lilacs. 'Honey chile,' I told her, 'you done good.'

'Mama Pearl, I've done well,' she started back at me, 'and all because of you.'

'Hush, now,' I say to her.

'It's all because of *you*," she say'd again. She aw'wes was a persnickety chile, my Melinda.

'Me? Oh no, chile,' I said. 'Wasn't me studied day 'n night. Wasn't me passed them fancy tests.'

'You're wrong, Mama,' she say'd.

'You give me pride, Melinda,' I tole her back. 'Ain't nothin' better a chile can give to her mama.'

'But don't you want more? For yourself too?' she akst me on her last visit home.

'Things down here are, are just plain assbackwards!'

'If ever'body leave here who got the good sense, how things ever 'on get right?' I tole her. 'Chile, you got a husband and someday you 'on have chirrens of yo' own. You don't need be fretting over me. That ain't 'posed to be your job, chile. Imagine me up there with them Yankee shop folks aw'wes in a such a hurry. What you think they say once I start drawlin' out my list the way I do?'

My Melinda, she say'd, 'Well, Mama, I'd tell them she talks slow but thinks fast, so you'd best be on your toes with this one.'"

WITH THE RAINS ABETTING, MOMMA thanked Ruby Pearl for watching over our boys.

"I 'ppreciate your time and trouble Misses Banks. Truly, I do. And I hope someday to repay your fine hospitality,"

"Aw. G'wone now, Missy. Truth be tole me 'n Cody hope you 'n them boys come back soon. Real soon," Ruby Pearl said flashing a broad, impish grin. "Don't we, Cody?"

Cody's keen and steady barks back left no room for doubt.

Momma smiled shyly.

I, on the other hand, emboldened by Ruby Pearl's proposal and Cody's furtherance blurted out, "How 'bout tomorrow?"

For the second time that day, Momma near swallowed her tongue.

Ruby Pearl's silly grin shriveled into a pucker as she placed one stout, crooked finger to her lips, forming a kind of a question mark. She jutted her jaw and turned her head side to side, slowly scanning the room. "You say sumthin' Missy?" Ruby asked, her eyes narrowed into slits as she rubbed away the goosebumps formed on the cushy flesh of her forearms.

Feeling her face flush again, Momma wheezed out a distracting cough.

"My, oh my. I do declare. I got me a tickle in my throat. Quite a tickle." Momma was talking to Ruby Pearl but looking at me in such a way that, at that moment, I was glad I was already, well, you know.

"Can I give you all a ride home?" Ruby Pearl asked, her finger tapping her lip now making a period instead of a question mark. "Yo' buggy there's busting at the seams an' I woudn't mind none," she offered as we all bustled from her front parlor and out onto the porch.

Here they go again. *Promenaaade, home.*

Momma hesitated but this time not for long. "Well, now. I reckon you could drive us far's the entrance to Tribesmen's."

Ruby Pearl looked even more puzzled, "Nonsense, chile. I'll just carry you to yo' door."

"But I'm afraid that mightn't be safe for you." Momma lowered her eyes. Overhead the sun was trying to push its way through puffs of bullheaded clouds.

"Ohh. Hmm. Ahh. I sees," Ruby Pearl said, a sad note left to linger on the stoop while we carried on with our departure.

In reverent silence Momma loaded the boys, overfed and overtired, into the back of Ruby Pearl's shiny purple pickup. Even they enjoyed the peaceful five-minute drive to just outside our woebegotten trailer park, which could have been near an hour's walk.

Up front, Momma and Ruby Pearl spoke warmly in hushed tones. Once to the outer limit of Miss Ruby's safe zone, a quieter quiet took hold as my momma stumbled over an apology she didn't have words strong enough to carry.

FOUR SLEEPY HEADS RESTED SECURE, snuggled alongside one another, crammed in their carriage with any more recent grants and gains stacked, packed, or wedged into the four-wheeled folding shop cart on loan from Ruby Pearl.

"Cieli Mae, I intend for us to have a nice little place of our own too someday," Momma whispered into me as she pushed that buggy full of boy with one hand, and, with the other—the bandaged one—she pulled along our overloaded shop cart.

This time around, I had to hustle to keep up with her.

Praise God and thank the Lord, my brothers fell asleep shortly after the transfer. Momma and I hoped only for time enough to put away our new acquisitions before all heck would break loose once again.

By the time we arrived at our trailer we'd already passed through and moved on from those other far-off notions. Heads cleared, we got right down to the business at hand.

CHAPTER TWENTY-EIGHT

Darkness was coming on fast, and Momma said we needed to be ready from this night forward.

"Ready for what, Momma?" I asked.

"For whatever happens our way, I reckon."

She slid the boys, two at a time, from the stroller onto the larger pallet and we continued on, hoping for the best.

From the depth and breadth of the cleaning supplies and hardware purchased earlier, I'd reckoned she was in for some hard labor.

Cleaning was mindless work, and I was grateful for the reprieve. My imaginings needed time to digest what had been set out. I pictured us all, fumbling around in a big dark house, with only one working lamp in each room, and but a weak current, unable to support more than one lighting at a time, making it all the more difficult to get from one room to another without stumbling.

Momma dragged out the old Hoover and unraveled the cord. Gently, she finagled its bent and sorry prongs into the wall socket and kissed a prayer up to heaven that it start. With duct tape she had attached the innards of a discarded roll of paper wrapping to its hose. Aiming her creation at the ceiling's four corners, that recycled cardboard tube sucked up spiders, webs, and whatever else had risen above our daily fray to a supposed safety.

Then tapping gently, she dumped the contents of the vacuum bag into the trash pail she kept tucked just outside the door and hidden amongst clumps of purple coneflowers and black-eyed Susans.

Any gardening efforts Momma made were more a function of camouflage than show. And although she'd tried every which way to coax the kudzu up the sides of our trailer as a cloak, somehow even those lowly vines knew enough to reroute themselves away.

Momma didn't subscribe to the newly popular theory of wastefulness. After emptying her "New and Improved" disposable vacuum bags into the outdoor garbage can, she'd shake them out, dust them off, and rinse them in the bucket. As long as they were still rugged enough to hold their own, she'd put them up on the line, after which they'd be used again, and then again.

As for those recently displaced critters, well, they found themselves free to search out better nesting spots for them and theirs.

"All God's creatures, even those itty-bittiest ones got a right, no, a duty, to protect their younguns and to live safe," Momma said, glancing upwards at the temporarily cloudless blue clearing overhead, imagining confirmation.

RUBY PEARL HAD OFFERED US a fine chair and some other whatnots left behind by Madame Lafayette's daughter.

"I tell you what, Missy. I ain't never seen a chile so stubborn in all my born days. 'I won't be wanting any of that ol' stuff,' she done tole me. 'And,' she say'd, 'I'll be damned if I'm gone out of my way to be there for the old woman just cause she's dying.'

Now, is that any way fo' a chile to talk?" Ruby Pearl said, dabbing at her eyes. "All that po', sick woman wandt was to see her baby's face one mo' time. I said, 'Miss Camille, maybe yo' mama just want to 'pologize?'

'My dear Misses Banks,' that young whippersnapper say back at me. 'It is too late for that.'"

Of course, Ruby Pearl was torn to pieces over it all. As her elderly benefactor clung to her last threads of hope, Ruby Pearl made up one excuse after another, day after day, as to why Miss Camille couldn't pay her mama a call today, after all.

"Oh, the girl paid me a visit soon after her mama's passing. 'Lookit here, Misses Banks,' she'd said with a sweetness I ain't seen befo'. 'She left you the house. Just keep all the rest too. I'd just a'soon take my remembrances in cash. Crisp 'n cold. Just like my mother. She was quite fond of you, Ruby Pearl. Quite fond. I visited with Attorney Binghamton just yesterday and signed the necessary papers. It's all yours. The house. The grounds. Good day, Misses Banks. I hope you are happy here. Lord knows, I never was. God bless you for taking such good care of her.'"

Ruby Pearl shook her head in a sad disbelief.

Oh, she could have sold the furniture and those other prized possessions intended for Miss Camille, made a pretty penny, and kept the money for herself. She could've, but our Miss Ruby would never do that.

Ruby Pearl's kind, giving nature left her wide open to any goodness in others and sincerely confounded by a lack of it. I suspect that is what she and Momma had most in common and was the true force that'd pulled us all together in the first place.

MOMMA SCRUBBED, DUSTED, AND REARRANGED what little we owned to make room for Ruby Pearl's much finer handovers, most especially that nice chair with the wobbly front leg. "Don't you worry none about that," Momma said, clapping her hands together in an unbridled happiness. "Such a fine, fine piece. I just need get my hands on a fresh batch of that wood glue. And some proper tools. That's all—"

"Don' know if they be proper or unproper, Missy, but you is welcome to whatever you might wandt from the shack out back." Ruby Pearl didn't need make that offer more than once.

Within the old-chicken-coop-turned-toolshed, Momma found herself a happy hunting ground of gadgets and whatsits. Utility knives to band saws. And most anything in between. Oh, some needed oiling, some needed cleaning, and some needed sharpening, but mostly all were at least functional. Momma could hardly contain her joyfulness.

First off, she aimed to fix that nice chair and place it by our window. That way, when the electricity went out, as it's been known to, there might still be enough light for book reading come the early evenings. With the boys huddled around, Momma could deliver noble Bible stories or happily-ever-after fairy tales without having to fret over dripping wax or kerosene spills.

"CIELI MAE?" MOMMA ASKED. "DID you notice how Misses Banks's kitchen table leans to the one side?"

"Yes, Momma. I did." But I'd reckoned it would've been rude to mention such in the face of Ruby Pearl's unrestrained generosity and gracious hospitality.

"Well, I intend to fix that for her on our next visit. I could do that one little thing, and she wouldn't even need to know." Momma dropped her voice to a hush. "'Cause then she'd try 'n pay me. And why, I just couldn't abide by that. Maybe Cody and the boys might could work up some kind of fuss and draw her out-of-doors. Shouldn't take me but a minute or two."

"That's a fine idea, Momma." After all, raising a ruckus is what our boys do best. There's no "might could" about that.

BY HAND, MOMMA HAD SEWN up a new hall curtain, using some of Madame Lafayette's leftover drapery fabric passed on by Ruby Pearl. JB had smashed up the partition Momma'd constructed that past year. I reckon she'd meant the new panel as a kind of a filter to blur whatever went on in the front room from the back, and vice versa. Needless to say, that original bedroom door had seen better days.

"There, now!" Momma gushed, stepping back to admire her handiwork, having carefully thumbtacked the finished product into place.

"Sure looks pretty, Momma," I said.

"You'll stay put, in the back room, tonight, and from every night here on. With the boys. I'll sleep out here on this chair. By the door. And y'all are to stay put. Back there. No matter what you might think. Or hear," she'd said, waggling her finger. "Unless I call for you, Cieli Mae, you will not come out here. Do you understand?"

"Yes, Momma. I understand," I said back, fretting over her intent.

IN FINE SPIRITS FOLLOWING THEIR afternoon with Ruby Pearl and Cody, James and Bootie laughed aloud while making silly faces and gently poking one another in the ribs. For once they didn't try even one little bit to disturb their slumbering baby brothers. It had been such a long time since those littlest ones'd had full enough tummies and as much fresh air. "Why," Momma'd said, "they might just sleep through til dawn."

"Momma!" Bootie called out, hopping up and down from one foot to the other like he needed to pee, "Me 'n James wanna catch us some fireflies!"

"Can we Momma? We'll stay out from under your feet so you can g'wone'n get somethin' done 'round here for a change," James added, cocking his head, mimicking her in his *don't be mad, I'm only just teasin'* voice.

"We'll be oh so quiet," Bootie interrupted, in hushed tones. "We swear it!" he added, looking excitedly at his twin, "Don't we, James?"

Strawlike tufts and wheat-colored ringlets bounced in tandem atop the nodding two-headed, towheaded monster.

"Hmmm," Momma murmured, finger-tapping her forehead, granting the decision more weight than it had any right to.

She pulled an empty jar from a low cupboard, poked small holes into the lid using the hammer and nails close by, and handed it over to the boys for sharing.

"Now then. Y'all stand still," she instructed. She tied a separate strand of twine, one each, from around one of their little waist loops to a hook on the porch rail. "These here strings got secret powers," Momma told them, sending a wink my way. "You boys don't want to find out what happens if you stretch 'em too thin!"

It'd be easy enough to keep an eye on them anyways while she worked on the new chain lock for the front door and cut down an old mop handle, which she'd later use to wedge the side slider windows almost shut.

"But Momma, I wonder how come you didn't just go ahead and buy one of them super deluxe deadbolt locks?" I asked.

"Why, sugar," she said pointing to the sorely splintered doorframe, "First off they cost more 'n I'm willing to spend. And second off, this here wood trim wouldn't never support such. 'Sides, and third off, I just don't have the time, nor the right tools on hand, to situate one of them proper.

At least with this chain back in its rightful place, even as weak as it seems, I done my duty to forewarn."

CHAPTER TWENTY-NINE

AFTER A LIGHT SUPPER OF Ritz crackers and Campbell's tomato soup, Momma decided they'd all done enough work for one day.

Years had slid from my momma's shoulders. With her face scrubbed clean and that unruly mass of cinnamon curls tumbling down the back of her white nightie, she didn't look even near her twenty-seven years. We checked Clayt for breathing noises, and we smiled over Eli's peaceful snoring sounds. After what all their little bodies had gone through in that week past, they ought be allowed to catch up, so we let them be.

Night fell gently this time.

Momma lit a candle. Somehow she'd forgot to pick up electric light bulbs, though I'd reminded her twice how they were on her list. I'd have sworn there were some in our cart at one point, but then I reckon not as they weren't there by the time we reached the checkout. I looked on as Momma, James, and Bootie held hands in prayer before she tucked them in, in the back room, in the dark, alongside the silent sleepyheads, Clayt and Eli.

Afterwards, Momma whisper-warned, "You remember what I said, baby girl? That door stays shut. Unless I call for you. You be sure 'n remember that."

"Momma? Wha—"

"Hush up and listen. Cieli Mae, I'm counting on you like never before. If something happens to me, promise me you'll find some way to tell Misses Banks. Or Doc. Or Sunny, even. Somebody got to know about how their daddy cain't be left to raise them boys up appropriate," she said flatly. "Mind me now, sugar, it's always best for a body to have a plan even if she don't want to use it. That's all."

"You thinkin' about the bad man again?" I asked.

She nodded, biting down on her lower lip.

"Don't worry, Momma," I hushed.

"Okay, baby girl," she whispered back. Oh, her body was here, but I could tell her mind was getting itself ready to head elsewhere. It had been a long while since one of her spells, and I needed to do what I could to bring her back before it got too late.

"Momma? You shut the windows, locked the doors, and loaded your pistol?" I asked. I knew she had. I was just testing her.

"Yes, I believe I did," she said. "I did all that and then some. Now please get on back there with your brothers. And Cieli Mae? I love you."

"I love you more," I said. My voice salty, but steady.

Momma's shadow smiled. "Baby girl," she whispered with a sigh, closing the door softly behind her, "that just ain't possible."

Outside the air buzzed with the raspy clicks and chirps of the Georgia thumpers and the bold, crazed mating calls of other forms of wildlife. It surely was stifling in that back room, what with the door closed tight and the windows wedged almost shut. Our boys tossed and turned in their discomfort.

Amidst obnoxious grunts and gick-gick-gicks of the pig and the cricket frogs, a close-up and unnatural rustling startled me some. But then again, back there, most anything could be expected. Our lonely rental was the last trailer in the park and as close to being a part of the woods as was possible, without it being a treehouse. And anyways, we couldn't expect the rest of Mother Nature's children to follow the same sleep cycle as our own hapless pack, as, even if they'd wanted to, ours would have been a hard schedule to pin down.

Momma tinkered about in the front room. She'd got herself all fired up, shuffling things about, making room for whatever other surprises Ruby Pearl might be rightly inspired to send our way.

The chain rattled now and again, but it was just Momma double-checking we were properly secured. She'd gotten into a habit of second-guessing herself as to whether she might have forgot to lock a door, to turn something off, or where she'd set something down. Lately things seemed to go missing or askew more often than usual.

"Cieli Mae? You seen my red blouse?" she asked just yesterday. "You know, the pretty one Misses Tilley gave me our last time out to Life Springs?"

"You checked the broom closet near the iron an' board?"

"I did," she said, scratching the back of her neck, her face wearing a frown.

"Hmm. That's where it was—"

"Well, I know it didn't grow legs and walk away on its own."

DRIFTING IN AND OUT OF my own contentment, I was halfway thankful Ruby Pearl didn't have any kinfolk of her own living in these parts anymore. I wondered if she might adopt us all. The boys could be her secretly longed for grandbabies, and Momma, of course, one more favorite daughter. I was beside my spirit with joy at the possibility of having Ruby Pearl Banks as a relation. That way we could all just go on ahead and live with her without even causing too much of a stir.

"Cieli Mae Jackson, you take a hold!" I scolded my spirit. "Ruby Pearl's got a right nice family. She worked hard to bring them up as such. Anything she does for us is out of a pure goodness and not 'cause she's supposed to." Besides, I didn't really think the clerks at the Willin County Court House would take kindly to such an arrangement. Why, whoever heard of a colored woman and a white trailer-park family adopting one another?

And JB? Well now. Then he'd be her relation as well. I felt bad for even wishing such a terrible awful thing on as fine a person as our Miss Ruby.

Ruby Pearl had offered to meet my momma the next day near the park's entrance. Momma was to bring a wagonload of our soiled laundry, and Ruby Pearl would take care of it for her. Ruby Pearl told Momma about her almost brand-new Maytag just waiting on such a challenge.

Claiming she preferred doing most of her own laundering by hand, Ruby Pearl told how she feared the washer might forget how to run if it didn't get more regular practice. That, in fact, we'd be doing her a favor. Though Momma had her doubts, she seemed glad enough to oblige.

After all, it would've taken her from here to kingdom's second coming to hand scrub all that on her old washboard.

My momma thought long and hard before asking me to ride along to Ruby Pearl's. Momma had been leaving me behind for short periods now and then. Sometimes on purpose. Sometimes on accident. But this was different. This time she'd be *sending* me off. Almost like just after JB chopped off her fingertip.

"I trust Misses Banks with my whole heart," Momma said. "And, it'd be of some comfort to me, knowing you'd be there for her, just for this little while. But only if you don't mind none."

"I don't mind none, Momma. You'll be all right then for just this little while?"

"I'll be all right then, for just this little while." And there she went again, smiling that smile.

Those mounds of dirty wash might've been too much to carry from our place to the park entrance had it not been for the boy's Radio Flyer— another of our Child Swap treasures, courtesy of Sister Anna and the Church of the Twelve Apostles.

The dead sparrow on our stoop that next morning took us all by surprise. Its missing feathers and little white neck, snapped like a wishbone, told us the poor thing had not flown into the side of the trailer on accident. This was no happenstance.

Momma lost all color and her feet quick-froze to the spot. She looked about. Left, right, left. She grabbed the outdoor broom and gently swept the little sparrow to one side and off the stoop so maybe the boys wouldn't see it.

Bootie smushed his nose up against the screen. Still rubbing the sleep from his eyes he asked, "Is the little birdy daid, Momma?"

"I'm very sorry, Booth. Yes, he is," she'd said.

"Can we bury 'im?" James asked, having sidled up alongside his twin.

"Of course, James," Momma said, "But Misses Banks is waitin' on me, and I just cain't leave her setting out in harm's way. We'll tend to the birdy here in due time. Y'all need stay put for now and look after your brothers."

Momma and I took a worn, well-traveled path, moving quickly through the maze of mistreated portable homes. Backing away from the chainlink fence, she hightailed it past the Burlson's Doberman. The large black dog, its shiny coat glimmering in the early day sun, circled her cage, sniffing for a challenge, while the scalloped-edged plastic bowl proved a sorry reminder of the night Bitsy had lapped up the tip of Momma's pinky, along with her water.

Matt Burleson had worked for the Butts County Corrections Department for forty long years before taking retirement. The Burlesons sold their clapboard house and bought this brand new doublewide. They'd settled here amongst the riffraff to be closer to their oldest son and his family. That side pen was sturdily built. Well secured. It surely wasn't Bitsy's fault, nor Mister Burleson's, what all had happened just a short while back on that last turn out of Tribesmen's.

Matty and Tatty Burleson were a nice enough couple who mostly minded their own business. "We don't mean nobody no harm. Bitsy girl's just here to make sure ain't nobody do us none neither." I reckon I'd understood all that. After all, they had no way of even knowing about Momma's severed fingertip.

We came upon hooligans, Whitey Fugate and Billy Jack Battle wasting their young lives away as usual, up by the front entrance to the park. It was not yet noon but there they were, scrawled on display for all the world to make note of, swilling corn whiskey from their brown-bagged mason jars as if they were grown-ups and shooting marbles as if they were kids. There're a lot of mixed up folks in this world I said to myself. Billy Jack shouted a taunt I could not make out as both juvenile delinquents dragged themselves upright.

Momma, anxious about getting back to our boys, was in no mood for any fool's shenanigans. "Now, then. Ain't ya'll got no home trainin'?" she said, staring them back down again. "Get out my way, 'fore I whip the stew out of you both."

It's funny what a broken sparrow on her stoop and a wad of dollar bills in her pouch can grant a woman. I suspect having that loaded pistol in her pocket didn't hurt none neither.

Those flustered scoundrels snickered uneasily, their heads down now. Momma walked on by with her nose in the air, strutting herself and our cargo out of the park with no further to-do. I did take one nervous look back just to be sure she hadn't, somehow, turned them both to stone.

As expected, we found our Miss Ruby with her engine running; Momma loaded up that truck in record time.

"Thank you kindly, Misses Banks. I don't know how to—"

"Ain't nothin', chile. Now get yo'sef back to them chirrens."

Quick as a wink I sent my momma a kiss and a secret smile, hoping she wasn't thinking second thoughts. "I'll be all right," I said, again. "You'll be all right too."

Momma nodded once my way, still not knowing for sure how to feel, before turning on her heels and rushing back down the path to tend to our boys.

Inside the cab, Ruby Pearl swayed to the gospel music pouring from her working radio. I thought to myself that today of all days, if heaven can truly be found in the cab of a pickup like they say in so many of those country songs, I reckon I might already be home.

CHAPTER THIRTY

OUR MISS RUBY COULD TURN even laundry detail into an interesting proposition. Sorting and Spotting: a game of salvation.

Truth be told, as she set about to scrub, it was as if Ruby Pearl might've been fixing to purge the devil from the soul of a lost relative.

As the belly of her wash machine filled with suds and warm water, Ruby Pearl spot-cleaned. Then she placed each item, one at a time, into the tub, mindful to spread the load out, nice and even.

She chortled, recalling aloud her first time out with her new Maytag before she knew enough to be careful about product distribution. "Dadgum contraption chased me halfway acrost the room!"

While she sorted and scrubbed, our Miss Ruby conversed with her dead husband and her grown but faraway children. Almost like the way Momma chatted with me, so's no one else would know. Ruby Pearl had peppered the wall opposite the Maytag with framed photographs of them all, in tones of sepia and in black and white. I imagine she enjoyed looking at them to whom she spoke. Maybe it helped her to be just a little less lonesome for them all.

"This here family be truly blest, with four healthy chirrens dirtying up these many clothes!" she'd said, fussing over the boys tattered undergarments, grass-stained britches, and dirt-smudged tee shirts. "Truly blest. Umm-hmm. They sho is."

It took a minute for me to realize Ruby Pearl was talking about us. Momma and our boys.

Truth be told, I didn't usually think of us as blessed. But our Miss Ruby had gone and done it again. She had shed her special light, allowing me to see us more clearly. Now, if she didn't let JB's evil ways and shenanigans taint her appraisal of my family's situation, then, gosh dang it, neither would I.

Once the Maytag's drum was fulled-up, Ruby Pearl turned her attentions back to her own family. I tried not to eavesdrop, not to be a Nosy Nellie, but before long curiosity got the better of me. Here is what I learned from Ruby Pearl's conversation with herself:

Teacher-daughter, Tiny, helps special children to learn whatever and however they can in a town called Vineland, New Jersey. Melinda, Ruby Pearl's married lawyer-daughter, and her husband work in the state of Pennsylvania as public defenders for the city of Philadelphia, "the city of brotherly love."

Ruby Pearl didn't talk much about the other one. Her boy. Seems Leslie'd been a handful since Mister Banks's, his daddy's, murder. Leslie had run off and joined the army, "Soon's he turnt eighteen."

Last she'd heard, her boy had settled in at Fort Bragg with the 82nd Airborne. But when the FBI came sniffing around, she just figured Leslie'd "up and got hisself into some worser kinds o' trouble than us'ual." Ruby Pearl doubled-down on her praying, all the while fretting day and night over her boy and his lost ways.

IT WAS JUST ABOUT NOON when Cody's raucous barking alerted us to the postman's arrival. Catching sight of Mister Rainey hobbling at a clipped pace up the graveled road, Ruby Pearl rushed down the walkway, past flowering shrubs and her glittering blue bottle tree, meeting him at the gate.

"Lookit here, Misses Banks. A letter from Phil-a-*del*-phi-a!" Mister Rainey removed his postman's cap and placed it over his heart, adding, "My, oh my. You look most 'specially lovely today."

"Why thank you kindly, Mister Rainey. How'd you like a nice, cold glass o' fresh squeezed lemonade? It is hot as blue blazes out—"

"Why, now. That sounds better then satisfactual, but I need be off right quick. Arvella Rose's great-granddaughter gived birth just this mornin'—"

"Praise Jesus!" Ruby Pearl said, raising both palms to the heavens. "Boy 'r girl?"

"I din' ask."

"She aw'wright?"

"Seems she's fine, but you know Arvella. Want me to fetch Doc, just to be safe. I wandt to make sure you got this here special delivery. Sure do hope it's good news, Misses Banks."

With a gentlemanly bow, and a tip of his cap, Mister Manfred George Rainey was on his way, but not without giving Cody a good ruffle under the neck.

THE CALLOUSED PADS OF RUBY Pearl's short, dark fingers trailed gently back and forth over the fancy script lettering scrolled atop a faux-linen finish. She waved the cream-colored envelope, like a dream in slow motion, sending the heady scent of lilac wafting through still air.

She breathed in, her eyes fixed in my direction. "You ever seen such fine handwritin' as this here?"

I wanted to believe she might be talking to me, but I knew that could not rightly be so. Could it?

"Why she spray my letters with her 'spensive perfume?" Ruby Pearl pretended to be irritated. "If I tole that chile once, I done tole her one hundret time, 'Save the good stuff for someone more 'po-tant.'

'Silly Mama Pearl!' my Melinda say back to me. 'There is no one more important.'"

RUBY PEARL SLIPPED THE UNOPENED envelope into her apron pocket before reaching up to pluck a bloom from the tree beside her.

"I wonder who gone read me my letter now?" she murmured, tucking the blossom behind her left ear. She turned from me and headed back toward her front porch.

"I will!" I shouted. "Me! I can do it!" Still trailing her close, I found myself wishing I could just tackle her for it.

She turned back around, cocked her head to one side, and clucked. "Ruby Pearl," she scolded herself, "There you go hearin' things again!"

My inner spirit itched so bad I almost couldn't stand it. I'd never expected to be charged with the reading of a personal letter. Especially one that was not Momma's. Still, I was game to try. But how might the process be begun? What if something happened to her fancy notepaper? Poor Ruby Pearl would be so sad.

"Oh, that's okay," she might say, not wanting anyone to feel bad. But then, when she believed no one was looking, she'd cry.

Ruby Pearl patted her front hip pocket and marched back down the lane with me attached, like flypaper, to the backs of her heels.

"I can read your letter Misses Banks! I'm a good reader," I implored. "Better than James. Better than Momma even."

As if to drown out something—her confusion, maybe?—she began singing aloud her version of "Onward Christian Soldiers" while one thick fingertip skated inside her pocket and around the edges of that fine envelope.

Warily, Ruby Pearl glanced back over one shoulder as she reentered the house. She closed the door behind her and stood in the entry hall shaking her head, thrumming one set of fingers against the door's oak trim and the other against her precious envelope.

"All in due time," she murmured.

Her broad face, wizened, but otherwise unlined by the years, showed a consternation as her full chocolate-berry lips pressed against the envelope's return address. She wiped a lone tear from her cheek and laid the scented page, flat open and smoothed, onto the desktop.

"What are you doing with that there letter? Don't you even care what it—"

"Shucks," Ruby Pearl murmured, seeming unusually perplexed by the void surrounding her. "Oh, I can't read nothin', baby girl. Someday you gone find that out and be 'shamedt yo' mama. But I can't think on that now. I need get the laundry done fo' Missy Vidalia and them chirrens."

More than an mile beyond frustrated, I was bewildered over how anyone as grand as Ruby Pearl Banks could think so poorly of herself. Then I remembered how many of the finer folks do that all the time. But why would she ramble on so about not knowing how to read? Well now, that just couldn't be. Could it? Why, she'd seen to the education and raising of a lawyer, a teacher, and a, well, that last one would just need be marked as uncertain. At least for now.

Who read to her children when they were little? Somebody had to've read to them. Memaw Veta Sue and Pawpaw Clyde Royce Kandal didn't talk much to my momma—or to each other, for that matter—but, "Come heck or high water," Momma once said, "one or the other of them read to me, every single day. And that's why I made almost all A's, until, well, until I didn't."

I REMEMBERED BACK TO THAT one proud morning soon after our first eviction. My momma, accompanied by me, and Missy Pickett Dandy, with whom Momma'd kept in touch on the sly, marched into the Willin Town Hall and Library. Momma had applied for and was awarded her very own library card, even though JB warned against such nonsense. "It'll be all right," she whispered to me once we were safely back in Purgatory and alone in our room off Gamma Gert's kitchen. "So long's he don't find out. We'll just be most 'specially careful about it. That's all."

Soon after, while helping out with our laundry, Gamma found that card in the pocket of Momma's housecoat. Gamma removed the card and tucked it under her flour canister which she kept on the top shelf of the bookcase my momma had made from some discarded hardwood planks. After Momma's frock had been washed and line dried, Gamma slipped the card back into that same pocket, folded the garment, and handed it over to Momma with a prideful nod.

Gamma never did breathe a word about it. Not to anyone.

Momma delighted in our story times. Library books filled the heavy blank spaces between her pregnancies and JB's comings and goings. She enjoyed my reading almost as much as I appreciated hers, and so we took turns with her always turning the pages.

"The only thing better than doing it yourself is learning someone else how to. That there's one gift you can be sure won't never go to waste."

That's what my momma said.

"WHHEWH-" RUBY PEARL PUFFED. HER whites hid behind heavy ebony eyelids. As she eased her own sturdy frame down into the cherry wood armchair, its velvet cushions sighed along with her. Within seconds, her quickened breaths had turned slow and deliberate.

I'd be darned if I could wait any longer. I reckoned it was likely not the rightest thing to do, and that I might very well go to hell in a handbasket, but maybe Ruby Pearl mightn't mind too much, not really, not after all. Didn't she say she wanted her friend to read it for her? Am I not her friend?

There are situations in this life, I'd begun to understand, which required a higher level of reasoning, as regular, everyday logic just does not suit every instance.

Ruby Pearl stirred and a gentle say-so floated toward me. *Read to me, angel.* But lo and behold, she was out cold. So I did the only thing I could do. I read that letter.

> *Dearest Mama,*
>   *I have the most wonderful news! My gynocologist has confirmed my pregnancy and that all is as it should be. I have only a minute, but I wanted you to be the first to know!*
>   *If I can be even half the mother you have always been, Mama Pearl, mine will be a very, very lucky child.*
>   *Melinda*

It did not take long to reckon I'd intruded on what should have been a private moment. Heavy with the shame, I wondered if this was how the three wise men felt on that first Christmas Eve.

I glanced back over at Ruby Pearl. There she was, no longer asleep in her favorite chair, but down on her knees with her head bowed, her fingers steepled in prayer. Her eyes squeezed shut.

Then, suddenly, her arms raised up and her spirit burst out.

Then, just as suddenly, mine became enfolded into hers.

"Alleluia! Alleluia! Lord God A'mighty!" Ruby Pearl cried. Round and round, we spun. "We's havin' a grandbaby!" she exclaimed. "We's havin' us a *grand*baby!"

Swallowed up in Ruby's jubilation I joined in her chants and we twirled, punch-drunk with delight. A mess of those happy tears ran down her cheeks leaving slick, translucent puddles on the just Spic 'n Spanned, black-and-white flooring. Finally we collapsed in one dizzy, delirious heap atop the glistening linoleum checkerboard.

CHAPTER THIRTY-ONE

Soon ENOUGH, WE RETURNED TO Tribesmen's. Our bushel full of clean laundry, still needing to be hung out to dry.

Ruby Pearl offered to help as Momma went about refilling the red Radio Flyer now lined with a crisp, brown paper shop bag, cut open, and trimmed to fit.

"Please, Misses Banks. You done too much already," Momma insisted. "Go on home now. You need be on your way."

Momma's forebodings might've sounded rude or ungrateful to any unsuspecting onlooker, but Tribesmen's, most especially at those certain times of day or night, was not a good place for our Miss Ruby.

"You don't need worry none 'bout me," Ruby Pearl said, peering back over her shoulder, "but I reckon I best get on my way." Amongst those white folks in residence here, a sour few were made up of that most dangerous composition: hatred, ignorance, and fear.

I watched both Momma and Ruby Pearl as a sadness stepped all over their words. "My door is aw'wes open to you and them chirrens, Missy," Ruby Pearl said. "You know that, don't you, chile?"

"I do, Ruby. And I cain't tell you how much it means to me. To us all," Momma sighed, uneasy, her eyes darting back and forth from the vehicle to the park entrance. "But dear, dear Misses Banks, you need be getting on now. Thank you ever so much—"

"Don't you think nothin' of it," Ruby Pearl said, handing Momma a flashlight. "I'd 'preciate if you could give this to yo' boys." Ruby Pearl told Momma she thought them little rascals might want to try it out some evening. Maybe tonight? All they needed do was shine it through our rear window come nightfall. That way, she'd said, she and Cody might know all was well. It was of some comfort to us that Ruby Pearl could see as far as our trailer as long's it was lit from within, once the sky outside went dark.

James and Bootie had taught Ruby Pearl some Morse code. They'd all wondered what would happen if they flashed the beam off and on out from our one particular window. Might Ruby really see their dispatch in shorts and longs from her own upstairs hall window seat?

That being the case, they could then message back and forth *good night* and *all's well,* the two phrases the boys had shown her that past afternoon. Ruby Pearl may've been unable to sound out printed words on a page, but she was still just about the smartest person I ever did come upon on this earth. As her truck pulled away, a powerful and lonesome sadness remained in its place.

Fresh as a spring rain, smelling sweet as boiled corn newly shaved from its cob, that wagonload of spanking-clean laundry buoyed Momma and ushered us both back to our realer place in time.

The wanton faces of James, Bootie, Clayt, and Elijah greeted us. Four pug noses up against the screen just as she'd left them. Why, it appeared they hadn't moved even one iota. For once they'd done exactly as they were told.

"Hey there, y'all!" Momma called. "Come help bring up this wagon. Hand me them wood pins so's I can hang the clothes. C'mon now!"

Spell released, the boys burst through that screen faster than a warmed knife in a tub of Crisco and out into the great outdoors. A brigade of eight little paws raised, each offering up one of the wooden clothespins just spilt from the bag.

"Pick mine first!"

"My turn, my turn!"

"Me first! Plee-ease!"

My brothers could finagle most anything into a competition.

"My heavens," Momma said, exasperated but grinning. Her smiles had been coming on at a quicker pace these days. A new assurance, sturdier still than a just issued army blanket, wrapped itself around her.

Even if she wasn't always right, Momma tried real hard to be square. I'd long since come to recognize the value of this and developed an appreciation for even her failed attempts. I wondered though, if her growing sense of justice in the face of all that little-boy cuteness was a byproduct of maternal instinct or a matter of survival? Some of each, I suspected.

A CERTAIN AMOUNT OF EVENHANDEDNESS should come in handy for a daddy of the proper nature as well. I needed to believe other daddies at least tried for such. To misjudge a population based only on my own vantage point, well, that'd be plain wrong.

Most other daddies appeared trustworthy and just. Surely they'd put the needs of their families before their own, at least a good part of the time. And while I knew my own was incapable of such regard, I stayed hopeful that my own personal experiences fell far below the norm of your average spirit child.

IT WAS MY JOB TO keep track of who did what, when, and how often. If one or the other of my brothers whined about so-and-so *al'wes bein' chosed first,* I quietly assisted by refreshing Momma's sometimes faulty memory.

Favor got doled out according to a timetable with a stronger sense of balance than any heart could keep. Each one of our boys had laid a claim to an equal chunk of my affections, and I loved them each in different ways, at different times, for different reasons. But even at their individual worsts, I never loved them not at all.

Those small wooden clips got passed and received in orderly fashion, according to an alphabet game Momma'd invented. She had it in her mind to teach the younger two their letters. We all sang the ABCs as my brothers handed over the pins. It was their duty to throw up a free hand at the mention of any letter in their own names—not their brothers'. This required more of a holding back than most folk might imagine.

Clayt, and even more so Eli, needed help. James and Bootie, on the other hand, were permitted no prompts. Momma said this was good practice for the older pair, and it was fun to see the youngest set trying their best. They all went 'round and 'round, and whenever a letter was missed, or one of them spoke out of turn, Momma forced a frown.

"I 'spect them're tired of being learnt so much in one day," Bootie had said, looking down on the two little ones with a kind of concern.

"I know I am!" James piped in, a mischievous grin plastered to his face.

"G'won then, y'all skeedaddle!" said Momma, shaking her head and waving them off as if her feelings had been hurt. But the boys knew better. Even Clayt and Eli.

As the last of the laundry went up and my brothers took to busying themselves elsewhere in the yard, Momma and I had a chance to chat. I told her mostly all about my wondrous day with Ruby Pearl. About the car radio, the blue bottle tree, and the dancing Maytag. Even the sweet tea with floating mint leaves.

Momma retold those stories to the boys, and they all had some silly fun. Egged on by James and Bootie, Clayt and Eli reenacted the story of the wash machine's jitterbug across Ruby Pearl's kitchen floor.

Clayt shook his little body so hard his britches fell! The rest of us enjoyed a hearty laugh at his expense—all but Eli, who tried to help him pull them back up even though good-natured little Clayt didn't seem to mind one bit.

Although it left me feeling unhonest, I did not share with Momma the part about Mister Rainey and the perfumed letter from Phil-a-*del*-phi-a. That was Ruby Pearl's secret to make known, when and if she wanted to. Not mine. Truth be told, I wanted to keep that part from Momma for just a little longer. I reckon my shadow had a dark side of its own.

Bootie was eager to show off the fancy *ci*-gar box. The one Momma had allowed him to use as a casket for the dead bird. That cardboard receptacle looked more than vaguely familiar, and I wondered by what demons Momma had become possessed.

While I didn't dare imagine what might happen if JB found out, I couldn't near stop myself from taking pleasure in her mischief. "In for a penny, in for a pound," as Gamma Gert might say.

Using the heel of her shoe, Momma marked off in the dirt a miniature burial site, just beneath the clothesline. James dug a shallow grave using Clayt and Eli's rusted toy shovel. Then, hand in hand, James and Bootie recited a prayer over the bird's corpse.

"Dear Jesus, only Son of God," James began. "Please look after this here l'il broke birdy and welcome him into heaven so he can sing with them angels what's awlready there." He looked over at his twin. Bootie, lost in his own thoughts, needed a good rib poke before chiming in with a benediction.

"And sir, Jesus God, it'd be right nice if you could put back his feathers and fix his wings so he might, if he ever got the notion, fly around again someday. And maybe pay us a visit, you know, down here. On this earth. Amen."

The duo placed the mangled creature into that ill-fated cigar-box-turned-dead-bird-coffin, and with solemnity due a higher purpose, Momma closed the lid and placed the poor dead birdy into its plot. Properly solemn, the boys covered it as best they could with fistfuls of dry, brown-red clay dirt.

James fashioned an awkward cross to mark the spot using two long-discarded popsicle sticks and a rubber band. Clayt and Eli sang to the tune of Momma's processional hymn, making up words as they went along. Bootie picked a mess of wild honeysuckle and buttercups and spread them slowly and with great respect over the fresh dirt mound.

It didn't take long for that late afternoon sun to scorch through the boys' grief, and Momma still had ironing yet to get done.

James and Bootie helped Clayt and Eli rinse their hands in the tin bucket, and I agreed to watch over them all awhile longer as they finished up a game of Red light, Green light, guarding them with my thoughts.

A hearty breeze was just about coming into its own. Soon enough they'd all be rushing here and there, gathering the freshly washed clothes and linens from the line.

Momma came bustling out amongst us just as the syrupy sky filled to its brim.

"Time to warsh up for supper, y'all. But first we'd best put down that laundry."

Once again, our boys formed an assembly line. James handed bunches of the pins to Clayt, who passed them to Eli, who placed them, one at a time, back into the bucket. There was no hurry in Elijah, God love him. Everything that child did, he did with purpose.

Bootie set about to sorting the socks, tossing each matched pair into the smaller straw basket. Momma started out folding bedclothes but soon hastened her pace, stuffing whatever else was left into the larger basket to be tended to later on, inside.

The rumblings from above grew louder and louder as the sky darkened to a shade of huckleberry deep enough, almost, to be black.

James and Bootie headed for the trailer while Momma grabbed Clayt, who'd been trying to drag his twin, but Eli, so mesmerized by the off-colored sky, wouldn't budge. Momma just shrugged. As long's he wasn't afraid she could see no harm in letting the boy be but one moment longer. She'd retrieve him in a bit, as one of them always did.

After depositing Clayt alongside James, Bootie, and the partially filled laundry bushel, Momma headed back outside to round up any stragglers.

Crisp foliage and cogon grasses rustled amidst squeals of awakened nocturnals. The retching of those pig frogs made the downy hairs on Momma's arms stand at attention. Hurriedly, she grabbed a lone clothes-pinned sock from the line with one hand and scooped up little Eli with the other.

Like the sound of a flatbed driving over a chuckhole, a loud *pop* visited a frightful notice upon us. Momma's body jerked too quick toward the sound of JB's Saturday Night Special.

"Da?" Eli chirped, another little birdy wounded in flight.

His cherry lips glimmered, parted with glee and upturned in an open smile, even as his baby blues narrowed to slivers.

The other three screamed as one. Front and center, blood surged geyser-like from Eli's forehead.

Blood spurts with each heartbeat. Gushing is a good sign then, right?

Willing her knees to hold her upright, Momma clutched Eli closer. "Nooo!" she shrieked heavenward, unable to move from the spot. "Oh no, You don't. No! You don't even dare!"

Unaware of me, Bootie stepped up. Herding the other two to safety, he yelled, "Run, Momma! Git in here!"

His instincts were good. Thoughtful Bootie. Doubtful James. Calamitous Clayton. Sweet Elijah. Sweet, sweet Elijah.

"You need get ahold, Momma," I implored. "Eli needs you. We all need you. Please—" Momma, unblinking, ran for shelter. James slammed the door shut behind her and flipped the hook into its latch, and just like that, Momma shoved her own self aside.

"Bring me that basket, James. Bring it here, quick! Eli? ELIJAH? It's me, your momma, sweet boy. You hear me, don't you? Open your eyes, child!"

Eli made no response.

Momma gulped back sobs, that being the best she could do.

The contents of my heart overflowed their supposed boundaries while my brothers supplied her a steady stream of freshly laundered, almost-dry, little-boy socks, tee shirts, and bed linens. But even as Momma pressured Eli's wound with all the might she could muster, that little innocent's blood wouldn't stop flowing.

On the verge of losing herself, Momma cried desperate prayers and promises to whomever might be listening. "Mary, mother of God, I don't know what to do!" she wailed. "Sweet Jesus! Please. Tell me what I'ma 'posed to do."

"Lookit there. Eli's drawlin' breath," I hushed. "You always watched close when Doc tended you. You know what to do, Momma. You got what all you need, right here, right now." Momma scowled, looking harder upon me than ever before. But that didn't stop me none. "Go on. Go fetch that 'mergency kit you got hid. And your pistol too. Eli's gonna be all right. It's all gonna be all right, Momma. I promise. But you gotta do what you gotta do. And you gotta do it right now!"

Momma nodded. She wiped the wet from her face and placed Eli onto his older brother's lap. She hurried to the back room, her bib apron smeared with blood, her hair glowing like embers.

She'd be back, right quick.

I wasn't struck by lightning or recalled and ascended into heaven over what all I'd said so far, or what all I was thinking, but I said a quick prayer for forgiveness anyways. What I was meaning to do went against all the rules, and I wasn't sure how long my temporary pardon might hold.

I had to work fast.

I spoke words, quick and clear, into our baby's ear, "Eli, honey pie— you don't know me, and you won't never remember none of this, but I'm your big sister. Someday we'll be together, that is true. But not today. C'mon back now. It's not your time, Eli. Not yet. We both know that, don't we, little brother?"

The thick, moist veil of lashes fluttered, then went still. Again.

"I know you hear me, Elijah Percival Jackson. C'mon you little rascal, take a deep breath. You know how to do it. That's right. There you go!"

The bleeding had all but stopped. Eli's lips wrinkled into an pucker. Slowly, one eye opened. And then the other. From his mouth came a whimpering, which simmered for a short while before rising to a full, rolling boil.

Bootie and Clayt hovered. James stroked little Eli's soggy cheek, and his full-throated mewling bubbled over into a wheeze and then a raspy chuckle.

The sounds brought Momma rushing back into the room. Four pairs of blue-eyed bewilderment looked up at her—to her—for what to do next.

Eli's eyes danced across her face, gathering her in. Momma mirrored Eli as his tiny, dry, Cupid lips upturned into a smile. Within seconds, my brothers' timid tee-hees exploded into great gales of laughter, reabsorbing our little family back into its unit, upended but unbroken.

CHAPTER THIRTY-TWO

"LOOKIE HERE, MOMMA. LOOKIT ELI. I held him jest right. See?" James proclaimed. "He ain't even bleedin' no more." If James' shirt had had buttons, he'd a busted them all.

"Yes, James. You did good. Y'all did real good," Momma said, praising her troops, her happy tears free-flowing. "Scoot over some," she said, easing Eli gently from his big brother's protective grip and back into her own. "Lemme take a closer look."

"Eli's gonna be aw'right now," Bootie whispered. "Ain't that right Momma?"

"Oh, yes," she said. "Yes, sirs. I expect your little brother's gonna be just fine. Let's get him warshed and taped up some. Bless his precious li'l heart, he surely don't need lose no more blood."

Bootie nudged James and the two placed one hand apiece under each of Clayt's little armpits lifting him up so that he, too, could see his twin.

"Hoo-ray for Eli!"

"Ya-a-ay!"

"Yip-ee!"

The boys squealed with delight, clapping their hands together. Why, they jumped and bumped like a business of ferrets doing a weasel war dance. By then, Eli had overcome his confusion and was getting anxious to join in the celebration. Momma brought forth her emergency kit. Sending a wink my way, she mouthed the words *thank you.*

Cleaned up, Eli's wound looked no worse than what lay behind

Momma's own scarred tissue. She already knew full well how to fashion the appropriate dressing.

About three years past, not long before our fateful getaway to Cousin Arlis and Aunt Patsy's farm in Tuscaloosa, JB had pitched a wire hanger into Momma's face. Split the skin open between her eyes. Her blood spilled like Eli's had just now. It was, as Gamma Gert might say, just one more of those straws piling up on the camel's back.

JB had told her he was bringing an old football buddy, Hopie Mungin, back to the trailer that evening. "That dimwit is willing to pay fitty bucks just to lay down next to you, Vida Lee," he'd said, shaking his head.

"You take leave of your last senses?" Momma fired back. She emptied the water sprinkle jar into the sink and unplugged the iron, holding onto it a moment longer than necessary before setting it down on the hotplate. "I'm your wife. The mother of your childrens, JB. And I'm pregnant—"

"He don't care about that."

"I'm not listening no more, JB. You're talkin' crazy."

He grabbed ahold of her hair. "Well, now. Ain't that just like the pot callin' the kettle black. You keep the lights out so Hopie don't get too good a look at you and change his mind."

JB didn't stop there either, even though he must have known he should've. "Don't be lookin' at me like that, Vida Lee. And don't be getting no ideas neither. Hopie's got money, and he ain't real partic'lar, but he don't take kindly to whores. And hear tell," JB snarled, backing her into a corner, "he likes little boys just as well. You understand what I'm saying, Vidalia? A buck's a buck. A body's a body. He got bucks. We got bodies. Don't make no never mind to me either way. Ain't gone matter to that horny bastard, neither—"

Momma had grabbed up the closest heavy object she could reach. She clipped him in the back with the still-warm clothes iron.

For a long second he just stood there staring at her, open-mouthed.

As if pressed down by her own actions, Momma slumped to the floor, "I'm sorry JB," she said, spitting her words. "I do my part. I do more 'n my part. We're broke cause you won't never do nothing to support your own family. You cain't go expectin' me to lie down with Hopie Mungin cause you cain't hold a job."

JB snatched that wire hanger off the door hook and flicked it, catching her smackdab in the middle of her forehead. Blood spewed everywhere. Just like in those 3-D horror films showing at the Peeples Theater and so popular with city kids these days.

I feared he might kill her right then. Most likely he would've if old Hopie wasn't waiting on him down at Picayune's.

JB stormed out, yelling back over his shoulder, "I'll be sendin' Hopie around soon's it gets dark enough. You be ready."

After he left, Momma cleaned herself up as best she could. She tied her hair in a freshly pressed silver-blue ribbon so it wouldn't get all stuck in the bandage she'd fashioned, changed into her clean dress, pinched her cheeks for color, and dabbed on some lipstick.

"What're you doin', Momma?" I asked, incredulous.

"Hush, Cieli Mae," she whispered. "I ain't got no time to chat."

Momma packed her biggest bag, grabbed up the babies, and at half past seven that same evening, off we set for the bus depot, stopping by Doc Feldman's on the way, her head wrapped and bandaged under her bonnet. A trickle of blood made its way as far as her left eyebrow, trying to give her away. She fibbed to the doctor anyways, saying how that all was on account of her own clumsiness.

Doc noted the stuffed carpetbag by her side but pretended he didn't. He showed her how to fashion a proper butterfly bandage and as matter-of-factly as possible, he handed over a small leather pouch containing a jar of bee salve, a six-ounce bottle of peroxide, and a white envelope stuffed with extra dressings.

In addition, he'd offered her an amount of just-in-case money which Momma accepted this time—but only a portion of—without putting up a fight. She swore she'd make it up to him soon's she'd figured out how, and Doc let that stand, though he ached to tell her there was no need. Murmuring, yet again, it was the least he could do.

Wasn't long before JB tracked us down, explaining to Momma how he was only just joking with her about old Hopie and begging for one more last chance. As it turned out, after many complaints lodged by his girls and several regulars, Pat Picayune had tossed Hopie out on his ear while a parade of bullets escorted the unwelcome lowlife, with his peculiar set of likes, to the edge of town. And that was the last anyone in these parts had seen of or heard from Hopford Mungen, JB's old buddy from his glory days back at Coggins County High.

SO FOCUSED ON OUR LITTLE Eli, it was a good five minutes before any of us noticed the gentle but steady rapping at our door. Momma shushed the boys, and with nary a sound she passed Eli back over to James. Not one single body took a breath as she approached the door. Her pistol ready to go in her apron pocket, she peered through the side window.

At the sight of a fidgety Doctor Feldman, his trusty black valise in hand, Momma could hardly hold herself in. Relief flooded from her like bathwater pouring over the lip of a stopped-up tub with its faucet left running.

Again willing her knees to hold her upright, Momma turned the knob, opened the door, and stepped aside.

"Why hello, my dear," Doc said, his carefree intent betrayed by the heightened pitch of his voice. "Vidalia? What is it? Is everything all right?" A chill rushed at him through motionless air as he observed the spoils of our day: the recognizable bulge in her pocket, mounds of bloodstained laundry strewn about, and the well-stocked first aid kit with its contents scattered. Our boys squirmed under the scrutiny.

Momma's face flushed scarlet.

"Have I come at a—" he restarted. With no warning, Momma burst into a fit of giggle-laughter, doubled over, and lowered herself to the floor. The boys sat, wide-eyed. Doc swiped his brow with a white starched hankie. Then, he carefully refolded the cloth square, stuffed it back into his chest pocket, and helped Momma to her feet. "Have I come at an, an inconvenient time?" he asked, still riding the fence.

Taking one deep breath in, Momma turned serious. Gently, she maneuvered her bandaged baby boy from his brother's arms and held him up for inspection.

Doctor Feldman nodded. "Well now," he whispered, leaning in closer. "I don't know what transpired here, my dear, but I see by the quality of care administered that you've been paying attention." Doc gave Momma's hand an awkward squeeze, trying his best not to frighten her and the boys further. "A most excellent butterfly, Vidalia. Most excellent."

Doc uprighted the stool and pulled it closer to Eli. He checked the boy's vitals while the patient grabbed playfully at his stethoscope.

"Vidalia Lee, I'm very, very proud of you," Doc said, his voice wavering over each word. "But what happened? What happened to—"

"A shot rang out from the woods. I turned too fast," Momma said, cutting him off. "Must've been that terrible, awful bad man we all been hearing about."

"Ah," murmured Doc. "So you saw him?"

"No, sir. Not exactly. But I heard a sound. A sound of something dropping. *Ping*, it went as it hit his boots. Those ones with the steel toes."

"The kind JB wears?"

"The kind JB wears," she'd said, nodding slowly, staring down at her own bare feet.

"I see," Doc said, the concern rising in his words. "I'm going to have a look out back Vidalia. Keep an eye on Eli, of course, but I am confident our boy will be quite fine before long." Doc patted her hand, but not in a patronizing way.

We all spent what was left of that evening entertaining the injured party while Doc Feldman nosied around outside. When he came in, he gave both Momma and Eli another once-over.

"Is it loaded, Vidalia? It is a .38 caliber, correct?" he asked, his eyes locked on hers.

"That's a funny question, Doc," Momma answered.

"What? Oh, well. I always carry one in my valise. For varmints and such. When I'm making my house calls. Never know what I'll come across. You know, I'm not due back at the hospital until early morning. Perhaps you'd like me to stay the night? I could sleep here on the chair by the door," Doc offered, pointing his chin toward Momma's newly leveled reading chair.

"Thank you kindly, Doc. But I got it all covered from here on. And, yes, sir," Momma said, gently patting her pocket, "she's loaded."

"Just the same, Vidalia, I've got some time on my hands—"

"Would you like a cold Co-Cola before headin' out, Doc?"

"Why, no. No thank you, my dear. I believe I'll just sit outside awhile. That is, if you don't mind?"

"You go on 'n set as long as you like," Momma said, through a tight smile and gritted teeth. "But don't fret none. Like I said, I got it covered."

"Oh, of course. Of course, my dear," Doc waved one hand, dismissing her urgings as if fretting had been the furthest thing from his mind.

"Now, Doc. We all 'preciate you lookin' after us the way you do. I mean that truly. Thank you."

"Think nothing of it," Doc replied, smiling. "It is the least I could do." Momma's eyes searched the older gentleman's face though I'm rightly sure she didn't know what it was she was looking for. Doc took a step toward the door, "You'll lock up after me, Vidalia? And it might be a good idea to position something sturdy up against the door."

"Sure thing, Doc," Momma called after him, then commenced to wondering, once more, over why he felt with all he did that all he did was the least he could do.

⟨⁓⟩

CUTTING SHORT OUR BEDTIME RITUALS the boys took to their pallets more readily than usual, books, blocks, and gangly understuffed animals in hand. Eli whimpered time to time as his stubby, little fingers reached up to pat his hurt spot.

"We cain't let him sleep, boys. Not just yet," Momma cautioned.

The brothers watched him closely, disrupting as needed any hint of slumber with whatever silly nonsense came to their little boy minds, while in the front room Momma scrubbed and fretted, and fretted and scrubbed.

I peeked in on her for good measure. I reminded her how the boys and I were on guard and that she ought to try 'n get herself a some shuteye.

Momma shook her head. "I'm fine, Cieli Mae. I'll take a break, maybe soon. G'wone now."

Alone again, Momma bowed her head and leaned her palms together, pressing the tips of her fingers against her forehead. She spoke in a voice flat and steady. "I thought I was ready," she'd said, softly, "I got caught off guard. I will not be caught off guard of him. Not ever again."

Night passed into day with no further upsetments. Doctor Feldman had fallen asleep just outside on a partly webbed aluminum lawn chair, between woods and door. His weak back—strengthened some now by staunch intention—pressed guardedly against our trailer's warped siding. Awakened by Misses Bysa's roosters, Doc had just enough time to make it to Lafayette General for a previously scheduled surgery.

Sleep had crept in for the boys as well, and Momma, too, just before the morning light. To see the sun rising up in all its glory, why, no one would suspect what all we'd gone through while this world was turning.

That same morning, Misses Ruby Pearl Banks awakened with a start. What she called her "uneasy feelin'."

"Why din't them boys flash me no message!" But they were only just boys, after all. Maybe they forgot? Our Miss Ruby didn't think so.

CHAPTER THIRTY-THREE

Ruby PEARL PARKED HER TRUCK a full block away, wrapped herself in her shawl, drawing it up awning-like over her head, and pulled its sides across her back and down her arms to her knuckles.

The hem of her flowing housedress barely brushed the high tops of her red P. F. Flyers as a pair of overextended anklets struggled to rise to the occasion. She hoped the lazy bums who might take issue with her presence were still sleeping off their previous night's misdeeds, but today was not a day to take chances.

That she'd crossed paths with a flustered, exhausted looking Doctor Feldman on her way to us only fueled her suspicions.

Might the doc have been rushing from an overextended social visit with friends? Our Miss Ruby didn't think so.

As the sun rose behind our trailer, there she was, on our stoop, in all her Ruby Pearl splendor. Knocking on doors. Tapping on windows.

An orange mesh shop bag bulging with goodies and other lumpy, bumpy delights hung from the crook of a camouflaged elbow and bounced at her side as she wriggled handles and peeked between cracked window slats.

James was the first to spy our Miss Ruby, a friend indeed. He summoned his twin and together they pushed aside the stool Momma had wedged up tight against the door. On tippy toes, Bootie flipped the flimsy hook latch up from its eye, and oh so slowly, he turned the knob.

After a mild Ruby-scolding the trio went about their business as quietly as a chorus of church mice.

Momma awakened to find Ruby Pearl in command. Water boiled for tea as she soothed my brothers with melt-in-your-mouth biscuits warm from her oven, slathered so generously with her own blackberry preserves that all four pairs of their little lips had turned a bluish-purple.

They knew better than to resist Ruby Pearl, not that any of them would've wanted to anyways.

For Ruby Pearl, Cody or no Cody, the boys fell into line right quick. Eli was unaware why his boo-boo could be of interest to anyone other than ourselves, but of course it was such to our Miss Ruby.

For Eli's sake, and Momma's as well, Ruby Pearl quieted her anger, taking it out, instead, on the bloodstained dry goods scattered hither and yon. The boys helped her scoop it all back into the basket from whence it had come, spotless and fresh, just hours past. Tsk-tsking to herself, Ruby Pearl laid the wicker hamper right by the door so she couldn't forget to take it with her.

Our process of reparation had begun.

With mealtime cleanup underway, Momma and Ruby Pearl needed some "growd-up time" to talk. Exiled to the back room, the boys made sheet tents. James, as usual lately, took the lead, which was just as well, as I was in no mood for childish games of make-believing.

One finger pressed to his chin, Bootie studied the bedding, figuring the best mode of attack. I assumed my post and kept watch over the boys, but truth be told, my focus, as pre-ordained, was trained on what all was being carried on in the other room.

"The Good Book tells me to 'turn th'other cheek.'"

"Mm-hmm. That's right, Miss Vidalia. That's what the Good Book says."

"But it wasn't *my* cheek this time, Misses Banks," Momma said, smoothing out imaginary wrinkles from her apron skirt.

Ruby Pearl stayed silent as if she had no response, but Momma knew better.

"And what about that other verse," Momma continued. "The one not spoken of in the church halls, 'An eye for an eye'?"

Ruby Pearl took a moment. She inhaled slow, then exhaled fast. "Don't drag yo'self down to there, Missy. That ain't what's inside you—"

"Oh dear, dear Misses Banks, you don't know—"

"Don't you be tellin' me what I don't know, chile," Ruby grumbled.

"But you don't know what's inside me."

"Oh, yes I do. A whole lotta strength and whole lotta goodness is what's inside you. You can't let nobody take that away. That belong to you—"

"Now, Misses Banks, I don't mean no disrespect, but—"

Ruby Pearl tilted her head, studying the being in front of her. "You is me, chile. In a different wrapper is all."

"I don't understand," Momma started.

In a way larger than life Ruby Pearl threw back her head, her wide eyes in search of something higher up. "My Ruben was a fine man," she said. "A fine man. Workt hard at the Feed 'n Seed near ever' day o' his growd life. An ever' day, Missy, he took that same route home. Ever' day he picked me a blossom off the tree at the fork in the road down by the crik. He'd get home and I aw'wes be in the same place, standing over at the stove.

"I acted surprised, cause that's what he expected, an' I'd try 'n shoo him away. But he'd just go on kissin' my neck folds, whisperin' sweet somethin's in my ear while fixin' that flower into my hair.

"I'd tell him, you go on now with yo' sweet talk. I need get back to my cookin' or you an' them chirrens gone have one burnt supper.

"Maybe a time or two, while the chirrens was playin' outside and din't take no notice of their daddy's homecomin', that supper did burn, but they din't never go hungry. My Ruben woun't hear of such a thing.

"One evenin' we was dryin' dishes—we aw'wes dried the dishes together, Missy—cause my Ruben, he said I workt too hard as it was, cleanin' and toilin' so for Madame Lafayette. Ruben tole me his boss's wife comedt by the store. He felt bad for that girl. She aw'wes lookt so sad. That Mister Greenley, he was a nasty sort. I tole Ruben that kinda thinkin' was just gone get him into big trouble someday.

"'Them's bad men,' I warnt him. 'You best be careful.' And don't you know what, Missy? I ain't never been so right.

"One day Misses Greeley showdt up, her arm in a sling. My Ruben, he made the mistake of akstin' after her. 'Why, Ruben,' Mister Stuart said back, 'I wonder why you is akstin' after a white man's wife?'

"My Ruben 'pologized. Tole Mister Stuart he din't mean nothin' by it. But then all day Ruben tole me, he had his uneasy feelin'.

"After that, Bud Greenly and Jeb Stuart spent a lot o' time out behind the Feed 'n Seed. Actin' mo' strange than usual.

"Bud Greeley's boy, you knows young Master Greeley?" she asked Momma.

"I believe I do," Momma said. "A year ahead of me and Sunny in school. A quiet sort, if I remember correct. Stammered some?"

Ruby Pearl nodded, slowly. "Mm-hmm."

"Had nice eyes though. Green. Light 'n dark at the same time," Momma said with a wistful smile. "Like a watermelon shell."

Ruby Pearl rubbed her chin some before bringing herself back on track. "That evenin', Missy, just when I's 'spectin' my man to sneak up aside me, here come young Master Greeley, runnin' up the dirt path, screaming his fool head off, *'MISSES BANKS! MISSES BANKS!'*

"That chile, he was trippin' so bad over his words, yellin' over how his daddy and them cracker friends o' his went chasin' after my Ruben with wood bats and hammers and such.

"'You gotta come quick, Misses Banks!' he said. 'My daddy, he yelt out, IT'S HOG KILLIN' TIME! and then all them white robes and pointy hoods took off after Mister Banks. I yelt at him to run but he couldn't hear me.' The boy whispered, 'Them bastarts hurt him, Misses Banks. They hurt him bad.'"

"'Oh, Lordy!' I cried out. 'Where is he boy? Where's my Ruben?' That po' boy lookt up at me, tears spillin' all down his chin. 'I'm sorry, Misses Banks,' little Master Greeley tole me. 'I let him down. But I had t' leave him 'neath that tree. By Old Macomb Bridge. I'm sorry, Misses Banks. I'm sorry for what my daddy done. I'ma fetch Doc Feldman, and I be there s-soons I get hold of 'im, I s-swear on my mama.'

"My po' Ruben, there he layt, in a pile. Threads of rope stitched into the sweat 'n dried blood around his neck."

Ruby Pearl squinted, laboring to swallow back the acid in her words.

"They kilt him dead, Missy," she said in a coarse whisper, tugging a hanky out from between her breasts. Ruby Pearl dabbed at her eyes and bowed her head. "Hung him from a tree. Them savages kilt my Ruben. Put a hole in my soul. Shot a cannonball through my belly."

"I'm so sorry—" Momma started.

Taking Momma's hand in hers, Ruby Pearl said, "Ain't no need fo' you to be sorry. You din't do nothin'."

"Those men was monsters, Ruby. You must'a wanted to—"

"I did. At first. But then, Me 'n Him," Ruby rolled her eyes upwards, "we had a *loong* talk. Decided it best if'n I left it in *His* hands."

"God? Are you talkin' about *God*? How could you still believe in a god who'd make such a thing happen?"

"God din't make that happen, Missy. Them fools done it all on they own."

"Where was *He* when them bastards beat your husband? When they hanged him, Ruby? Where was *God* when—"

"God be ever'where, Missy. In my chirren's faces. In yo' chirren's faces." As Ruby Pearl paused to inhale, I wondered how much she could truly see and whether or not I might, in some way, be included in her observances. "God want what's best fo' us, His chirrens," she went on. "But Vida Lee, *we* got to want it, too, even mo' than Him. See, Missy? He had to leave some of it up to us, oth'wise they woun't be no cause fo' heaven.

"Most folk do right," Ruby Pearl'd said, nodding. "And some folk do wrong cause they don' know no better, and them? Them's gone be forgiv'd. But some folk? Some folk know better and do worser anyway. It's them that's gone be sorry."

Momma wrung her hands and shook her head, ever so slowly. She didn't fully believe the last of what our Miss Ruby had said. But she didn't fully not believe it either.

Ruby Pearl cleared her throat, "Me, Doc, and the boy, we drug Ruben's body out from under Ol' Macomb. Then Doctor Feldman went with young Master Greeley to the sheriff's office. There sat Mister Bud Greeley, bold as gold and brazen as a raisin, hollerin' over how his boy made it all up! 'Lock him up, Coots.' Mister Greeley sneered. 'I'll be back to get the little faggot next week. That boy needs be learnt a lesson!'

"Back then, Bud Greeley had the town in his hip pocket. Sheriff Cooter 'n his good ol' boys wasn' no 'ceptions.

"Mister Greeley left the town hall lookin' fo' trouble as if he din't already have enough. Found his wife packin' a bag for her an' her boy. Greeley beat that po' woman to near death. After that, he called a 'mergency meetin'. I followed after him, Missy, even though Doc warnt me not to.

"Greeley preached like they was a hun'red people in them woods, though they was only seven. 'Them federal marshals is making a big fuss o'er in Mississippi. Get your weapons ready boys!' He screamed louder and louder, as if he wasn't already bustin' folks' eardrums. Actin' mo' and mo' crazy with each word comedt out his face! 'Them goddamn Yanks got no bidness here, but they're comin', and we got to get rid o' any evidence!' he hollered."

Ruby Pearl shook her head in disgust. She pushed back from the table, rose to her feet, and paced, her pointer finger aimed on high.

"'Lord', I said to Him," she told Momma. "'Bless my soul. I need answers and I need 'em quick. 'Cause, between You 'n me? I'm 'bout ready shoot them sonsabitches dead. Ever' last one.'

"But if I done that," she went on, "them'd lock me up—or hang me from a tree like they done my po' Ruben—and who was gone be lef' to look after my chirrens? Who was gone watch out fo' that boy?

"Oh, Lord help me. I wandt to kill them peckerwoods fo' what they done," Ruby Pearl glowered. "But I prayed instead, 'God A'mighty, hold me back. Tie my hands, Lord. Let me let Your will be done.'

"After their meeting, after ever'body else went on home, Greeley sat there, still stewin'. He pulled a big jug from out his trunk and chugged down the rot-gut inside. Ev'ry last drop. 'I reckon I besst destroy the ev'dence myssself then,' he slurred, doing what he could to adjust hisself inside his pants.

"His club foot chomped down on the gas pedal, and that dumbass cracker drove his truck hard and fast into that sad, sad oak. The branch, that one they strung my po' Ruben from, still hangin' limp and heavy under the weight of what it done, comedt down hard, crashed through the rusted roof of Greeley's cab and crushed the skull of the boogey-man inside. 'Divine re'bution' was what Doc later called it.

"And God's will, Missy? Oh, it got done, aw'right."

CHAPTER THIRTY-FOUR

THE SKY WEPT WITH A vengeance after having threatened such all that morning. Hard rains pounded the trailer's rooftop and grayed rivulets ran down every other corner where walls met ceiling.

Our sadness was tempered by wonder over how this world works in such strange and roundabout ways.

Once Ruby was out of earshot, my momma bent down and whisper-asked, "Ain't it so very strange, Cieli Mae, how the more a person knows about this world, the less they understand it?"

"Maybe that's the way it's 'sposed to be, Momma?" I asked back.

Momma sighed and headed for the reading chair. She put down her dust rag, picked up a book, and assumed her post, holding in her healed left hand, *The Book of Bible Stories for Young Children,* courtesy of little Sister Anna and the Church of the Twelve Apostles.

Clayt, still on guard, plopped onto Ruby Pearl's lap alongside Eli, waiting on the others to join them.

Once James and Bootie settled in, too, we left our own universe behind for other worlds where goodness and fortitude always triumphed over evil. The boys seemed satisfied to know there was such a place, even if it could only be seen with their mind's eyes.

As Momma read the story about how David slew Goliath, Ruby Pearl pretended she wasn't listening.

Momma read until she went hoarse. It was hard to get her started sometimes, but once she got going, she wouldn't stop until she had to.

Ruby Pearl, whose capacity to sit still in one place for too long had been exceeded, excused herself. She puttered about, clanging pots and pans and other items pulled forth from her bottomless mesh goodie bag.

Later, in the early evening, once the rains abated, they all cozied up in the kitchen to a spread of refried ham slices and fresh-made johnnycakes fixed from cornmeal and the jar of pork fat Ruby Pearl had brought from home.

James and Bootie cleared the dishes from the table to the sink while little Clayt, his jaw clenched tight, guarded his twin.

Momma touched her hand lightly to Clayt's furrowed brow. "Eli is gonna be just just fine. Don't you worry none. We're all gonna be just fine." She then declared it bedtime for all little hooligans as she needed to finish tidying up from supper.

"And get yourself home safe, Misses Banks," Momma pleaded, "before them crazies slither back out from under their rocks."

Then she and the boys said their goodbyes, thank-yous, be safes, and see y'all soons, to our Miss Ruby while she gathered up her belongings. Momma shooed the boys to the back room and walked Ruby to the door.

"You hear me, Missy," Ruby Pearl said in a hushed but insistent tone. "You hear me good this time. That man don't got all what's comin' to him. Not yet. But he will. Mark my words. Yo' only job fo' now is to keep them chirrens an' they momma safe. Not nothin' else."

"I'll think on that, Misses Banks," Momma said, her lips a thin line. "I promise I will. Now please, get on home to Cody."

MOMMA TUCKED IN THE TWINS, kissing them all double and then again, and she whispered to me a reminder to stay put, and to see to our boys, no matter what.

We hadn't heard from JB in a long while, and he was nowhere to be seen. Fortified by his mispresence, we maintained a position of watchful hopefulness.

CHAPTER THIRTY-FIVE

THE MOON CAST A SALLOW blanket over us all as I struggled to regain focus. Bold voices cut sharp edges into my musings.

Two sets of twins tossed and turned, innocent in their state of hibernation.

The outside door had been opened, allowing in a gust of wind, altering the sense of balance we'd labored so hard to put into place.

"How'd you get in here, JB?" Momma whisper-shouted from somewhere close beyond.

"'Scuse me? This is *my* house, woman. You think some old guard bitch Negra woman and some two-bit locks is gone keep me out my own house?"

"I sent Misses Banks home long ago," Momma said, adjusting her tone. "She's not still out there is she?"

"Not no more she ain't. Told her to haul her black ass back to where it come from or I'd do it for her."

"How dare you disrespect her. I'm warning you," Momma hissed, straining to stay level. "You best leave. You best leave, now."

"Well, I'll be a sonofabitch."

"You heard what I said, JB."

"Goddammit, girl," he said dragging his feet. "I was only just tryin' to scare you—"

"By takin' potshots at my childrens? You coulda killed Eli."

"Well I didn't did I?" he yelled, inches from her face.

"Go, JB. Just go. And don't come around here no more. It's over, JB."

"Fuck you, Vida Lee. It'll be over when *I* say it's over!"

"I mean it. You cain't come around here. Not no more—"

"Fuck you with a river stone, whorebitch."

"These childrens deserve better, JB." Wearing her conviction like armor, a strong certainty coursed through her veins.

JB looked down his nose at Momma, his head cocked back like a drunk rooster, giving him a drop-dead, ugly, stubbled double chin. His cigarette-holding hand grasped tightly onto his left forearm. "It's all your fault the kid got hit."

"My fault? What're you talkin' about?" Momma asked, taking two steps back from him. Even I was confounded.

"Was but a warning, Vida Lee. 'Sides, I was aiming for you. But hell, you moved. Let the kid take it for you," he said, rubbing his hand up and down one arm and across his chest. He snatched up his cigarette from the kitchen countertop and flicked its ash onto the freshly scoured linoleum squares. "Girl, just lookin' at you gives me pains in my—"

"I got a gun," Momma replied. Her voice dull and matter-of-factual.

"Well, now. You think I'm stupid or somethin'?" he sneered. "I done emptied that chamber long ago."

"I reckoned you might'a." Momma's voice wavered but one little bit. Her pinched lips gave way to a nervous grin as she mimicked his attitude, mirroring his sneer. "But I done filled it right back up again."

Tiny silver-saffron squares seeped through the one intact window screen, showing off a hazy, grid-like perspective.

It was just past midnight. JB's face had taken on an ornery shade of gray. I could not see much nor too clearly, but I did see that.

"You don't look so good," Momma told him.

"That's cause I'm all backed up inside, and that's your fault too," he snorted.

A chair scraped linoleum. The table toppled along with any leftover emergency supplies.

I heard the clink of JB's belt buckle. A swoosh of muffled sounds, then a thud. I listened hard, awaiting summoning.

I'm ready, Momma. I'm here. Just call for me Momma. Call for me, dang it!

Awake now, James and Bootie cowered in our doorway.

"What we gonna do, James?" Bootie clutched his matchbox cars, his little pink knuckles now white.

"I don't know Bootie. I'ma 'feart he's gone hurt her—"

"He's gone hurt her bad."

James swallowed back a hot burp. "I wish she'd shoot him."

"Momma wouldn't do that—"

"Wish she would though."

"Me too. I wish she'd shoot 'im."

"Maybe then he'd go away and not never come back?"

"I wish she'd shoot him *daid*—"

"Hey, Bootie. What's Misses Banks doin' out there?"

The outside door had been left ajar. And there she was. Our Miss Ruby.

I expect I should've been alarmed about Ruby Pearl mixing into this fray, but instead a quiet calm washed over me. Like somehow this was all going to work out, and that Momma and the rest of us would awake tomorrow none the worse, now that our Ruby was here. That same quiet calm must have poured over my brothers as well.

"Aw, James. We best git back into bed now 'fore Misses Banks sees we up. It'll be okay now."

"I reckon."

The two sleepyheaded cubs crawled back onto their pallet, under the cover. Reality, as it is meant to be at their age, only a temporary intrusion.

"Now be nice, y'all. Put that gun away, Miss Vidalia," instructed Ruby Pearl. "An' Mister Jackson? I believe you best take yo'self a nice, long walk."

"What the hell! When the *fuck* did we get us a mammy?"

"Mister Jackson, sir. I believe Misses Jackson's got 'nuff bullets in that pistol to blow yo' fool head to kingdom come. An if she don't, I do," Ruby said, stroking both the left and right pockets of her housecoat. "You best take a minute 'n think about that walk, Mister Jackson."

On that note, the door sprung open again surprising even Ruby Pearl. There stood a wild-eyed Doctor Lewis Feldman, his revolver drawn. Why, I'd never seen the doc's hair standing on end before. I expect it might've been an amusing sight in a different place or time.

JB turned around fast. "What the fuck! Goddammit! I'ma kill all y'all!" He lunged at Momma, grabbing her by the throat. What remained of his lit cigarette went flying, the butt landing in the waste can beneath the kitchen sink.

Ruby Pearl took hold of the lone lit lamp, smashed it over JB's head, and the room went dark. I thought back to the shop cart and the missing lightbulbs, and I was glad for Momma's forethought.

One gun discharged. Just like in an old-time crank movie, its flash froze the room's inhabitants in awkward positions. Momma in recoil. Doc steadying himself in the one corner shaking the sound from his brain and taking aim, with Ruby Pearl just about to.

Another explosion. This time from Doctor Feldman's corner.

And then another. This one was Ruby Pearl's.

Pop. Pop. Pop. Like that first afternoon in Ruby Pearl's kitchen during the storm with the rains pounding away at her tin roof, but different.

JB lay there like an empty peanut shell. Brittle. Spent.

The boys awoke. Clayt and Eli started screaming. James and Bootie, their ears still ringing, reassured each other, and then saw to the little ones, ushering them into the closet for safekeeping.

I wished Momma hadn't made me make that promise.

Ruby Pearl was first to rebound. "You aw'right, Missy?"

"I'm fine, I think," Momma coughed out the words with one hand massaging her sore neck and shoulder. "Where's Doc? I cain't see Doc—"

"Here I am, Vidalia. It is dreadful dark in here, but I suspect we may've just caught that madman-escaped-prisoner, that one we've been hearing about all over town."

"Why, Doc Feldman, sir. I do believe you might be right!" Ruby Pearl said, doing a quick hand wave over her heart.

"I came by with the intent to check on little Elijah," Doc proffered. "The door was ajar. From outside I heard voices. Loud, agitated voices. And I, well, yes. I was duly concerned and confused as to the state of affairs inside—"

Just then, Mister Burleson and Bitsy ambled in breathless.

"Y'all awright in here? Bitsy and me was out for our walk an' heard gunsh— Well, I'll be. What in the tarnation!" Matt Burleson exclaimed.

There lay Momma in her white dressing gown, one recently discharged .38 by her side. She'd left herself and had collapsed in a heap next to the lifeless body. Doc stood by, a smoking snub nose in his right hand. Ruby Pearl gasped and dropped her still-warm pistol at the sight of the Burleson's Doberman. And then she, too, fainted dead away.

"The bad man," a small voice murmured in the darkness.

Mr. Burleson ran back to his trailer to ring for the sheriff who'd been on his way home and already close by.

"SHERIFF TRUITH HERE! I'M ON the inside! Don't nobody move!" Truith's voice rang out almost as loudly as the gunshots. What with all the confusion, the sheriff had forgot to adjust his ear speaker.

Peering through darkness and lingering smoke, noting inert bodies and fumy odors, the sheriff let his fingers fumble along the wall. He flipped the light switch, but nothing happened. He flicked it again. Nothing.

By now, Momma had come to and pulled herself upright. Knees against chest, curled in a tight hug, she stared at the back of the collapsed man's head.

"Cieli Mae, please come out here now?" Momma murmured the words, more of a wish even, than a request.

And there I was. "Momma," I whispered. "I'm here."

Sheriff Truith reached into his holster and pulled out a flashlight. He snapped it on and shined it directly upon the victim's face. Confounded, he bounced the beam back and forth from the injured party to my momma as her wide eyes, too, darted back and forth from Truith to the victim.

"That weren't no escapee got shot here, Vida Lee. That there is your husband. And he don't look to be breathin' no more."

With that, Momma shut her eyes and toppled to a mound on the floor again, right aside JB. Ruby Pearl had just revived her own self some and stood there like a cat who'd just ate the canary, feathers and all, as a fog of gun smoke loitered in the air. The heat of the sheriff's gaze seared into her.

"Well now, Misses Banks," Sheriff Truith yelled, forcing our Miss Ruby to take a step back. "I got questions what needs answering. You all're gone need to explain what in the hell happened here!"

Truith's request met with yet another loud *thud*. For lack of any better option Ruby Pearl had, once again, dropped to a dead faint. Deputy-on-call Riser had entered just moments earlier and I almost felt both his and the sheriff's eyes to be closing in on me.

Next thing I knew my spirit had collapsed in a heap alongside the others. Not that anyone noticed.

Waiting for the thick, dizzy feelings to pass, for the fog to rise, and for breathing sounds in the room to return to a normal rhythm, I considered what all had happened and reckoned maybe this was just a vision. Only thing is, I didn't want it to be.

THE DOC, AS CALM AS you please, in a voice bolder than his own, went about explaining to Truith and Riser how he'd rushed in to the sounds of a struggle between Vidalia Lee and a, who-he-believed-to-be, crazed stranger.

"Well, my kind officers of the court, what was I to think? I could see, but just barely, mind you, the hands of the character in question wrapped tightly around the young mother's neck. Without a doubt, his intent was to do grievous harm. With Vidalia gasping for breath and Misses Banks issuing ultimatums and babies screaming in the the background, why, it never occurred to me the midnight marauder might be Vida Lee's own husband."

Truith just stood there pulling at his chin hairs, fiddling with his one hearing aid. Whether or not he truly heard all of what the doc had offered up seemed to be of little consequence.

Our boys could be quieted no longer. Shushes, cries, and whispers, ricocheted within their hiding place. I reckoned I should get back to them but didn't dare to take leave of my place with my momma. Not just yet anyways.

"I drew my weapon and fired at the perpetrator," Doc continued. "Now what thinking man—and I ask this of you Sheriff Truith, as I know you are a thinking man—what thinking man would have, could have, reacted differently? Especially with all we've been hearing of late about the recently escaped prisoner."

"Why, Doc," Truith said, handing over his notepad to the deputy.

"That sick son-of-a-bitch's been caught and put down. Call came in just about the same time as Burleson's. Now, then. Ain't that a kick in the balls."

Doc frowned. His mouth opened, but I reckoned he was having some trouble finding the right words because nothing came of it. Either that or his voice was temporarily tired out.

Truith shook his head. "My Katrina come home from the beauty parlor the other day fussin' all over me about a story of a madman on the loose and why didn't I have the good sense to warn her? Well, now," I tole her, "I don't know nothing about that." Truith stopped to swat at the gnats that'd started congregating. "But, I reckon," he went on, more thoughtful than usual, "there'll be more than one mind in Willin put at ease some, after this here odd turn of events."

In the meantime, Doc Feldman had gathered up his thoughts. He repeated clearly, but with not so much gusto this time, how he had only come by this evening to check on little Elijah, having been unable to get around to it earlier. That he'd heard an awful commotion from within before he even had a chance to knock. And how he'd heard Ruby Pearl already on the inside, heartily advising the alleged intruder to leave the poor girl be.

"Gentlemen," Doc said, addressing the two lawmen on hand, careful to aim his words directly at the sheriff's better ear, with a tone of seriousness most usually reserved for a deadly diagnosis. "I could only assume an unknown and evil presence had invaded this humble domicile, threatening those within." And then the purposefully misguided medicine man described how he'd rushed in, pistol cocked, ready to defend.

Doctor Feldman insisted, "In this instance, the women fired as caveats, whereas, if any one bullet struck the 'victim', it was my own. A warning shot has a very different agenda, kind sirs. A very different intent," he said. "*My* intent, was to defend my d—" Doc sighed, taking one more long, thoughtful pause. "My patient. At what cost to the perpetrator? Well now. I must confess, his safety was not amongst my concerns."

Momma's weapon was loaded and the safety off, as was Ruby Pearl's. Both had been discharged. All three pistols involved, were, in fact, .38s. The puzzle at hand then would seem to be from which pistol which bullet was fired, and which, if any, had dealt the fatal blow.

Long before Lewis Feldman was appointed the county's medical examiner, he had taken an oath to do all in his power to protect.

"It was the least I could do," he stated as a matter of the facts and turned his back on the body currently in question. The one he'd just pronounced dead.

SHERIFF TRUITH PACED THE ALLEGED crime scene. His day had been long enough to tire a mule, and now he and his deputy had to wait on the coroner and then look after the remaining suspects, once they all came to.

"Gentlemen, you're both weary and rightly so." Doc spoke utilizing his best bedside manner. "I would consider it not only my civic duty but an honor and a privilege to remain in your stead and look after the young widow and her charges. I'll do my best to assure the scene remains undisturbed. You have my word."

Hopeful, the doc looked from one appointed officer of the court to the other.

"Well then. I reckon we could come on back in the morning. Whatd'ya say, Riser?"

"Yes, sir. It don't look as if anybody else gone be gone nowhere anytime soon anyway," Deputy Riser agreed.

I wondered, *And why not?* Doc had nothing to hide, he'd already confessed. Not quite self-defense, but it came off looking pretty much the same.

And it *was* dark. And there wasn't one working lightbulb to be found. And the sheriff and his deputy were tired. After all, it would be daylight soon enough, and, for sure, it'd take more expertise than was in that room to get to the bottom of this dilemma. To gather evidence, samples, statements. To compare the spent casings with those bullets lodged helter-skelter throughout the trailer.

I'd only counted three shots. But I supposed in the confusion I could have missed a few.

"Just don't nobody move nothing," Truith directed. "I need to finish drawlin' the chalk lines to mark the spot and cover up the body. Riser, fetch me that mattress cover out the car."

"The one with the zipper, sir?"

Exasperated, Truith looked at the deputy. "We only got but one, son."

"Yes, sir. Sorry, sir."

"We'll stay put til the coroner gets here. My good sense tells me there's a bullet in him, but I'll be gosh-darned if I can find it. I'ma leave that up to Lazarus. After all, that's what he gets paid for. When he's done, we'll all get the heck out of here."

EVEN THOUGH DOC STAKED CLAIM to responsibility for this "disastrous and unfortunate event," so too did Momma and Ruby Pearl. It was no secret they were, each in their own right, accurate marksmen.

Each was, as well, protective of the other, asserting it was his or her own doing.

That at best, and at worst, they shared equally in answerability.

To and amongst one another they'd supposed an accident might still be considered such, even when the outcome had been one long fancied.

For any one of this here blessed trinity of crack shots to have missed at such close range with other intentions, well, now, that there would have been the only true accident—a near miracle, as far as I could see.

AFTER A SHORT WHILE TRUITH took both Doc and Mister Burleson aside. He explained how he and Riser had best be getting on their way and that even though Momma and Ruby Pearl had come to, no further investigating would be going on around here. Not until daybreak. And that he needed some time to buck up, as Gertrude Kaye hadn't yet been notified.

By then, both sets of twins had rejoined our posse of mourner-suspects, providing some needed distraction, while the sheriff and his deputy shored themselves with one cold brew apiece courtesy of our newly attentive neighbors.

Coroner T. W. Lazarus came, saw, and carted off the dead body-in-a-bag.

Matty and Tatty Burleson shepherded us to their place. Tatty served consolation refreshments in the form of warm sugar biscuits and cool fresh-squeezed lemonades. Miss Bitsy, safely caged out of doors, paced in her pen.

Matt Burleson, schooled in the ways of the local penal system, advised us all why the authorities needed wait on an autopsy to declare cause of death.

"That there is the only sure way of knowing if there's something else that needs be known."

The origin of the "aforementioned coagulated blood splatters found within shouting distance of the body" was yet to be determined. Sheriff Truith and his deputy weren't the only ones wondering over where, oh where, was that critical point of entry.

A rancid smell leaked in on stiff air and then, *Shh-boom!* All heads snapped easterly and looked out the Burleson's window. There went the roof of our rental trailer in a flash of fire and a puff of smoke, leaving behind only the charred remains of truths—as told by Momma, supported by Ruby Pearl, and verified beyond any reasonable doubt by Doctor Lewis Feldman.

The warning bell for Fire Engine Number Two clanged in the near distance.

CHAPTER THIRTY-SIX

SURELY THAT NIGHTMARE-TURNED-INTO-DAY called for a conniption fit of some sort, but Momma would have none of that.

The boys had brought along their favoritest stuffed animals and whatnots, so, other than fretting over the state of her books and Ruby Pearl's pots and pans, Momma was doing all right.

All right, that is, until I finally got hold of her attention. "Momma!" I shrieked, forgetting myself and startling her. "What'ya gonna do about Gamma Gert?" It was a question more important than any posed to her by local law enforcement.

Momma gasped. "Oh, my heavenly stars. That poor woman—"

Ruby Pearl waved her hand over her heart like a flag in surrender, murmuring "Oh, Lordy. Good God in heaven."

All eyes rested on my momma as she struggled to put thoughts into words, "Did they find her yet? Has Gertrude been told?"

Tatty laid her pitcher in the sink and led the boys to the easy chair in the parlor where she wrapped them all in the one quilt and asked what lullabies they might like to hear.

Doc left the kitchen, as well, intent on carrying on his pacing out-of-doors. Back and forth between the Burleson's doublewide and our smoldering rental, he kept careful watch over what was going on in both camps.

"Truith and Riser drove out to Purgatory," Mister Burleson explained to Momma, his voice low and reassuring. "Searched up and down for Gertrude Kaye. Made calls to neighbors and whoever. Turns out Gertrude left for Belle Isle just yesterday mornin' to look after her pa. Somehow

Grady Bo had gone 'n got hisself stuck under a loaded cattle trailer. Seven cows. But eight inches 'tween him and a concrete floor. Broke ribs, a busted shoulder, and a mess o' lesser cuts and bruises."

"But did they find her? Did they find Gert? Does she know? Poor Grady Bo, bless his heart—" Momma broke down. Genuine salt tears now floating freely along her cheeks.

"Ole man's dinged up pretty bad. Be needing some time for healing but says he'll be fine soon enough. Gert was out runnin' her errands so Truith needed to tell what needed tellin' over the phone, to Grady Bo. And Grady Bo says, now get this, Grady Bo says 'I'm lucky to be on the right side of the dirt and seein' this day, I'll handle it from here on, Truith. Thanks for calling, and you have a blest day.' That's what Grady Bo said, then he hung up on the sheriff!"

In a slow motion, Momma excused herself to the front porch swing. There she sat, overwhelmed with the sadness. And there she stayed, still, but for the shaking, her arms wrapped tight around her middle, holding herself together. Ruby Pearl filled the tea kettle and fussed about in the Burleson's ample kitchen, washing up dishes and wiping down counters.

By now, Sheriff Truith and Deputy Riser were back and trying their darndest to piece the puzzle together by the time Fire Chief William B. Nill from Hollow County, accompanied by their rookie Ballistics and Arson Specialist, arrived on the scene for a look-see.

Who would ever have reckoned our misfortune of sorts could've created such far-reaching commotionings?

Momma assumed her role, a portrait of melancholy, for the benefit of family and friends alike, but mostly, for the various law enforcement officers now at hand.

Doc Feldman remained on duty and attentive, a variety of pharmaceuticals at the ready, though, tell you what, Momma didn't appear in need of any of them.

"It seems best, my dear, that you limit your conversations during this trying period," the doctor advised her. "And don't you worry about the boys. They're in good hands. Your delightful friend, Sunny Beauregard Knight, came calling when she heard the news and is caring for them all. And, Vidalia, please remember, you need not speak further with these strangers. They have our sworn statements."

Ruby Pearl also did her best to isolate Momma from the scrutiny of this legion of unfamiliar muckrakers. At a safe distance from the hustle and bustle, and with an aura of sanctity reserved for confessionals, Momma and Ruby Pearl fretted back and forth.

"But I meant to do it, Misses Banks. I wanted it to happen. Ain't that just as awful?"

"You is worrin' around the problem, chile. If you meant to, you would'a."

Before excusing herself for one minute, Ruby Pearl offered up kindly that, for the time being, Momma and the boys ought all come stay at her place.

"Forgive me, Cieli Mae," Momma said in a low, earnest voice once the coast had cleared. "The honest truth is that, ever since he hurt Eli, every ounce of flesh on me, and every bone in my body, too, wanted JB gone from us, wanted to shoot him daid."

"Then what happened, Momma? Why din't ya?"

"I 'spect maybe, my spirit made a different choice," she'd said, her gaze dripping with confusion.

"But, why'd you fire your weapon then?" I asked, but not to be smug. I was curious is all. I'd always reckoned she didn't have it in her to commit M-U-R-D-E-R , but I was unsure what other choices she had in the moment, all things considered.

"Killing is a awful wrong, but it would be even awfuller still," my Vidalia said softly, "to let the doc or Misses Banks take the blame in my defense. For my failings." Shaking her head, she stared at the floorboards. "Are you ashamed of me, Cieli Mae?"

"Why no, Momma. I ain't ashamed," I hushed to her. "Truth be told, I ain't never been so proud." Through her tears, Momma's eyes beamed brighter than the lights of a new automobile being driven off the car lot for the very first time.

⌒

"THEY'LL BE MORE QUESTIONS FOR y'all, so please don't none of you think about leaving town. At least, not for a good while," the specialist from Hollow County warned the saintly trio.

Assuming the role of spokesperson, Doc Feldman responded with a crisp nod. "You have my word, officer. I've known Misses Banks and Misses Jackson most all of their born days. Please remain assured there will be no journeying by any of the parties involved. Myself included. We are pleased to be at your service, sir."

Embarrassed, the young man sputtered, "I'm sorry Doctor Feldman, I d-didn't mean to suggest nothing about you. Or them neither."

⟨⟩

IF I TELL IT STRAIGHT, of the three, Momma had a best chance at shooting JB dead if that was her intention. Even with all the goings-on, and even with Doc's sudden, dramatic entrance.

A flash of moonlight caught the commotion in its glow just afore JB took his last tumble. But there was too much of it, commotion, I mean, as his body hit the floor like a sack of rotted produce.

Not much blood spilt though, as noted by those witnesses to the scene after the fact—Sheriff Truith, Deputy Riser, and Matt Burleson—and properly supported by Coroner Lazarus's report.

Officer Greeley had his suspicions and speculations but sent the previously-found dislodged bullets to the lab, for confirmation. On the scene, Lazarus, the medical examiner, indicated a lack of any point of entry worth its salt, strongly suggesting natural causes as opposed to, I reckoned, those of a more supernatural nature.

With an autopsy pending, the investigations continued on to "solidify and confirm all aspects of whatever findings were found," according to Sheriff Truith. In the meantime, charges against Momma, Doc, or Ruby Pearl had been dubbed "most unlikely" as this was not a "killed-by-gunshot" kind of death.

"Don't you fret, Misses Jackson. I'll get my colleagues and the rest of these other folk out from under your skin s-soon's I can," the young officer informed.

"Oh, it's fine. They don't bother me none, sir," Momma replied, while her nonstop toe tapping and fidgety fingers called her words into question. "I reckon they're just doing their jobs, same's me and you. And Doc and—"

Rookie Greeley nodded. "You need take some time, Misses Jackson.

And then get on with your life. Hear tell, it ain't been easy for you, b-but that could all change now."

Through her many truths and confusions of late Momma saw him again, almost as if for the very first time. Yes, it was him.

"I'm s-sorry Misses Jackson. I've overstepped," he'd said. "What I meant was that some folk carry their damages in their heads. Some bury them in their hearts. Shoot. What I'm meaning to say is that I'm right s-sorry for your loss, ma'am."

"My wh—? Oh. Oh, yes. Why thank you. I 'ppreciate your kind words, officer. Truly I do."

"Not at all, ma'am," he said, shaking his head. A warm flush of color crept from his collar, up the back of his neck, and snaked around toward his face. "If I can be of service of any kind, just give a holler. I may not look it, but I got strong shoulders."

Momma bowed her head but by some kind of magic, black or otherwise, her eyes were drawn up to his. And vice versa. Like magnets. The rosy blush spread across his cheeks now and to the tips of his ears. His lips pursed in a dry grin, and his forehead glistened with a nervous sweat. "I 'spect I b-best let you get back to your grievin', ma'am," the young man spluttered, turning quickly on his heels.

"Oh. I'm so sorry! Excuse me," he'd said after bumping into Ruby Pearl during his hasty retreat. A lesser woman might've been knocked to the ground.

"Kenneth? Kenneth Greeley? S'that you? It's me. Ruby. Ruby Pearl Banks."

The young officer paused, all circuits frozen. An is-she-talking-to-me look glazed his now paled face. Maybe he'd considered stopping, turning to answer, but he didn't.

Ruby Pearl sighed, then frowned and pursed her lips like if she'd been sucking on a lemon. "Maybe not. Sure do look like him though."

Misses Banks followed the young officer, finally tapping him on one shoulder. "G'wone over there then Mister Whoever-You-Be. Talk to her!"

"I'm s-sorry, ma'am?"

"I seen you lookin' at her boy. Seen her lookin' at you just the same." With both clenched fists planted firmly on her hips, Ruby Pearl dared him to go against her counsel.

"For goodness's sake, Misses Banks. With all due respect, we are investigating her husband's death."

"Thats right, boy. So g'wone over there an' do some investigatin'. What you *think* I meant boy?" And there she went again, getting all puffed up.

Just then Momma strutted by carrying a plate of cookies.

"Why, excuse me," Momma purred, like a cat with questionable designs. "I hate to interrupt y'all, but Misses Banks, have you seen my boys?"

"I'll help you round up them li'l scoundrels Missy Vidaliaaa. Ohh, on second thought, I reckon this fine gentleman here could help you find them boys. Young man, woun't you like to help Misses Jackson here find her chirrens?"

"Heck yeah. Oh, I mean, of course. Of c-course I'll help her. May I, Misses Jackson?"

"Why thank you, Kenneth. I'd be most appreciative. It is you, right? Little Kenneth Greeley? And all grow'd up, I might add—"

"Uh-huh. I mean yes, Vidalia. I mean, Misses Jackson. That is correct." With a measured reluctance, the officer had finally owned up to his name, his legacy, and his face drained further with each word to that end. "It's me. Officer Kenneth Greeley at your service, ma'am."

Momma lowered her eyelids while a flush took over her face, making up for whatever color he'd lost. *Oh my. Oh my,* I sighed.

Ruby Pearl rolled her eyes.

Momma and the young officer left the scene to wander the worn path toward the roughly-treed, prickly shrubbed piece of earth which separated Tribesmen's from the rest of this world.

"You and Misses Banks been through ever so much," Momma began, just as if she might be fixing to tell him a fairy tale. "Why cain't you just talk to her? That's all she wants, Kenneth."

"Geeze, Vidalia. When the call came in, when I heard the names involved in this, it was like a Sunday punch to my gut. Brought back all kinds of recollections. I prayed nobody here'd remember me or my daddy. Especially not my daddy."

"Just cause your pa was one way, it don't mean you gotta be that way too. Right? Look me in the eye, Kenneth. Tell me that's truly true. Why,

I just couldn't stand if it wasn't," she said, pleading on her own account as much as his.

Kenneth Greeley exhaled, long and slow. "How could Ruby Pearl not hate me after wh—"

"She ain't like that, Kenneth. You know she ain't like that."

"But I know she didn't forget. How could she ever near forget?" he asked Momma as if she were a window, and he was looking through her. "I haven't forgot. Not one thing. It's why I do what I do, Vidalia. Tryin' with all that's in me to make something up to somebody."

His words landed with a soft thud. Momma nodded in her most understanding way, and Kenneth took in a deep breath. "Well now," he said running a shaky hand through his hair. "I reckon we best get to roundin' up them boys of yours."

"My boys are fine," she replied. "Cody's watching after them." Twisting her hands first this way and then that, keeping his eyes fixed in her sights, she continued, "I believe it might help for you to talk about it some, you know? About what all happened back then to Mister Banks. A body cain't just Band-Aid a wound as big as that one. Not without cleaning it out first. You got to air it. Else it's only gonna fester. Everybody knows it weren't your fault. You were just little. And you tried to help as best you could. Near ever'body knows that. You know that too, don't you?"

Kenneth shrugged and my momma straightened, pleased with herself. "Well now," she went on. "That's what Misses Banks told me. And Misses Banks wouldn't lie. Not about something like that."

Kenneth dropped his head into his hands and slunk down onto what was left of a felled oak whose trunk bore rings, much like his sorrows, too many to count.

Momma went and sat aside him, placing a hand gently onto his shoulder.

"That afternoon," he said, toiling over each word, "me 'n Ma rode down to the Feed 'n Seed for supplies, her arm still in a sling. She'd tried to hide the bruises on her temple with a sun bonnet even though it was raining." Kenneth's left eye twitched and his voice dropped to barely a whisper. "Pa watched the whole time, never saying one word to us. Never once lifting a finger neither. Then Mister Banks asked, could he help us.

"After loading the last sack of feed into the truck, Mister Banks told my ma how every night him and his Ruby Pearl prayed that the Good Lord protect her and me. Ma was grateful in her heart to hear a near stranger wishing us well, but we just we drove off without her saying even one word back to him. Not even 'thank you.'

"Once, on accident, she'd told Pa, 'Why, that Ruben Banks is a fine gentleman.' Pa's face shook with a spitting rage and quicker than blue murder Ma added, 'For a Negra, I mean, Bud. That's all I meant.' Pa then busted her jaw, and she didn't never say nothin' nice about Mister Banks or any other Negra ever again. But Ma'd never stopped thinkin' what a good and kind man Mister Banks had always been. And she bet he didn't beat on his wife nor stand over her with a belt while she stitched up costumes for his stupid meetings, then beat on her again cause her fingers near bled all over those white sheets.

"I saw how Pa had been watching Mister Banks real close lately, so I started following after Ruben as he set out for home each night after quitting time, with him unawares.

"Then, one evening he saw my pa's pickup, half-hid down the road apiece, under the bridge. Mister Banks kept on walking, awlrighty, but with his head down like he was looking to his work boots for what to do now.

"Pa and Bear Stuart along with one more hooded coward came out from the bushes to the one side of him. Poor Mister Banks understood all too well that if he ran they'd shoot him in the back so he'd stayed put, greeting his gutless stalkers. 'Why, howdy, Mister Greenley. Mister Stuart. Mister Tate. Somethin' I can do for you alls?' he asked. Through proud but sorrowful eyes Mister Banks was pleading for his life, the life of his wife's husband, the life of his children's father.

"But them fools rushed him. First they whupped him 'til he was good an' raw. And then they hanged him. I was t-too much a yella-belly to speak up," Kenneth sobbed. "I didn't say nothing to stop them. I wanted to. But the words just wouldn't come out. So I snapped some twigs and rustled some bushes. To spook them. And they ran. Those cowards just rushed off and left poor Mister Banks hanging there, bleeding, his neck broke."

Kenneth recoiled when Momma reached for his hand.

"But you were just a boy back then," she said again, even more softly this time. "Wasn't nothing you coulda done. They'd a' killed you too. And you knew that. And then poor Mister Banks wouldn't a' had nobody to—"

"Do you reckon there's some truth to that Vidalia?" he asked, hopeful to a point, wagging his head. "I stayed hid until I was sure they'd all gone, then as quick as I could, I scooted up the knots of that old trunk. Then I shimmied along the branch until I was close enough to work on that sinful rope with my pocket knife.

"The old branch strained under his weight, but I didn't mean to let that stop me. And I surely didn't mean to leave Mister Banks hanging from no tree. That sorry limb creaked under me. Its bark scraped the skin off my arms, but I didn't even notice none of that until days later. Oh, it took some doin', but that branch held up enough to let me cut through that rope. Mister Banks's body dropped. It hit the ground with a thunk that turnt my stomach.

"He looked so bad I wanted to tear off my own skin and cover him with it. Instead, I took off my bloodied shirt and put it right over top of his ripped chest. 'I'm sorry for allowing you fall like that, Mister Banks,' I told his lifeless body. 'But I didn't know what else to do.' Somehow I thought maybe he could hear me. 'I'ma run for Misses Banks. And then I'ma fetch Doc Feldman. He'll know what to do.'

"Oh, I found Misses Banks," Kenneth said, nodding, tears still raining down his face. "I sent her on to him just like I said I would. But it was too late."

"You did the best you could," Momma said, her voice breaking, her heart full.

Just then my brothers came barreling toward them both, yelling and tripping over one another. "Misses Banks is packing up, Momma! C'mon now, it's time for us to leave!"

It'd been a long short day and we all were so very happy, especially Momma, the decision to go home with Ruby Pearl had already been made. That, for tonight at least, we knew where we were headed.

CHAPTER THIRTY-SEVEN

A SERIES OF APOLOGETIC RAT-A-TAT-TATS to Ruby Pearl Banks's front door intruded on our slumber. The sun shined bright, and the birds chirped ever so sweetly. *If we all pretended to wish yesterday a bad dream, I wondered, might anyone be fooled?*

The townsfolk had heard slowly but surely about our tragedy of sorts. Alms and other forms of benefaction presented on Ruby Pearl's front porch. Baskets full of clothing and buckets stuffed with staples, the likes of which none of us ever imagined, appeared overnight.

Mister Speight brought over a dented but almost new Philco console to replace the one we never had. Mister Treloar himself dropped off four cans of paint in Momma's favorite shade of buttercup. He knew we had no home of our own left, but she'd once told him how the color yellow left her feelin' happy.

Doc returned that morning, followed by Sheriff Truith. The results of the arson investigation designated a cigarette butt in the waste can by the gas stove as cause of our trailer's timely explosion. "The Butt of the Corpse," according to Truith's official report.

Ruby Pearl raised her brows, acting surprised, while under her breath she purled, "Umm-hmm. Tole her so."

"As luck would have it," Sheriff Truith announced, stopping to adjust his testy ear speaker, "there was but one casualty on that night. And he was already daid."

Grady Bo had filled in some blanks with what he knew of his grandboy's medical history. Doc called in a few favors and got the county coroner's report rushed through necessary channels, its autopsy findings confirming suspicions. It was all done on the up and up, as Doc Feldman wouldn't've had it any other way. Though JB's liver, for certain, had seen better days, it seems a previously undiagnosed genetic heart defect was held "directly to blame for the victim's demise."

Undetected heart defect? Now then. I had no medical background or training to speak of but I could have told them all there was something wrong with JB's heart. And I was pretty sure anyone else who knew him had already reckoned as much.

~

ASIDE FROM THE MORE MORBID details and those gloomy comings and goings, it was a fine morning. A right fine morning indeed. Ruby Pearl prepared a hearty breakfast for us all using the just-laid eggs left by Misses Isla Bysa and the generous slabs of bacon courtesy of Mister Pacinos. And, of course, Ruby Pearl's melt-in-your-mouth biscuits smothered in a special red-eye gravy, her own savory mixture of coffee and cooking greases.

Momma and the boys bathed and dressed after sifting through the baskets of clothing left for them, and we then loaded ourselves up into Ruby Pearl's truck and headed down to the Goodenough's Funeral Parlor to make final, final arrangements.

"Oh my dear, dear Misses Jackson," clucked Misses Goodenough. "It pleases me to tell you this, most especially with what all else you got going on, that you don't need to worry your pretty little head none about expenses." Earlier that same morning a benevolent donor, with strictest of instructions to remain anonymous, had made a most generous contribution on behalf of the Jackson Family. With Ruby Pearl steadfast by her side, my momma sniffed, appropriately grateful, into whatever tissues were offered her.

They were all just about to commence with the planning meeting when the Wild Women burst into Goodenough's with Gamma Gertrude Kaye in tow. Braced upright by the unruly posse, Gamma sobbed uncontrolled, split down her middle like a weeping willow twice struck by lightning. Unable to bear its weight, Gamma's spirit spilled out. It covered the floor, climbed the walls, and dripped back down from the ceiling, causing the sad, sad cycle to begin all over again.

Misses Goodenough ushered those Wild Women along, escorted Gamma to the planning room to join Momma and Ruby Pearl, and then snuck away to call for the doc.

"Why din't nobody do nothing? Why?" Gamma bellowed. "This is all my fault, ain't it? I shoulda been there for my boy. I shoulda," she blubbered. "Maybe I coulda saved him, just the one more time."

My momma's heart reopened to an anguish which, in a time not that long ago, had been her own second nature.

Mister Goodenough spoke slowly. "We are all sorry for your loss, dear Gertrude. Please take a seat here, next to Vidalia. I will explain everything as best as I can."

Betty Ann Goodenough returned bearing a gleaming silver tray with five tall tumblers of iced sweet tea and an equal number of shot glasses, filled to their brims.

"Now, Gert. Don't that blackberry brandy smell good? G'wone dear," Misses Goodenough said with a practiced empathy. "Let's us have a sup."

Even with five shots under her belt, the coroner's findings only nudged Gamma closer to the edge of her bluff.

"It *is* my fault then," Gamma moaned. "JB's daddy done took leave of this world near about the same age as him. I got word when Clayton Sr. croaked, but I just din't have it in me to tell JB his pa wasn't ever coming back. The boy didn't never forgive me for losing his daddy that first time around." Gamma shut her eyes tight, scrubbing a hand over her face. "I only done what I done to protect my son. I was just trying to protect my boy, but—"

"Now, now, Gert. Ain't no buts about it. You did the best you could do. A body cain't do no more than that," Momma said in her warmest voice, trying her darndest to be convincing.

Betty Ann Goodenough chimed in with her two cents worth. "Well now. There surely ain't nothin' to be gained in playin' the blame game."

Ruby Pearl leaned in, her fingers loosely clasped in her lap. "Wasn't nothing nobody shoulda done different," she confirmed, looking directly at Momma. "Them all said so."

I reckon there're some people, like Memaw Veta Sue and Granny

LuLa, who can't feel a stomachache unless it's in their own gut. But my momma wasn't one of those. And neither was our Miss Ruby.

"My boy, Jamerson," Gamma muttered, a sorrowful quaking in her voice. "He was a right fine husband. And a good daddy, too."

Momma straightened, focused only on Gamma's overwhelming sadness. "A fine husband," she echoed, unblinking. "And a good daddy, too."

"Them boys, they ain't gone soon forget our Jamerson," Gamma blubbered on. "And all what he done for them."

"Ain't that the truth," Ruby Pearl grunted with attitude, waving a hand over her heart. Momma caught Ruby Pearl's eye in rebuke but our Miss Ruby wasn't interested and looked away still waving.

"'Course not, Gert," Momma whispered, nodding gently. "No child forgets what their daddy done."

"Amen," said Ruby Pearl, setting her jaw in a hard line.

ALL ALONG, GAMMA HAD AIMED to protect, in the only ways she knew how, those she loved whether they deserved it or not. Especially now in her state of shock, her efforts plum outweighed her.

Momma held Gamma's shrunken face close to hers, one arm draped protectively around her shoulders. Cheek to cheek and ever so softly, Momma stroked Gamma's hair, gone grayer and finer overnight.

After a long while, Gamma calmed and my momma eased her grip some. In that one instant Gamma slid through Momma's loosed embrace and any other manner of possession. There was no hold big enough to contain Gamma's woe.

My heart overfilled up alongside Momma's with a knowing: In times such as this, no matter what a child has been or done, every mama has the inalienable right to lose her mind in any way she sees fit.

CHAPTER THIRTY-EIGHT

THE GOODENOUGHS LIFTED GAMMA GERT onto a gurney and wheeled her, flanked on either side by Ruby Pearl and Momma, to the Fainting Cottage out back.

Suited for such occasions, nestled amid spindly scrub pines and sourwoods and shrouded in kudzu, the little shack housed a divan, an embalming table, and other seemingly sordid but necessary amenities.

Doc arrived soon after the aggrieved, administering kind words and an injection.

Gamma, aided by Doc's choice of pharmaceuticals, grew quiet for a time, but then woke with a start. "It's back," she mewled, ashen-faced and bolt upright. "That voice. There I was caring for my pa while that voice called after me, hollerin' for help. 'But I'm tired!' I tole the voice. 'I'm way tired.'"

Upended beyond reason, Gamma carried on for the better part of that afternoon and so much so that Doc needed administer stronger and stronger sedatives until one kicked in. Still in an upright sitting position, finally, Gamma's eyes closed. Her head flopped forward and her chin dropped to her chest. I reckon she couldn't hardly absorb as much downheartedness, and surely not at the one time, without some kind of help. After all, she'd been treading water for long enough. Any might Gamma Gert had had left in her went toward just keeping afloat.

Momma's eyelids weighed heavy under her own mix of uncertainty, fortitude, and understanding. A guilty melancholy. For all that he wasn't, Jamerson Booth Jackson was Gamma's baby, and Gertrude Kaye Jebbit Jackson had loved him the best way she knew how.

EXCUSED FROM ANY PARTS OF this day's exercises, my brothers busied themselves in the Goodenough's manicured courtyard.

"Lucky them little rascals 're too young to know what all happened," townsfolk surmised, drawing back from the situation. "That there's the best thing to come out this whole mess."

Tell you what, our twins understood more than they should've, and I suspect Ruby Pearl, Doc Feldman, and even Momma figured as much.

Ruby Pearl had brought her friendly border collie along to help keep the boys in line. Under Cody's wary and shepherding ways—with the Goodenough's gardener providing backup—James, Bootie, Clayt, and Elijah played together, mostly unaffected.

Comforted by my brothers' overall gleeful resilience, I rejoined the grown-ups now back in the vestibule where Momma held court. She had taken gentle yet absolute command while sipping sassafras tea, sniffing into her handkerchief, and nibbling politely on buttered sweet biscuits.

Having sized up the seven coffins on display and then circling them all again one last time, Momma made a declaration. "Please don't take this personal Mister and Misses Goodenough, but I have decided I will be providing my own box for JB's burial."

Oh, she was willing to let the undertakers do whatever else, and charge whatever else, but their offerings came across as more decorative than practical and not nearly as sturdy as her own fine, hand-hewn pieces.

Though Ruby Pearl, Doc Feldman, and I were all on hand and growing more fidgety by the minute, Momma didn't look to any of us for support. Or advice even.

"Misses Jackson?" Mister Goodenough appeared confused.

"I'd built us a nice tall bookcase," Momma explained. "Right after we all moved in with Gert. She still uses it for storing her canned goods and preserves. It'd always been one of my husband's favorites."

"Surely, I do not understand," Mister Goodenough replied, eyeing Momma with the suspicion of an unethical lawyer. Tufts of his shoe-polished black hair stood on end.

"All's I need do is take out the shelves and give it a proper cover. And a padlock. A nice, strong padlock."

Mister Goodenough scoffed, lifting one overgrown eyebrow. "My dear, *dear* Misses Jackson, that would be highly unorthodox." The seasoned veteran now sounded like he might be fixing to have a come-apart of his own.

"My dear, *dear* Mister Goodenough," Momma said, speaking each word clearly, her nose just inches from his. "I'll still need y'all to add padding and lining. You can even charge us double for it. Now, how's that sound?" Affecting a shyness, she paused just long enough to cock her head and smile sweetly. "Surely, my mysterious benefactor won't mind getting some change back. Or maybe y'all should keep whatever's left over, you know, for your troubles. I wouldn't mind none. And 'sides," she added, "what righteous husband wouldn't die happy, just to be laid to rest in a product of his beloved wife's design?"

With Misses Goodenough looking on, Mister Goodenough couldn't nearly argue with that.

JB HAD PASSED ON WEARING his knotted face, and no measure of mortuary magic could change that. Ever since he was just a boy, Gamma'd warned, "Son, if you don't stop that scowlin', your face is gone freeze that way. You mark my words."

Gosh darn it if this time she wasn't right.

Dissatisfied with Mister Goodenough's prickly efforts at the table, reenergized, Gamma got herself into the act. After shoving more cotton into her dead son's cheeks, she massaged his temples to loosen him up some and plied this way and that at his cold, cold lips. Poor Gamma tried so very hard to slacken JB's features, but for some odd or unearthly reason, she couldn't get them to let up.

After a while Momma, Gamma, and the Goodenoughs agreed upon other specifics and that the bookcase-casket should remain closed. No one, aside from Gamma, of course, anticipated much of a crowd anyways.

"I'll work through the night if need be," Momma said, doing some figuring in her head. She'd take measurements, make adjustments, and restructure the pine cabinet into a coffin with a rugged lid and a sound lock. Time was passing at a warped speed now, and Momma wanted for our private family time to take place sooner rather than later. The Goodenoughs concurred and mapped out the remaining details.

By that following evening they were all near ready. The Goodenoughs weren't any bit happy about the change in JB's final accommodations, but after seeing Momma's fine workmanship first hand, Mister Goodenough softened up some. Why, he even hinted at the possibility of commissioning Momma to carve up some of those convertible bookcases for resale for the funeral parlor, someday, at a time more appropriate.

During our pre-wake vigil, Gamma pulled out two gilt-edged, framed pictures from a grainy flour sack bag. In the one larger photo of JB, from before he and Momma met, a smiling face promised a different sort of fellow. To this day, no one could deny Jamerson Booth Jackson was as handsome a hound dog as they came.

The second photograph caught him and my Vidalia on their wedding day, with Momma looking over her bruised shoulder while JB dumped two burgled bottles of buckeye bark into the punch bowl.

"These here pictures could set right aside your bookcase, Vida Lee," Gamma proposed. "That way folks can remember my boy like he truly was."

Ruby Pearl turned away and mumble-grumbled something not meant to be overheard.

⌇

I SNUCK A PEEK INSIDE that finely hewn pine pall. Not long after, when no one else was looking, Momma lifted the lid and did the same. Seems we both needed reassurance that he was still inside, that this was not another fake out, like when Momma thought we'd gotten away clean to Cousin Arlis's in Tuscaloosa.

It'd be just like JB to be sitting there on Ruby Pearl's front stoop, waiting on us after his own funeral, with a posy of oleander in hand and the sweet talk sliding off his tongue.

He would laugh agreeably, offering up a strong handshake while he explained to Sheriff Truith and company, "Vida Lee's just having another one of her spells. She be aw'right once I get her back home."

Then, turning to Momma, he'd coo, "My sweet Vidalia, don't you be sad no more. I didn't really leave y'all. I's just messin' with you. Teachin' you a lesson, is all."

OUR BOYS SPILLED INTO THE hall, grabbing up treats meant for the bereaved. Pecan shortbread cookies, assorted fruits, lemon bars, and raisin biscuits. By the end of that week, all eight little sunken cheeks had grown so full you'd have thought someone had taken a tire pump to them.

Memaw Veta Sue and Pawpaw Clyde Royce came by to drop off their respects. Pawpaw inspected the bookcase-coffin. Admiring Momma's handiwork, he gave a quick, hard tug on the padlock she'd affixed to it and told Momma she was gonna be fine. That she was better off without the shifty sonofabitch. I wondered why a person might feel the need to tell another person what that other person had to've figured out by then.

Taking heed of this newfound family bond, Ruby Pearl excused herself. "Well now, Missy Vidalia," our Miss Ruby said in an exaggerated huff. "I'ma take Cody on outside for his walk. But I be back soon 'nough."

Pawpaw looked over at Momma and, without even asking Memaw Veta Sue's permission, went and offered up their services. "Me and Veta Sue can stick around some, Vidalia. We'll give you a hand with them boys."

Memaw Veta Sue nodded in affirmation. My momma's mouth fell open, but she shut it right quick, trying to hide her surprise. Then Memaw added onto Pawpaw Clyde Royce's offer. "Me 'n Paw got something we need talk to you 'bout anyways, Vidalia Lee. After that we can carry y'all to wherever you want."

Ruby Pearl pulled a deep breath and looked around some before taking her temporary leave.

All this day, off and on, Memaw Veta Sue had been sipping on something from a little flask, giving Ruby Pearl one of her uneasy feelings. Oh, Memaw'd been helping herself most generously, but she didn't seem tipsy, just less unyielding than usual, as she settled herself into one of the Goodenough's comfy chairs with little Eli tucked onto her lap.

Why, Memaw near wooled that baby to death, hugging on him like as if she'd never hugged on anybody before.

I was afraid I'd have to figure some way to wangle his release, but in the nick of time, she let him up for air. Eli didn't seem to mind it at all though, beaming his special melt-your-heart smile. Memaw's eyes glittered in the afternoon sun as she pulled him back into her again and hushed into his unruly mop of yellow ringlets, "I aw'most had a little boy of my own once."

Bootie, James, and Clayt lined up, front and center, as they watched her in awe, waiting patiently on their own turns, just as we'd seen the Catholics do over at Twelve Apostles. It didn't matter how long the line, you never saw anybody try to cut. They just all stood there waiting on their holy communions like a legion of saints-to-be waiting on their canonizations.

My little brothers knew this here was something special. That although there was no altar in sight, this was no less a sacrament.

On any other day Gamma Gert might've been overtaken by the green-eyed monster seeing how Memaw Veta Sue was fussing so over *her* grandboy cubs. On this day, though, poor Gamma had a hard enough time seeing through the holy waters streaming down her own face that nothing else much mattered.

With Pawpaw standing to her one side, Memaw Veta Sue beckoned Doctor Feldman over to join them. Once close enough, she held Eli out to him. "Here you go, Doc," she whispered. "I reckon they're just as much yours as ours."

Looking on from across the room, Momma narrowed her eyes pretending to be pouring herself a cup of lemonade. Fretting in her head, she hoped with all her heart Memaw Veta Sue wouldn't go starting trouble with the doc after all he'd done. A burning sensation welled inside while the oddest of confusions took hold. Her lips tight, my momma approached the trio to within listening distance.

"I'm sorry, too, Lewis," Memaw whispered back, handing little Eli over to him before scooping up one of the other grandboys just waiting to take his place. "What's done, been done. Time to quit the blaming and the hating over it all."

Momma had never heard Memaw Veta Sue utter one civil word to the doc, let alone call him by his given name. And she'd never seen Doctor Feldman cry. Not in all her years of knowing him.

"What's going on here? What's wrong, Doc? Maw? Paw?" Momma asked.

Just then Ruby Pearl poked her head back into the room. "Come on along now, you all," she said, drawing the boys to her. "Me 'n Cody got a new trick to show you outside."

She stole a look at my momma and blessed herself, making the sign of the cross, which was not amongst our Miss Ruby's regular habits, being a natural born Baptist and all.

Once Ruby Pearl and the boys had disappeared down the hall, Pawpaw Clyde Royce cleared his throat, rested one hand on Momma's shoulder, and nodded in the doc's direction. "This here's your real daddy, Vidalia," Pawpaw Clyde Royce said, his voice calm but shaken.

"Paw?" Dazed, Momma cut her eyes from one man to the other. "What exactly d'you mean, Paw? You're my daddy—"

"You and the boys got to be mine through a backdoor and a slight o' hand. The good doc here," Pawpaw said, speaking his words with a soft resignation. "He's your real pa."

"Maw? Doc?"

"It's true, Vida Lee," the two answered, almost in unison.

"No. No, it's not. Clyde Royce Kandal is my real daddy," Momma said, aiming her words at Doc. "He is my sons's real granddaddy. Even as much as I appreciate all you done for me, for us."

Momma then took two steps back and shook her head nice and slow, finally disposing any of her leftover supposes.

CHAPTER THIRTY-NINE

HEADING ON HOME HERSELF, RUBY Pearl provided for Doc a shoulder and a ride back to his office, which was almost on her way.

Momma and my brothers stayed behind with her folks a while longer.

Memaw Veta Sue looked after the boys while Pawpaw helped Momma apply one final coat of preservative to JB's bookcase-coffin. Once they'd finished the job to their mutual satisfaction, they packed up, piled in, and drove off in Pawpaw's automobile to our predetermined destination, Number Five Sherman Oaks Road.

Pawpaw waved his goodbyes to my momma and his grandbabies, warmed by the notion that maybe, just maybe, he had done something right in his life. Memaw Veta Sue blew tear-filled kisses out the window of their sky-blue Galaxie 500, its front headlights jutting like fish fins as it skimmed over the half-graveled road with its rusted rear bumper dragging on behind, leaving a tattletale trail of sparks in its wake.

Done with our own waving and happy goodbyeing, Momma and the boys turned toward Ruby Pearl's house. For as many times as we'd visited, or just in passing, even right after a storm, Ruby Pearl's front lawn and flower beds had never ever looked as dissheveled.

A miniature lighthouse tipped to one side amongst color-crazed blooms, parched and straggly, in the fuchsia tire garden. Nearby, a second deeply colored planter flooded over as water poured out from a hose left running. Once sturdily rooted plantings now floated, hopelessly upended.

Half-open seed packets dotted Ruby Pearl's front lawn with an overturned metal watering can acting as a final punctuation mark. A firm breeze swooshed the ashy scent of burnt biscuit our way.

"That don't much smell like Misses Banks's cookin', James," Bootie grumbled, wagging his head.

"Sure don't," whispered James, as he leaned in toward his twin, sniffing at the seared air.

Wide-eyed, Momma looked around, dry-washing her hands. Little Elijah burst into tears.

Momma grabbed Eli up, and with him hanging from her hip, she rushed by Ruby Pearl's bottle tree. By now, under her breath, she'd begun shushing up prayers instead of questions. "Dear God. Something ain't right here."

It wasn't like our Miss Ruby to let anything interrupt her gardening. Or her cooking. Not any more. Those days were long gone.

"Lookit, Momma! Here she come!" yelled James, bouncing on the balls of his feet and pointing a chubby finger at the freight train rushing in their direction.

Wiping her hands on her apron, limping at a steady pace, a fresh gash visible on her right shin, Ruby Pearl barreled toward us all causing the boys to scatter like pigeons. With the back of one hand like a wiper on her truck's windshield during a hard rain, she swiped her forehead, back and forth, back and forth. Her cocoa eyes now red, raw, and tender. Her two plump cheeks glowed like chunks of coal smoothed from a burning. She paused only to hitch up her calico skirt while the outline of a tall individual loomed large on her front porch.

Momma handed Eli to James, but her eyes remained fixed on the dark, lanky stranger. Fumbling in her pocket, she broke from us, running full speed ahead toward Ruby Pearl. "Misses Banks!" Momma cried out. "What happened? Are you all right?"

"'Course I'm aw'wright, chile! I'm—" Ruby stopped in her tracks, donning the biggest, strangest smirk. Bigger and stranger and more smug than any I'd seen on her in all my days on this earth, and that's saying something.

Steeling her grip on Ruby Pearl's shoulders, my momma gave her a shake. "Who is that man?" she demanded, maintaining her sense of alarm. "What all happened here?" Then Momma paused. Leaning her head to one side, her voice softened and she whisper-asked, "Misses Banks?

Who is that strange man on your front porch? Why's he smiling like that? And why's he waving at me?"

"Why, that ain't no strange man, Missy," Ruby Pearl sang out, full of joy. "That there's my boy! Comed home, safe 'n sound."

"Your boy, Leslie?" Momma asked, finally relaxing her hold of Ruby Pearl's shoulder. One hand dropped to her side, but the other went right back to her pistol pocket, just in case. "Are you sure?"

"I believe I knows my own son, Missy," Ruby Pearl said in a huff, soon followed by the sheepish smile she could no longer hold in. "Can't wait for you all to meet. I done tole him 'bout how you and the chirrens was on yo' way!"

Our supper in the oven, Ruby Pearl had been out watering her flowers. She'd been fixing to plant some new ones, but then Mister Leslie just showed up.

She said she didn't know whether to smack him upside the head or smother him with kisses, what with all the worries he'd caused her over the years. Of course, being Ruby Pearl, she'd opted for the latter. She went at the young man so hard she knocked him, and pretty much anything else in her path, to the ground. Why, she was so fired up she didn't even notice the rip visited upon her leg by the roughly pierced nozzle of her watering can.

We all hurried to the house to meet this Mister Leslie and to see to our Miss Ruby's injuries. Leslie Ruben Banks was a sight to behold in his crisp uniform with a glorious blaze of multi-hued ribbons parading across his chest. He had Ruben's smile, Ruby Pearl's eyes and her Auntie Gearline's light, toffee-colored skin.

And there was one mighty fine supper awaiting us all.

What we had smelled from yards away, only the remnants of the first meal—the one she'd been working on up until the moment her prodigal son appeared in her garden and she'd temporarily lost her mind.

Spread out on the table atop Ruby Pearl's best linens sat a honeyed ham and a roasted chicken, corn bread, cowpeas, an unburnt batch of buttermilk biscuits, speckled grits, and fresh shucked corn.

Our Miss Ruby had outdone even herself with everything but a fatted calf laid out on that table. I reckoned had there been one of those available, she'd have slaughtered it with her own bare hands and cooked it up in honor of her boy's homecoming.

Almost looking like one of our boys grown up, Leslie was fair-skinned and light-eyed. My idea of having Ruby Pearl as our relation was not so far fetched after all, leaving me to expect all good things might indeed be possible.

Over the course of our evening meal, Momma peppered poor Mister Leslie with question after question. It was more of an inquisition than polite conversation, truth be told. She could not understand how it was that he'd just run off and enlisted against his mama's wishes. "But you are her only son, Leslie. Why in tarnation would you ever do such a thing."

"Like I told Mama Pearl, Misses Jackson, it was only a matter of time before the draft would get me. And, besides, I needed to do something. I needed to change. To be better. To do better. And I did. I worked harder and longer than any of those other recruits, black or white."

No more running with the wrong crowds, no more stumbling home pie-faced, no more getting arrested and dragged off to the pokey. Leslie wanted to make his mama proud, for at least this once.

"The chile always did have a chip on his shoulder," Ruby Pearl said, nodding. "Praise the Lord, he finally put it to some good use. My boy got hisself akst into the Special Forces," she said, busting her buttons. Leslie smiled, eyes glistening.

"And that chip Mama Pearl always so fretted over? Well now. That got took care of right quick," he guffawed. His merriment, deep and heartfelt.

"You have yo' daddy's laugh," Ruby Pearl said, looking down at her bandaged shin, pretending to be studying the makeshift footstool Momma'd fashioned for her on the spot using some bricks and a spare couch cushion. Then she reached down the front of her housedress, pulled out a hankie, and dabbed lightly at her eyes.

"But why the blue blazes didn't you never let your mama know your whereabouts, Leslie?" Momma asked, still shaking her head. "I'm sorry. I just don't understand—"

"Now, now, Missy," Ruby Pearl warned, placing her hand on Momma's forearm.

"It's all right, Mama Pearl," Leslie proposed. "Well now, Misses Jackson, I reckon I just didn't think of it that way. My mama'd always had a strong fear of strange places. If she'd known where I was going, what I was doing, why, she'd justa' worried more. Mama Pearl already had more'n enough heartache for one lifetime," he said in a flattened-out kind of voice. "And my team flew under the radar. My men. Our locations. Our missions. Everything was classified."

Ruby Pearl reached out and grabbed onto the unspoken apology floating her way where it got all tangled up in her heartstrings. "It's awright, son. You here now."

After supper, Momma and Leslie wiped down dishes while Ruby Pearl tidied her yard and the boys ran about chasing after Cody.

"I was 'sposed to be a man by then, Misses Jackson. It was high time I started acting like one. What happened to my father was wrong. Beyond any doubt. Reasonable or otherwise. But I wouldn't be doin' anything better with my own life than those cowardly hooded bastards if I kept on going down the wrong paths."

And now, Staff Sergeant Leslie Ruben Banks had returned home to his mama, still all in one piece. With the education and training he'd received, courtesy of the United States government, our Mister Leslie expected he'd get a better job, lead a better life. His was a good decision, rightly made, and in honor of his daddy's memory.

"Yo' daddy would be proud, son. So proud," Ruby Pearl said, wearing her own pride like a neon sign.

Ruby Pearl was happy.

It'd been a good day after all.

CHAPTER FORTY

Misses Bysa's roosters woke us early, with a hard wind blowing their cock-a-doodle-doo's our way.

That previous evening after the cleanup, Ruby Pearl had pulled Momma aside. "You want to talk 'bout it, Missy? About yo' Maw and the doc?"

My momma let out a heavy sigh. "I'll sort it all out in due time, Misses Banks. Right now we got more pressing matters to tend to, don't you think?" Momma squeezed Ruby Pearl's hand, planting a kiss lightly on her cheek. "Thank you, though."

While Momma said night prayers with the boys, Ruby Pearl and Mister Leslie rooted through the newest charity bushels brought in from the front porch. They'd found four small pairs of almost-new knickers and one not-so-almost-new white shirt apiece for each of the boys. Not that it mattered, but I spied something pretty I might like to've worn for JB's interment as well.

Ruby Pearl worked her magic, banishing some of the most foolhardy stains she'd seen. "An' I done seen some foolhardy stains in my day," she said, throwing back her head, tsk-tsking, but any fool could see she was thrilled by the challenge.

Leslie helped his mama with the scrubbing, but only so much. I don't rightly know how she did it, but before Momma even finished up with the boys, our Miss Ruby had got those shirts spanking clean and even dried enough for a pressing. Momma grabbed up Ruby Pearl's steel-bodied Sunbeam and the bright blue spray can of Faultless and took to her job like a rattlesnake with rabies.

Less than one hour later in the room off the parlor, I did my best to help, spurring Momma on as she turned one man's necktie into four of the tiniest bowties ever. We wanted our boys looking sharp for the event, shoes, or no shoes.

Marigold Sun Beauregard Knight stopped by with a box full of dresses and accessories from which Momma could choose her ensemble. As Momma'd never had an ensemble before, Sunny had to help her. Why, Sunny was so much more full of light than usual that she gave Momma's hair a much needed trim, style, and tease at no charge.

"Now then, Vidalia Lee. This is a big day for all y'all. I want you, in particular, at your very best. A gal don't never know who she might be seein' at events such as this. Why, you might meet some nice fella—"

"Sunny Beauregard Knight," Momma said, trying to appear flabbergasted. "You do remember this is my husband's funeral we are preparing to attend?"

"Don't you go pitchin' no fit, girlfriend. It don't make no nevermind to me, now, but that husband of yours, let me see, how should I put this? That husband of yours was one low-down, knee-walkin' drunk sonofabitch who didn't deserve the—" Sunny went on absentmindedly rifling through her purse. "Hah! Lookit here what I just happened to happen upon. A box of rouge and a couple extra lipsticks, hardly even used. I want you to have them, Vidalia. Why, they ain't even in my color palette, but they are in yours! I took a course, you know, so I'm certified to recognize such things."

Momma thanked her and they hugged long and hard before Sunny dashed off to do an emergency restyling for one of her regulars, and Momma set about to downsizing her new updo.

THAT NEXT MORNING CAME ON quick, filled with anticipation. According to the weatherman, the day would be a rough one. A tornado had touched down in Leland, just up the road apiece, with roofs ripped from houses and trees toppled by winds and rain. One scruff pine barely missed the Burlesons' trailer.

The Goodenough funeral car was to come for us in one hour. Of course, Ruby Pearl had insisted on shoring everybody up with a good breakfast. Leslie protested. He was still full from last night's feast. Clayt and Eli were so fortified by that point Momma fretted they might burst.

They'd put up a bit of a stink, but Momma and Ruby Pearl had finally got the first set of twins stuffed into their laundered knickers and starched shirts. Buttons buttoned, zippers zipped, ties tied. Then they started in on the second duo. Long wary of structured clothing, our boys were none too happy.

"My neck scratches somethin' fierce," James howled. "An' I cain't hardly turn my head."

"Me neither," cried Clayt.

"I cain't move my arms none!" Bootie squawked, hopping up and down and side to side. A jumping bean in a straitjacket.

"Hmm. Ain't that a shame," responded Ruby Pearl, giving them all the fish-eye.

Quietly patting his twin's crisp shoulder, only Eli, with his slow, gentle ways, seemed to reckon it'd all be over soon enough.

A smarter-looking quartet would have been hard to come by. The sight of them all gussied up like that caused a surge to my heart. Its seams stretched to breaking, and a sense of satisfaction oozed from between those split stitches. I wondered, is pridefulness a sin?—which I expect it is—and whether it's a mortal or a venial. I wished I could have asked Sunny, as Momma always said she was an expert on such matters. And that even if she didn't know for sure one way or the other, why, Marigold Sun Beauregard Knight would make up an answer on the spot just to put a person's mind at some ease. She was just that kind of gal.

A vision in turquoise, Ruby Pearl donned the feathered pillbox hat and hand-beaded, hand-tailored daysuit made for her by Madame Lafayette's personal seamstress for just such occasions. Our Miss Ruby had worn the fancy-dancey getup with her black patent church pumps to her former employer's funeral as well.

"Madame Lafayette turnt into good folk after all," Ruby Pearl said. "But one who had her own way to the finish." Lila Antoinette Lafayette had insisted that her Ruby look every bit as regal on the outside as she'd known her to be on the inside.

Genuine peacock feathers trailed in Ruby Pearl's wake, *swoosh-swooshing* side to side, as she gathered up any necessary items for the day—umbrellas, slickers, sweaters, and even a tarp—and shoved them all into her sturdy orange mesh poke as Momma finished up tidying the sink.

"You look pretty, Momma," I said to her. And she did. Though pale and thin, as she hadn't had the same appetite as our boys, my momma radiated a soothing shimmer, pouring over our new world, bathing us all in its soft, warm glow.

Her eyes brimmed now, not with the chilled droplets of yesterday, but with real, warm saltwater tears. "Cieli Mae," she whispered, "I am truly sorry. What with all the stir and bustle, I ain't paid you much mind of late."

"Hush, Momma. That's a good thing," I said. "We both know that's a good thing."

THE GOODENOUGH DRIVER STOOD AT attention, waiting on us all alongside a baby-blue stretch limousine as we filed out of the house with Momma in the lead and Ruby Pearl and Mister Leslie bringing up the rear. Like an overextended rubber band, Ruby Pearl snapped back to reality and pulled Momma to her. "You sho it's aw'wright if me 'n my boy ride with you all?" she whispered, unsmiling. "Me 'n Leslie'd just a' soon take the pickup."

"What? Why? Don't be silly, Misses Banks. Of course y'all will ride with us," Momma replied, her head cocked to one side. "Look at that automobile. Why, there's room a'plenty."

The driver helped the boys climb in and over one another. In a low voice, with a head nod in the direction of Ruby Pearl and her war-hero son, he asked Momma, "Beggin' your pardon ma'am, but how're them folks gettin' there?"

"Why, in the car with us of course," Momma replied.

"But thems colored folk, ma'am," the driver responded. Momma dragged her eyes over the chauffeur, a Negro himself, in a kind of disbelief.

The man looked down at his shoes as he continued in a whispered tone, "Ma'am. My instructions are that the car is for family members only."

The veins in Momma's right temple twitched as she glanced over at

Ruby Pearl in her feathered finery and Mister Leslie with his chest full of medals. Using her best voice, Momma begged the driver *his* pardon. "Misses Ruby Pearl Banks is my family as sure as this day is long. And you see that fine lookin' officer standing next to her over there? Well now, he is her son. So I reckon that makes him family as well. Sister Ruby?"

Without missing a beat, Momma stepped back, motioning for Ruby Pearl and Leslie Banks to enter before her.

Momma held the door open and smiled at the driver. Why, that poor man didn't even dare to question her further.

From within, the boys jockeyed for position.

"Sit here, Mister Leslie!"

"No, sit next to me!"

"*No!* Sit here, next to me."

"Here you go, Mister Leslie. Sit here!"

Leslie Banks was the first man in uniform they'd seen outside the pages of Doc Feldman's old *National Geographics.* Once settled in they peppered him with questions, asking after every little thing, from "Don't them boots hurt your feets?" to "How'd ya get all them ribbons?"

Staff Sergeant Leslie R. Banks looked downright dandy in his Grade A dress uniform, green wool beret, and black boots polished to a high gloss. He promised to answer all their interrogations, "But one at a time, grunts!"

James pointed to the beribboned area just above Mister Leslie's left breast pocket.

"What're them for?"

"Well, private, these here are my unit ribbons. 82nd Airborne," he responded, targeting the area above his heart. "And this," he said, aiming a little higher, "this is what's called a Combat Infantry Badge, and these over here are my Jump Wings, my Parachutist Badge."

"You jumped out ae-ro-planes, din'cha, Mister Leslie?" asked Bootie, his eyes as wide and bright as last night's full moon.

"When I grow up, that's what I'ma do," squealed James, in awed wonder. "I'ma jump out ae-ro-planes like Mister Leslie."

Momma knitted her brow and flashed Leslie a frown, but it was easy enough to see she was trying her hardest to keep the edges of her lips from curling up.

After they'd settled in, I took my place on the floor by the door next to Momma.

And there we all were. Smushed together in the back of that funeral car. One big, happy family. I didn't want to count how many sins I might've committed on that day. The day of JB's funeral. Truth be told, it was kind of fun being carried in the big baby-blue limousine, even knowing where we were going in it. And why.

Through the tinted windows the town passed by in varying shades of gray. Even the sky and even the trees. I enjoyed watching my brothers as they noted with glee, one filtered distortion after another.

Upon our arrival at River of Hope Springs Eternal, we found the lugging of JB's remains the topic of a most heated deliberation. Pat Picayune, the only one of JB's peers to've volunteered as a pall bearer, never showed up. Brimley Curtis-Mahoney came by with a bad back and news of keg-tapping problems down at the pub.

Pawpaw Clyde Royce got drafted against his wishes. Mailman Mister Manfred Rainey stepped up, politely informing Ruby Pearl of his qualifications.

"'Scuse me, Misses Banks, but might I offer myself up to your cause? A man can't help but get strong muscles carrying sacks of mail day after day, year after year." Mister Rainey spoke softly and without a hint of boastfulness. "I'd be most honored to oblige, if your little lady friend over there don't mind none."

Why, even Great Granddaddy Grady Bo didn't object when called upon, but—and this is the honest to God's truth—he appeared right pleased to provide some brand of comfort for his Gertrude. Seems after sixty-some years of living clean, and even after his recent run-in with the cattle trailer, Grady Bo was in as good a shape as any of them.

Still short one carrier, Mister Goodenough, wearing a thinly veiled question on his face, looked to Momma. Momma looked to Ruby Pearl, who looked to Leslie, as if they were all just playing a silent game of whisper down the lane.

"Of course, Mama Pearl," Leslie said with a nod, shoulders back, head high. If he could handle prisoner snatch missions in South Vietnam, he could surely handle the transport of this one lone rat-bastard sonofabitch to his final resting spot.

CHAPTER FORTY-ONE

So THERE. WE HAD THEM all. Our unlikely sentries—Granddaddy Grady Bo and Ruby Pearl's mailman admirer-friend on the right, and Pawpaw Clyde Royce and Staff Sargent Leslie Ruben Banks with his chest full of medals on the left.

Gamma Gert's ladies-in-waiting had been up since before dawn. They'd prepared and set out the coffee and juices, breakfast casseroles and cobblers, cornbread and biscuits, and coffee cakes and sugar cookies to be served in the inner sanctum immediately following the cemetery burial. Other folk—but not many, mind you—milled about.

Transformed overnight by the Wild Women, the River of Hope Springs Eternal Church and Pool Hall hardly resembled itself. Swathes of black fabrics draped this way and that over tables and chairs. Lilies, their petals lightly browned along the edges, left over from a previous day's funeral service across town, had been scattered about. Streams of dappled sunlight bobbed through the cracked and partially stained glass window overhead as dark clouds hovered like moving targets.

Not too many townsfolk were in attendance aside from the loyal fragments of our extended family. Brimley Curtis-Mahoney hung around for the service after hearing there'd be any number of refreshments offered at conclusion.

Strangely enough though, there was that young man from the county. Kenneth Greeley sat all by his lonesome in the next to the last of the portable pews. Sunny Beauregard Knight arrived late and snuck in beside him. Sunny'd had an emergency makeover to perform and that was why she was late, she explained to him, though he surely hadn't asked.

Up front at the piano, Misses Jones's fingers struck each key, both the faded blacks and the yellowed whites, with an equally sobering significance. A stone-faced Margaret Speight turned the pages of the hymnal.

Off to the side, Sarah Jean Peeples belted out "Amazing Grace."

I couldn't help but wonder at the seemly nature of it all thus far.

Preacher Tidwell, perspiring profusely despite cool winds passing through, approached the lectern with a rare timidity, an uneasy braid of apprehension, lowliness, and fear.

Tidwell had a fondness for our Gert who, by anyone's reckoning, was the most loyal and active sheep in his flock, and he wanted to do right by her irregardless of the worthless inclinations of her offspring.

In effort to avoid the truth of the matter and fill the time slot with more venue-appropriate commentary the preacher focused, for the most part, on the potential of JB's potential. He also employed a few choice *what ifs?* and quotes because, as anybody knows, a decent *what if* or a good enough quote can cover a multitude of sins.

"Amen, amen, I say to you. He who exalts himself shall be humbled. And he who humbles himself shall be exalted. Blest be the Lord day by day, God of our salvation who carries us. Our God is a god who saves. Our God is a god who crushes the skulls of the enemy. In You, Lord, I take refuge, but what if I put You to shame? What if I no longer deserve to be called Your son?"

Once he'd found his rhythm, Tidwell kept at it. After a slight pause to mop his brow, taking one more gulp of the amber-colored liquid from his mason jar, and noting the combination of shock and awe on the faces of his parishioners, the preacher man redirected his energies.

"In Your justice deliver us, we ask," he petitioned in softer tones. "And the Good Lord says, 'I am concerned about you.' And in our repentance we say, 'Father, I have sinned against You and against heaven.' Call to mind, oh my brethren, that our Bible is full of stories of them that are lost. And so," the preacher said, staring and nodding at those more dubious-looking members of the assembly, "I leave you, brothers and sisters, with one question. After all is said that can be said, Christianity is about forgiveness, is it not? Amen."

Even Pawpaw Clyde Royce, ever mindful of most words of scripture, appeared confounded by the preacher's interpretations and the confusion of psalms, proverbs, books, and chapters invoked during his filibuster at the lectern.

As noted by more than a few of the bewildered rank and file, this service was lacking in the personal touch for which—aside from those pesky, lickety-split, shotgun weddings—this man of the cloth was so highly regarded.

Through it all, Gamma Gert sobbed loudly, overtaken by that for which there are no right words. Regardless of anyhow or anyway, it is and always will be beyond the limits of any human reckoning that any mama should outlive her child.

And although there never was any love, lost nor found, between himself and Jamerson Booth, Great Granddaddy Grady Bo Jebbitt, too, yielded to the sadness of the moment. This gentle giant of a man wept undirected, torn up all over again by his inability to make things right for his only offspring.

No matter how big or strong, cunning or protective, smart or witty, a ma or a pa might be, there are certain matters beyond a their jurisdiction, and that there might be the most difficult of all of life's lessons.

So she could carry out in her own way the motions required by the occasion, Gamma's spirit disconnected from things of this earth. Somewhat numbed by a few sups of the corn whiskey meant to wash down the tranquilizers provided by Doc, she carried on. The blessing being she couldn't have rightly processed what nonsense the preacher had put forth in his bootlegged attempt at a sanctification of her boy.

Gamma collected whatever bits of herself she could and stepped forward from the portable front pew.

Grabbing Tidwell's hands in hers, she planted dry kisses on his smooth knuckles before raising her eyes to meet his. "Most folks had a missed understanding of my boy. Of his ways. But you, bless your heart, you always got him down to rights. Thank you, from the bottom of my soul."

The preacher flushed one, two, three, four shades of red, so deeply shamed was he by the purity of Gamma's gratitude.

Their collar starch melted some, our boys started in on a rambunctiousness. Arms went flying and legs wriggled and jiggled. They tumbled and mumbled, pushing and pinching and tickling and taunting one another, while wagering found pennies on "Who's gonna sit next to Mister Leslie on the way home?" and "Who's gonna jump out a aeroplane first?" Soon tired of themselves, they set off in search of those tasty treats prepared by Gamma's Wild Women and meant to provide distracting sustenance to those few mourners and the many mourner-watchers immediately after the lowering of the casket.

Momma heaved deep breaths while keeping her eyes at half-mast and a hanky pressed to her cheek as she leaned into her dear friend. Our Miss Ruby, our unwavering, shimmering, befeathered Miss Ruby, held Momma upright and together for us all.

There wasn't much left to be said after the sermonizing, even for a preacher.

The sky grew darker than it should've been, and the wind kicked up some. Ruby Pearl left Momma's side, grabbed her bag loaded with outerwear for her charges, and we all, accompanied by Gamma this time and four boys with their pockets stuffed full of gooey sweet treats, piled back into the big blue whale.

Some of JB's stool-hugging associates were on the scene when we pulled up to the cemetery.

By the time we'd disembarked, those crackers had already drowned most of their own sorrows in the drink even though it was just barely ten o'clock in the morning. It was near impossible to know for sure whether JB's boys Catfish Tyrell, Possum Stinson, and Slick Stevens were in the throes of a bereavement, or a fit of hilarity as they bumbled about, tears spilling down their grimy cheeks. But theirs weren't the only reactions difficult to gauge in this gathering of the misspent, the mistook, and the mistaken.

"Will y'all lookit me," Gamma blubbered, approaching the grave site. "I'm shakin' worse than the leafs on them trees."

And she was.

Fortified by Ruby Pearl's hold, Momma did her best to brace Gamma, even as her own slight frame trembled in tandem. The ripple effect set our Miss Ruby to thinking ahead.

Ruby Pearl shivered at the sight of the hole dug deep into the ground. I suspect that uneasy feelin' must've sprung up in her yet again. She let go of Momma and right quick grabbed up two disheveled urchins in each arm, holding them at eye level like lost kitties just found.

Poker-faced, Ruby Pearl started in with her most raspy, most threatening voice. "See that there line?" she said, lifting her chin toward the freshly scooped burial plot. "Any one o' you chirrens dare to crost over it, mos' likely, yo' gone fall down." Her voice still full of sand, grit, and gravel, she continued, "Down into that hole with yo' daddy. Just you 'n him passin' time while the rest us be cryin' over our goodies." Ruby paused, letting her seeds take root while she set those little kittens back on solid ground. "But don't worry none. Mos' likely somebody'll come back 'n fetch you all up 'fore mornin'."

Little brows purled as wide eyes darted back and forth from Ruby Pearl's face to the area between them and that big hole in the ground. The boys nudged shoulders, demanding in chorus, "What line? We don't see no line!"

"You all sees that line as well as I do, don' you?" Ruby replied. "Well, it don' matter much one way or 'nother if you sees it or if you don'. So longs you all know what's gone happen if you crost over it."

Not wanting to tempt the fates further, now lined up like baby ducklings all in a row, not one little muscle, hand, head, nor foot moved amongst them. That is, not until the pine box was lowered into its abyss.

The sky grew even darker. Eli shuddered at its purpleness, a harsh reminder of another ominous sky in his memory bank. "Da!" he cried out, just as he had then.

Those who didn't understand but thought they did, including Gamma and her sidekicks, clucked amongst themselves.

"That poor child."

"Tsk-tsk."

"Maybe he gone miss his daddy after all?"

"Tsk-tsk."

"Breaks my fool heart."

"Tsk-tsk."

Momma closed her eyes and sniffed into her hanky.

The motley trio hurried to hush Eli as visions of black holes and breached caskets danced in their heads. Ruby Pearl nodded, smiling Madonna-like and ever so pleased with her own creativity and forethoughtedness.

CHAPTER FORTY-TWO

SOME TIME LATER, BACK AT the River of Hope Springs Eternal Church and Pool Hall , Ruby Pearl stood off to one side. Her heated gaze seared into the fidgety newcomer. Motioning with one crooked finger, she drew him to her.

"Kenneth Greeley. Why you been payin' me no mind, boy?" she asked, more dare than question, arms crossed, chest puffed, toes tapping.

"I'm sorry, Misses Banks. I-I didn't have nerve enough. I reckoned how much you m-must hate me," he said, taking one big gulp of air after another. "I don't blame you ma'am. No, I do not." He shook his head forcefully.

"Chile. All these years I bin worryin' about you and yo' mama—" Ruby let her lips, now tightly pursed, carry the rest, *like I din't aw'ready have me 'nuff to fret over.*

"You can s-slap me now, ma'am, if you want. In front of all these people. I deserve it."

"Oh hush, chile. I ain't gone slap you! You ain't yo' daddy. You is a good man. You was a good boy. I aw'wes knowd you was gone be a good man. Ruben, he tole me so. And my Ruben was aw'wes right about such things."

Kenneth Greeley's own thin, pink lips disappeared into a smile-grin, and his eyes, as green and slick and shiny as the inside rind of a newly scooped honeydew melon at a picnic, danced a jig in a sea of gratitude and affection.

"And how is yo' mama doin'?" Ruby asked, unexpectedly altering the air between them.

"She died, Ruby. The Cancer got her. Last year. I was there when—" His eyes now dulled to a clumsy waltz. "When she passed. In her sleep. I was there. Holding her hand. It was all so peaceful-like. I don't know how much she suffered. My ma had got real good at hiding that k-kind of thing. She had p-plenty of p-practice."

"Come here, boy," Ruby Pearl said. Though her words were sharp, her manner was anything but. "Come on over here and give ol' Ruby a big hug."

Like the scared little boy she remembered, Kenneth swiped at his eyes with the back of one hand. "I've missed you somethin' awful, Misses Banks."

Ruby Pearl grabbed him up in a mama bear hug so that he near disappeared. From clear across the room, like a Buffalo Springfield Steamroller on a dirt road in need of leveling, Leslie headed their way at full throttle. I wondered, was our Mister Leslie still resentful? Or was this going to be something much worse?

Ruby Pearl stiffened. Backing away from the young officer, she dropped her arms to her sides. "Oh Lordy," she murmured, flashing back to the days before Leslie's turnabout. Ruby Pearl held onto her breath, not sure what might be going on inside her son's head. "Come on over here, Leslie," she said, grabbing at his arm. "I gots somebody here fo' you to—"

"Ken Greeley!" Leslie crowed, his right hand outstretched. "Well, I'll be a son of a gun. What're *you* doing here, man?"

"Lucky Leslie!"

A gentlemanly handshake turned quickly into one of substance, immediately followed by single-fisted shoulder punches and a hardy helping of backslappings.

"Well butter my butt and call me a biscuit," Ruby Pearl blurted out, one palm pressed to her heart.

"Me and this here brother," Leslie began by way of explanation, "we went through training together. And—"

Just then my momma walked by them all, turning back only to return a passing glance, catching Kenneth Greeley red-faced, the slightest of smiles on her lips.

"Ah . . . what? I'm sorry." Like a pickpocket caught in the act, he redirected his gaze back to present company. "What were you s-sayin' Leslie?"

"I was just tellin' Mama Pearl how we did our training together—"

"Oh. Y-yes ma'am, Misses Banks. We sure did. I finished one behind your son, Misses Banks. We were stationed together overseas for a while too. But not in the same company, though that would've been swell."

Momma walked on by them again, more slowly this time. She was getting pretty good about pretending she wasn't noticing being noticed. Kenneth's face edged two shades deeper as that uneven flush returned, creeping its way up the back of his neck. Something had passed in the air between them, and I spied a similar color spreading out onto my momma's cheeks. I'd always found Momma extra pretty when that happened. This time was no exception.

I wasn't the only one making note of the phenomenon. Why, I could almost smell sawdust as the wheels whirred inside Ruby Pearl's head. I just hoped I wouldn't need find a way to remind her that this was, first and foremost, a funeral. That this was meant to be a most solemn occasion. That there were hugs to be received and condolences to gather. Hands to shake and hankies to dampen. Sympathy cards to read and appreciation to express for those comforts, both large and small, put forth on our behalf.

Momma worked the room like a pro. Like it wouldn't have mattered one bit if I wasn't there. Or the doc. Or even our Miss Ruby.

Ruby Pearl and Doctor Feldman stood off to the side.

"She gone be fine now, Doc," Ruby Pearl hushed, signaling with her chin.

"Without a doubt, Misses Banks. Without a doubt." Lewis Feldman pulled in a deep, satisfied breath, confirming Ruby's diagnosis.

"MOMMA," I SAID TO HER. "Everything's gonna be all right."

My momma didn't say anything back to me. She just smiled her softest smile and nodded sweetly. Knowingly.

Momma had found her lost wings, almost all on her own.

And me? Well now. I'd like to say there were trumpets blaring and a host of angels sent to carry me on home, but that's not how it happens. No, I just closed my eyes. Closed my eyes and ever so slowly melted away into Momma's calmed waters.

Epilogue

Choice / n.

a decision to choose one

course of action over another

Momma visits my burial site often and always with a tied bouquet. She loosens the twine and places the freshly cut flowers in the palm of the concrete angel now guarding my plot. Lighting the candle perched in the statue's other hand, she hums one of her made-up tunes.

It had taken Momma over a year of saving most every penny she'd made with her new Build-a-Bookcase-Casket business to purchase my marker. My monument is flanked by five little crosses. Mementos of another kind.

We watch out for Momma and the boys from here—Alexia, the others, and I. As reckoned, they'd been waiting on me.

Kenneth Greeley wants to marry Momma, but she says no. At least for now.

Ruby Pearl dedicated her back property to Momma's notion of a safe house for women and children in need. Cecilia's Sheltering Garden. They named it after me.

Ruby Pearl spends much of her free time with Manfred Rainey, which sets Ruben to bristling. Nonetheless, Ruben is proud of the fine job his Ruby has done since his departure—almost as proud, I suppose, as I am of Momma and our boys.

Truth be told, if my Vidalia ever does turn around, she'll see the world she lived in back then served its purpose. And that yes, Momma, the spirit always has a choice.

ACKNOWLEDGMENTS

MOST ANY REWARD IN LIFE begins with effort and ends in gratitude. Thanks to my good pals and early readers: Beth Brodecki, Liz Grage, Laura Farjood, Colleen Fillar, Lana McBride, and Jamie Miles.

To my wise and witty critique group, The Forum Writers, and especially to those members who, more often than not at the drop of a hat, have gone above and beyond: Brenda Lowder, Dr. Doris Huggins, Gary D. Henderson, Harmon Snipes and John Wiseneski—thank you for your patience (even while speed reading) and good counsel. To The Peachtree Corners Forum Barnes & Noble, thank you for hosting us.

To Marianne Benz and Jean Ryckman, thank you for your friendship and never-ending support both on and off the mat. To Susan Crawford, thank you for your guidance, camaraderie, and uncanny memorization skills.

Cheers to the most supportive fellow book-clubbers ever: Donna Heinzelmann, Elaine Bogage, Charlie Anderson, Maria Villarreal, Jeannine Moore, Ginger Foretich, Karen Ploder, Karen Anderson, and Diana Burger.

Thanks to the Atlanta Writers Club, with a special shout-out to George Weinstein and Clay Ramsey. Kudos to my incomparable team at Turner, especially Caroline Davidson, Stephanie Beard, and managing editor Jonathan O'Neal, who arrived late to the dance but didn't miss a single step. To my lovely agent Janell Walden Agyeman, thank you for your faith in me, and for believing so strongly in this story.

Last but not least, to my home team, my family, my greatest treasure.

You are my inspiration, my touchstone. I can't imagine doing this without the comfort of your unconditional love and support. To my children Cara, Dana, and Brock, you've made me a better person from day one. Thank you for your encouragement and understanding, pep-talks, reads and re-reads, and for walking the walk and leading by example. To my husband, Tino, you are my own personal super-hero. Thank you for recognizing a rhetorical question for what it is, for bringing home take-out on a moment's notice, and for always, always having my back.

Deborah Mantella, August 2015